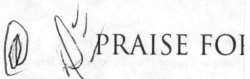

PRAISE FOR

"Baxter Kruger [is] a truly gifted writer. This story is riveting and entertaining. My eyes have been opened." —Kevin Freiberg, PhD, coauthor of the international best seller *Nuts! Southwest Airlines' Crazy Recipe for Business and Personal Success*

". . . evokes the tradition and spirit of George MacDonald and C. S. Lewis . . . A feast!" —Brad Jersak, author of *A More Christlike God*

"I could not stop reading. I met Jesus in a whole new way!" —Darrell W. Johnson, DD, preacher, professor, author of *The Glory of Preaching* and *Experiencing the Trinity*

"Brilliant work by gifted theologian and storyteller." —Francois du Toit, author of *The Mirror Bible*, South Africa

"With the clarity of a scholar and the compassion of a Southern gentleman, Baxter succeeds in opening eyes and hearts as he methodically dismantles the lies that have dominated much of modern theology. *Patmos* is a gateway drug to deep and engaging theology and transformation!" —Wm. Paul Young, best-selling author of *The Shack* and *Eve*

"Thank you, Baxter, for recovering what has been so sadly, tragically lost to so many Christians." —Richard Rohr, best-selling author of *Everything Belongs*

"*Patmos* is a must-read!" —Paul J. Lavelle, CMSgt, USAF (Ret), founder of Operation Restored Warrior

"*Patmos* is a book packed with creativity, inspiration, and revelation." —Denis Miranda, Senior Pastor CCE, Managua, Nicaragua

"In *Patmos*, the resounding theme of union fuels this deep, inward notion that anything is possible." —John Crowder, Sons of Thunder Ministries and Publications

"*Patmos* is a captivating novel that is as entertaining as it is revolutionary. Baxter shares a message that has been lost for centuries in the Western church." —Dr. Patrick Emery, MD, Wahpeton, North Dakota

"With the riveting plot of a master storyteller coupled with the deep but accessible truths from a renowned theologian, Kruger carries the reader deeper and deeper into a clear understanding of our Papa's love. I predict you won't only read it but you will gift it to others." —Steve McVey, author of *Grace Walk* and *Beyond an Angry God*

"In this riveting vision story the author allows us in to his inner struggles with searing honesty." —Ray Simpson, author and founding guardian of the international Community of Aidan and Hilda, Holy Island of Lindisfarne, UK

"It's so good I had to read it again! *Patmos* took me a thousand miles in my journey to recognize God's voice." —Mark Holloway, author of *The Freedom Diaries—God Speaks Back*, New Zealand

"Like morning dew on the pages, droplets from Baxter's enormous reservoir of theological knowledge sparkle through the plot, sheening the adventure in life-enriching truth and beauty." —Sherrilou McGregor, author of *Beings and Doings* and *Last Boat to Capri*, France

". . . eye-opening . . . And like a well-aged, single malt scotch, once you have tasted the glorious vision distilled through this finely crafted narrative, you will long to savor its intricacies again and again and reflect on its meaning for years to come." —Michael Lafleur, Director of The Infusion Network, Oakville, Canada

"This thinly disguised autobiographical novel reveals the remarkable and costly journey Aidan/Baxter has undertaken on his quest for the truth." —St. John of the Motherland, aka the Reverend John H. Walker, Associate Minister, St George's Church, Leeds, UK

"You will laugh and cry and never be the same after reading this mind-blowing tale! *Patmos* is a timeless gift for the ages and oh, so greatly needed by all of us." —Nan Clemmons, a mother, wife and grandmother

For More Information, go to:
PatmosTheBook.com

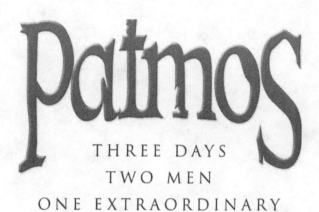

Patmos

THREE DAYS
TWO MEN
ONE EXTRAORDINARY
CONVERSATION

Patmos

THREE DAYS
TWO MEN
ONE EXTRAORDINARY CONVERSATION

C. BAXTER
KRUGER

PH.D.

PATMOS

C. Baxter Kruger

Copyright © 2016 by C. Baxter Kruger
Published by Perichoresis Press | P. O. Box 98157 | Jackson, MS 39298
Author is represented by Ambassador Literary Agency, Nashville, TN

Printed and bound in the USA
Cover design and interior layout | www.pearcreative.ca

ISBN: 978-0-9645465-7-8

For Kathryn,
our child of joy and color.
You are the daughter every dad wishes to have.

THE PASSAGE

Most Sundays that I am home, I sleep in as long as possible. But this Sunday had a mind of its own. A violent storm had raged through the night, and I hardly slept at all, which made me angry, as I needed rest after a two-week tour lecturing on theology. A little after six in the morning a strange silence—even more frightening than the storm—awakened me. I could feel the invisible war starting again. Although I had personally helped hundreds of people rise in their wars and find serious help, even victory, there was something unseen at work in my own life—dastardly evil that had a way of kicking my butt. I could see it coming like a dark cloud at sea moving toward me, but there was nothing I could do to stop it.

I knew sleep had vanished, so I decided to get up, throw on my khakis and a T-shirt, brew some coffee, and get the paper. I smiled thinking of how my wife, Mary, enjoyed real coffee—100% Arabica, she would say—but I loathed waiting for it to brew. It pushed my impatience button, like when the meter on the gas pump suddenly slows to a crawl for the last few dollars when you have prepaid. I vowed long ago to never prepay for gas, simply because I hated that feeling of being hindered. Somehow hindrance summarized my life. How many times had I gotten on a roll in my search for answers only to feel some damnable, unknown parachute open and jerk me back?

The blue flashing light of the coffeemaker startled me out of my thoughts. I pushed the button to start the brewing and dashed out of the kitchen to get the paper. I couldn't bear the insufferable wait. *Wouldn't it be great if you could text the coffeemaker and it would do the rest, and then it would text you when the coffee was ready?*

As I turned the corner into the foyer, I expected to see our front door, but what I saw was as shocking as something from the book of Revelation and the wild visions of the Apostle John.

Strange lights are not unusual around our door. It has twenty-eight panes of beveled glass, and sometimes in the winter the bevels will catch the sunlight and create a few colors. But on this morning the light hitting the bevels created hundreds of flashing prisms, all moving and passing in and out of one another as if alive, generating a spectacle of dazzling light and color a few feet in front of me.

Ever since I was a boy, prisms have fascinated me, but I've never seen or even heard about multiple prisms coalescing to create a larger one. But that is exactly what appeared between me and my door. Pulsating with myriads of colors, rainbows within rainbows, it all mysteriously joined together into one living canopy. I stood still, mesmerized by the vision. And then the canopy started moving—*toward me.*

I braced for some kind of impact, but when the canopy wrapped around me, nothing happened and I didn't feel anything at all. Then the world that I knew instantly vanished. Like someone had suddenly unplugged my house from existence. My house and all of planet Earth, everything I knew, was totally gone. In a split second I found myself alone in complete darkness.

"Oh, God," I screamed. *What just happened? Did I die? Am I dead? Where am I? What the hell is going on?* I checked my face, my head and chest, and then my body to see if I was still there—or here. My mind raced, but I was unable to think concretely.

Fear is not the right word. I have been afraid a hundred times in the woods at night, lost in briars with coyotes howling and strange sounds creaking in the forest, but there was always a sense of otherness that gave me some semblance of context. But in the unplugged universe of darkness that had suddenly taken over my life, I was alone, and there was nothing to give me a frame of reference: no dangling vines, no leaves rustling in the wind, no crickets chirping, no frogs croaking, not even a mosquito buzzing. One minute I was headed to my front door, and the next I was alone in a blackness so intense it seemed alive.

As odd as it may sound, I thought of a Scottish oatcake. The thought now makes me laugh, but that's what hit me. Understanding why didn't take long: the silent, dark world I had somehow entered was so devoid of *everything* that it was without taste, and compared to the humidity of Mississippi, it was as dry as sawdust. It cried out for something, *anything*—which even at the moment struck me as exceedingly strange given that my apparent entrance had been through so much beautiful color and light.

Such thoughts lasted only an instant as the darkness, which I swear was moving, pressed in upon me from all sides as if its intent was to swallow me alive. I could see nothing at all.

I panicked. *Where's my door? What happened to my house? Where's my family?* Confusion and terror, cross-fertilized with frustration if not outrage, rose from my insides as I realized my utter powerlessness. I didn't know what to do, which way to turn, or if doing or turning even mattered. It felt as if horror itself had morphed into an entity choking my very life. Maybe I *was* dead.

"Lord Jesus," I yelled, "what are you doing? This is not fair. *You* promised life, and I have searched since my youth—you know I have. Who on earth has worked harder? And *this* is the grand payoff?"

I heard nothing in response, no word, no sound, *nothing*, only the hideous silence of isolation in the blackest darkness, a nothingness I wouldn't wish even on the self-righteous Pharisees in my life.

"I have turned over every freaking leaf," I shouted. "For thirty years—my whole adult life—I wrestled my guts out trying to find answers. I carefully studied theology, even studied the *early church* and history and psychology, and I have been to therapy, in case you don't remember—*therapy!*—and now this *joke* of an ending? Is *this* the kingdom you announced? What else do you want from me? Tell me! You promised the river of living water, joy unspeakable, and I've scoured the denominations, even the charismatics for crying out loud, endlessly searching, but finding no real answers, and *now* my life ends in this *nothingness*? Is this all there is? Are you kidding me?"

I seethed with disgust as half a century of buried anger spewed from my heart. Fuming at the injustice of what was happening, I fell to my knees in desolation, emotionally spent, exhausted by the decades of words and definitions, of what was now clear to me, nothing more than empty ideas, the hollow forms and illusions and false promises of religion.

"I refuse to go out this way," I protested. "There must be more. This cannot be the end." *Whatever is happening, my life will not—I will not—end here. I will find my way home.*

As I sat in the forsaken dark trying to figure out what to do, I noticed a hint of gray in the far distance in front of me, like a light that was trying to be born but couldn't quite make it. Hope flickered in my heart but quickly died as my brain leapt to the thought of a train racing toward me in a tunnel. *Perfect*, I thought. *After all this damnable soul-searching, to be flattened now by a mindless train.* But there were no tracks, no sounds or vibrations. I noticed the weird smell of rotting cucumbers floating in the black void. I squinted, as if that could have helped me smell better, or see better for that matter, but it didn't.

I reached down to touch the ground with my left hand. Feeling fine powder like moondust, I said, half aloud and half to myself: *I must be on the dark side of the moon.* Unlike all my previous shouts swallowed by the void, this mumble echoed several times, so I figured I must be—now, if I wasn't before—in a cave. *Perhaps I'm in Arizona, and the train is the 3:10 to Yuma*, I thought, remembering the movie and desperately trying to bring a touch of levity to this most surreal moment in my life.

Determined not to disappear on my family and die alone, I rose and eased my way forward, instinctively toward the gray light. As I did, the light grew wider and seemed brighter. From a distance came sounds of marching, like a band practicing but with no instruments. The footsteps of the band got a little louder as I moved toward the light, but I still heard no drums or whistles or shouts.

It was so dark I had to move slowly; I made it only ten feet before I tripped on a rock—I think—and fell flat on my face. As I rolled over on my back, I felt pressure on my shoulders and legs pushing me down, like Gulliver being tied to the sand against his will, but something within me fought to rise.

Pushing myself up and dusting off, I shuffled toward the gray light. Like a zombie I inched forward, both arms held out in front of me, scared to death that at any moment I could fall headlong into an unimaginable abyss, as if where I was wasn't scary enough.

Eventually I made it to the mouth of what I discovered to be, in fact, a cave. Overcome with unspeakable relief, I strained to see as my eyes gradually adjusted to the sunlight. Before me lay an utterly treeless world as barren as Mars and as wide as the ocean. It looked like someone had filled the Superdome with orange dirt and then blasted it with a hundred high-powered water jets. The sky was Carolina blue, but everything else was orange. For as far as I could see or imagine, dramatic cliffs and hills and ravines and rocks littered the landscape, and they were all orange. I thought of the "Song of Moses" and his "howling waste of wilderness."

I stood speechless and immobilized until the sound of ocean waves broke the spell. Looking around to find the waves, I realized that the mouth of my cave was in the side of a cliff. Only a path, three or four feet wide, separated me from a serious fall; above me rose thirty feet of sheer rock. Where is this place? *Maybe I'm in purgatory*, I thought. *Or perhaps Australia.*

The marching sound reimposed itself on my consciousness; it was getting louder. I stood as still as a church mouse, trying to get a bead on the noise, when from out of nowhere a hand grabbed my right shoulder.

Before I could even scream, a voice behind me cried out, "Romans. Follow me now!"

I turned to catch the frame of a silver-haired man with an oil lamp in his left hand.

"Quickly! This way," he said with authority, motioning me with his right hand. When I realized the old man was leading me back into the cave and its darkness, I froze. "Wait a damn minute. What the hell is going on here?"

Without turning around he proclaimed, "Die without mercy, or follow me and live."

"Right behind you," I called out before thinking. *Whoever these Romans are,* I figured, *I can outrun this old man and buy myself some time if need be.*

As we moved with haste through the cave, I heard water bubbling in the distance, not a river but definitely more than a trickle. I tried to take mental notes of everything, but it was useless.

Eventually the old man turned into a room to the left and snuffed out his lamp. I caught a glimpse of his long beard and what looked like wineskins and a large basket before all was dark.

My breathing was heavy in the cool air. Again there was not a trace of humidity. I could hear him panting about three feet in front of me, but I could see nothing. *If something goes sideways,* I thought, *I think I can find my way back to the mouth of the cave and at least to sunshine.*

"They won't find us in here," he said calmly and with remarkable assurance.

"Sir, only God knows why I followed you back into this forsaken cave, but this charade has to stop. Who are you? Where are we? How did I get here? I am in no mood for any more mystery."

He took in a long breath and sighed. "All will be clear in time, young man. For now you need to know that you are safe here with me. Trust me."

"Trust? How can I trust an old man who appeared out of thin air in a cave in the middle of nowhere? I have no freaking idea how I got here, let alone who you are. I managed to find a little light, and now you have led me into the darkness."

"We are safe," he declared. Then enigmatically added, "The light shines in the darkness."

Having no clue what he meant, I sat in the black taking inventory, my body shaking as the double shot of adrenaline wore off. *At least I'm not alone. This old man poses no real threat to me, and he obviously knows his way around this darkness. That could prove helpful. For some reason he has shown goodwill toward me. But I want answers.*

His voice pierced the void. "Where are you from?"

"Me, I'm from Brandon," I replied. *At least I know the answer to that question.* "But the question is not where I'm from; the question is how did I get here, who are *you*, and what do you mean by Romans?"

He lit his oil lamp and slowly and confidently rose in front of me.

Several shadows bounced off the wall behind him. My first thought was *wisdom*, as I gazed at him. He was old as dirt and short and slight of build, but I could tell that in his day he had been strong—the lean type. (I had always wanted to be lean, but my Scottish ancestry had other thoughts.) His hands were still strong and larger than I expected, given his height. The old man's hair was long and white, almost glistening, as was his beard—both in stark contrast to the black of the cave. Crisscrossing his face were deep, ancient lines, each begging to tell its tale in the story of what surely had been an adventurous life. Not a trace of sadness appeared in his face. His eyes—framed by crow's-feet and eyebrows so bushy they had a life of their own—flickered with untamed intensity. That was the main thing that struck me: his deep brown eyes, vivid with light. They had that seasoned look of long-settled knowledge.

Clothed in a robe, he stood erect in the confidence of a vindicated visionary. A belt of well-worn leather, darkened by service, wrapped his waist. At some point in the past, I thought, the robe must have been white. Over his right shoulder hung an old brown satchel, obviously repaired a dozen times in the course of his adventures.

Something about this old man calmed me down. "Thank you," I said. "I'm shaken to the roots and terribly confused by what is going on here—"

"Aren't we all?" he interrupted. He rubbed his long beard and smiled. I noticed that he didn't have all his teeth and that most of those he still possessed had been whittled down through the years. But his smile made me think of a sanctuary. As bizarre as this world seemed, wherever and whatever it was, I felt safe. I was light-years from comfortable, but I was safe. He felt safe.

Still trembling, I managed to fake a laugh. "Sir, I was headed to my door at home when some weird stuff happened with lights and prisms, and I ended up in this cave."

JOHN

The ancient man led me out of the room and back to the mouth of the cave. Lifting his left index finger over his lips to let me know to be quiet—as if the gesture was needed—he made his way out onto the path. He moved with the stealth of a Cavalry Scout, so I reckoned he was a seasoned veteran of many wars. He stared at the barren land, listening like an alarmed deer, then looked to his right and above him. Apparently satisfied that all was well, he paused in what appeared to be an act of praise and then turned to me.

"My name is John," he declared, smiling. "I am glad to have you as a visitor, young man. Welcome to my world." He opened his arms in genuine hospitality.

"John," I responded, somehow smiling myself. "We named our son John, John Williams; I've always liked that name. I suppose it is good to meet you, but can you possibly explain to me what has happened? How on earth did I get here? And how do I get home?"

Surprise, I thought, swept his face as he took a deep breath, but I wasn't exactly sure of his expression.

"Sir, I was headed out my front door to get the paper when I ended up in this cave. Then you appeared, and—"

"The paper? Hmmm . . . ," he murmured, as if getting a clue to a mystery.

"Yeah, you know, like the Sunday paper," I said, my impatience rising.

The old man's countenance went blank with innocence. "What is a Sunday paper?"

I wanted to laugh but didn't. "I don't know where we are, but surely you have seen a newspaper before, even if you don't read the news yourself."

"Can't say that I have." Then, evidently lighting on the word *news*, he asked, "Is this newspaper about Jesus?"

His question caught me off guard, and I was not sure how to respond. "Well, sometimes there is a religious section, but that is mostly crap."

His eyes lit up with humor as he raised his left hand and declared, "*Skubala!*"

"*Skubala?*"

"It is Greek for 'crap.'" He chuckled.

Completely bewildered, I threw up my hands and turned to look out of the cave. "This is going nowhere; I'm going nowhere," I whispered.

"Young man, *skubala* is the Greek word for 'crap.'"

"Sir, you are trippin' me out. I barely meet you, and you have me running from the Romans. Now you don't know about newspapers, but you know the *Greek* word for 'crap.' Why don't we *cut the crap* and you tell me how I got here and how to get home." I could hear my mother saying, "There is no excuse for rudeness," with her patented look of disapproval, but I was in no mood for entertainment.

John shook his head, his long beard waving like a fish tail.

"What?" I asked.

"Young man, I have been around for a good while, almost more years than I can count, but I have never seen *that*."

"Seen what?"

"Someone cut crap," he replied, like a boy venturing his first curse word. "Can you do that?"

"Just an expression." He was funny, but I didn't laugh.

"Do they have a special sword to cut crap with or perhaps a tool they call the crap cutter?" He was clearly enjoying himself.

"Sir," I said, subduing my mingled exasperation and anxiety, "can you please tell me how I got here and how to get—"

"I believe that would be the Holy Spirit," John interrupted, his eyebrows moving like Charlie Chaplin's.

"I've never experienced anything like this. How could I go from my house to this cave? I guess my wife has been right all along . . ."

He waved his left hand, obviously humoring me.

"She's been telling me for years that I was losing my mind." I smiled wryly.

"The Holy Spirit," he persisted. "This has the fingerprints of the Holy Spirit all over it."

"But why? How? And how do I get home?"

"No one knows *how* the Holy Spirit does things," he said. "Such is a mystery beyond thought. But you are safe here with me. Take a few deep breaths, and try to calm down."

"But where is *here*? Where *are* we? And who are the *Romans*?" I pressed.

"I returned a few hours ago," John replied simply.

I struggled to hide my irritation. "Returned from *where*?"

"From Ephesus. Jesus asked me to make the journey back for a few days on a mission."

"Jesus? Ephesus? What are you talking about?"

"You do know Jesus, do you not?" he asked, shifting the conversation and still giving me no answer about the Romans.

"Yes, I do—I mean, I *believe* in Jesus. I'm a theologian, or at least I used to be, but I'm not sure about anything anymore."

"Have you not *met* Jesus?" His tone was serious. Almost detective-like.

"In person?" I asked.

"Of course," the old man said as if I *had* lost my mind, and in a way that gave me the strange feeling our meeting was not a shock to him.

"Well, no, not exactly. Jesus died and rose again over two thousand years ago. I have studied Christology for years, but I haven't exactly met Jesus personally."

He raised his white eyebrows.

"Wait a minute," I said hastily, latching onto something. "You say you came from Ephesus?"

"I did," he responded, as if this were quite unremarkable.

"Ephesus, like the ancient city in Asia Minor?"

"Ephesus, the city, yes," John declared, clearly puzzled by my line of questioning. "I used to live right here, but I was freed to live in Ephesus."

Oh, crap, I thought. "Where are we now?"

"This little part of the world is called Patmos, and—"

"Patmos! That's halfway around the world from where I live. Totally impossible. Is this some kind of joke?" I demanded, feeling helpless again.

"Believe me, there have been many days when I wished this was a joke, but it is not. Only the Holy Spirit knows how you got here, but you are here now, with me on the isle of Patmos, and—"

Before he could finish his thought, the realization hit me like a frying pan between the eyes. I shouted, "John! Patmos! Cave!"

He jumped back, his shadow dancing on the ground behind him, then slowly composed himself. As he did so, he turned both arms and hands upward, cocked his head, and stared at me as if thinking, *Well, bless his heart, the lights are on, but ain't nobody home.*

Staring back at the old man staring with pity at me, I thought, *Willy Wonka is looking pretty sane about now.* My heart grew frantic. "Well, John of Patmos, I guess you're going to tell me *now* that you are the son of *Zebedee.*"

He didn't have to say a word; I could see it in his eyes. "My father *was* Zebedee, a fisherman. I, too, was a fisherman and then became a disciple of Jesus. Some call me Elder, others Apostle."

"Yeah, right—and *I* am *Moses*," I exclaimed. "But I will have a little of what you're smokin'. We can call it 'tokin' on the Patmos.'"

He looked at me like I had an IQ of 0.2, which I countered with sarcasm.

"Well, John, son of Zebedee, Elder-slash-Apostle, I guess you'll tell me *now* that this is the Lord's Day and that you've been 'in the Spirit.'"

"It is," the old man responded, which astonished me. The cave seemed to shake, as if connected to his heart. "I *am*, and so are *you.*"

"I have no clue what is happening, but you have obviously been in some kind of spirits if you think you are *the* Apostle John himself and that this is *the* isle of Patmos."

"Young man," he answered, raising his voice slightly, "I do not know how you got here or why you dress in such strange clothes, but I am quite certain that I *am* John and that I am an apostle of Jesus—and that this," he concluded dramatically, spreading out both arms, "*is* Patmos."

"No! No! No! You can't be serious," I cried out, every nerve in me twitching, knowing that I had completely lost the plot.

"Of course I am serious," John said in a soft voice. "Why would I not tell the truth?"

His calm manner brought me a little peace. I got hold of myself, finally able to apologize. "I mean no disrespect, sir; forgive me. This is all kind of a shock and a mystery to me. I have traveled a lot, but I have never been to Patmos."

"You are here now," he said with a wink and a sanctuary smile. "Come sit. You must be tired from your journey. I will find my food and water. Then we can talk."

Sweat beaded on my face as I realized that he was dead serious, and I was marooned on some damned orange island with an apostolic head case, running from Romans. Adrenaline ran wild through me. My guts wrenched; it felt like I had caught a whale on a fly rod and got jerked off the boat. I grabbed my head with both hands—trying to stop myself, hold on to myself, or perhaps keep my mind from running out of my skull. *No way can this be happening.* My hands shook, then my body, and I lost it— lost control, lost everything—and fell to the ground like I had been beaned by a rising fastball.

SHE

Flat on my back, I came to hearing someone whispering above my head, but I couldn't make it out. After what seemed a few moments, the smoky halos in my eyes melted away, and the old man's face came into focus inches above mine, his long, white beard draped around me. Holding my head in his right arm, he gently wiped my face with a damp cloth.

Over a faint new undercurrent of hope, panic struck me again. Apparently this was not a dream. "What in the flying name of Jehoshaphat is going on? Where am I? Where is my family? This cannot be!"

"You are safe, my friend. You are safe," John assured me. "Can you get up?"

"I think so," I replied shakily.

He grabbed my hand and helped me up. *He is amazingly strong*, I thought, as he turned me around and slowly escorted me through the darkness to a small room just inside the cave and to our left, which I hadn't even noticed before.

"Sit here," he said, gesturing toward a flat rock beside what must have been his place to sleep. "I will get some more water. There's a fountain in the deep part of the cave." He padded off.

I glanced around. Dazed as I was, I was surprised at how small the room appeared. At six feet tall I had to stoop to get inside, but once I did the room turned out to be spacious. It was shaped like a bubble, the walls and floor and ceiling a monotonous earthy brown, not smooth but not jagged, either. Three simple oil lamps burned, exactly the kind you see in Sunday school pictures. They lit the room perfectly, although it crossed my mind that the room had more light than three oil lamps could possibly provide.

The old man's sleeping quarters—a pile of faded, dusty blue and purple and red rags on the floor, with no mattress or pillow—looked like they hadn't been slept on in years. I shook my head to get the cobwebs out, my heart sinking at the thought of anyone having to sleep on such a rat's nest. *Three lamps, two flat rocks—it looks like maybe he's expecting a visitor*, I thought. Then I noticed some writing on the walls in Greek and some in what appeared to be Aramaic. But before I could investigate, John returned with the water.

I had come to myself by that time, although no longer sure what "myself" really meant, if ever I knew. I laughed as I suddenly thought of my friend Julio and his favorite expression—"crazy as a road lizard."

"Here is some water and bread," John said gently. He knelt beside me, wide-eyed as I drained his whole pitcher of water.

"You don't have water in your country?" he asked, laughing.

"Forgive me. I was so dry I was pootin' dust."

A quaint half smile played on his ancient face. "Pootin' dust?" he asked, his eyes catching the light of the flickering lamps as he tilted his head.

"Just an expression, sir."

"What does it mean?"

"It means 'seriously thirsty.' Thank you for the water, and the bread." I was grateful to have both but the bread tasted like a stale water cracker. I nodded politely, handing back his clay pitcher with both hands. Then I ventured, "Did we just have the conversation I think we had?"

"Young man, only the Lord knows what goes on inside your head," he muttered, chuckling under his breath.

"Well, whatever's happening here, you're going to have to give me a few minutes—or days—to figure it out. Come to think of it . . ." I looked up, my face flashing sarcasm again. "If by some miracle you *are* the Apostle John and this *is* Patmos, how can you be speaking *English*—with a *Southern* drawl?"

At that the ancient brother rose and spun around, his eyes glittering with adventure. "So *that* is the language we are speaking. English, with a Southern drawl," he declared in an exaggerated accent, sounding like he had watched Foghorn Leghorn cartoons all his life.

I thought of asking him about the cartoon, but if he had no clue about newspapers, explaining a cartoon would be hopeless. So I sat quietly, eating a piece of bread, still trying to grasp what was really happening. "Sir," I spoke definitively, "I am quite certain that English with a Southern drawl was not spoken in the time of Jesus."

He perked up as if with another clue. "Do you *not know* the Holy Spirit?" he asked. I thought the room, or at least the air, shimmered.

"I have studied the doctrine of the Holy Spirit for years." I paused. "But I don't know what I know anymore."

The crow's-feet tightened around John's eyes as he squinted and quietly moaned. "Are you Greek?" He laughed as he sat down beside me. Before I could respond he slowly mouthed the words *studied the doctrine of the Holy Spirit*, with emphasis on each word. It struck me as a statement and as a question and something of a revelation all at the same time.

He tapped his finger on his lips, then said, "The Holy Spirit is no 'doctrine,' whatever that may mean. The Holy Spirit," he declared with considerable delight, "is a person, the lover of communion and *the master of communication*. Over the years I have spoken many languages, and most of the time I was not sure which one. I trust the Holy Spirit. If the Spirit wants me to speak your language, then your language it will be, Southern drawl and all." His eyes twinkled. "I am from southern Galilee, by the way."

It was obvious that he was fond of and respected the Holy Spirit, which I didn't think was impossible in itself, just different from my own experience and intriguing.

"That sounds like a pretty cool miracle," I ventured. "I'm in on that."

"You do know," he said with a wry smile, "that when you say things like that, the Holy Spirit takes them seriously?"

"Things like what?"

"I'm in on that."

"Did I say something wrong?" I felt a sudden wave of dread, as if I'd opened a door to an even more bizarre world.

"Not at all," he answered. "The Holy Spirit never ignores our wills. She nurtures us in our blindness, and when we give her an honest moment, she can make a lot of good things happen. I don't know how she does it, but she can even work backwards and forwards in our lives at the same time."

She? "Hold on, dude. Wait. It is a stormy Sunday morning, or at least it was. I'm headed to get the paper when by some crazy serendipitous twist I end up in this cave with you. All I want is to get home, and then you hit me with Patmos, John the Apostle of Jesus—and now the Holy Spirit as a *she*."

"Does that surprise you?" He turned away, pondering and apparently ignoring my quest for home. "What is this word *dude*? The Spirit does not give me a translation of it."

"Just an expression, like 'man' or 'brother.'"

"Is it good?"

"It can mean a lot of things, depending on the context, I suppose, but I use it in a good way. You could substitute your name in place of 'dude' and get the point." Then I added for good measure: "I mean no disrespect."

John stood up, rubbing his beard with his left hand. "It always intrigues me when she doesn't give me a translation," he finally murmured in wonder, turning back towards me. "I think I understand why. She likes names, actual persons. She is not so fond of words like *dude*."

"To be honest, I've tried to stay away from the Holy Spirit. But in any case this is not the question on my mind at the moment."

He looked as if he could hardly believe his ears. "Why would anyone try to stay away from the Holy Spirit?"

"I don't like ghosts," I blurted, with more force than I intended.

"Ghosts?" he exclaimed, his white eyebrows springing so high I thought they might come off his face.

"Um, 'spirit' is translated as 'ghost' in the Scriptures I grew up reading."

At that the old man grabbed his face with both hands, spun around, and shouted again, "Ghost? Horrible translation. Who could possibly find assurance with a divine ghost? What kind of comforter can a *ghost* be?

Young man, you must get that changed." Then, at the sight of my stricken expression, he said more quietly, "The Holy Spirit is no ghost. She is a beautiful person, the most beautiful of all, too beautiful for our thoughts."

"Well," I replied, rallying, and managing in the irrationality of this day to find my theological bearings for a moment, "if the Spirit is so personal, why weren't we given a name to use for the Spirit? You know, like Jesus and Father?"

"We *are*," he whispered, his face alight.

"That name is not in the Scriptures—not even in any of the writings of John the Apostle." I rose, my shadow now dancing against the wall. "But I repeat, that is *not* what we need to talk about at the moment . . ."

"Her name is spoken everywhere," the old man replied with simple authority, ignoring me again. "She speaks it to every person. Most can't hear it or say it yet. You, too, have a name known only to the Lord, which the Holy Spirit speaks to you always. One day you will hear it clearly, and then you will know who you are—and you will be able to say her name as well."

I sighed. "Can the Holy Spirit get me home?"

"Perhaps that is why you are here," John said, smiling as if he understood something I didn't. "The Lord likes threes."

"Threes?" Now I was utterly baffled.

"Jonah. You know."

"You are enigmatic, sir. Yes, I know the story of Jonah, but what does it have to do with me being here or with me getting home?"

"I have a hunch," he said in a tone of anticipation, "that like Jonah in the whale, you will be here with me for three days."

"So after three days, I can get back home?"

"Or *find* it," he answered mysteriously.

"Find it? What is that supposed to mean?" My body flinched as I asked the question as if it was trying to tell me something, but all I could think of was Jonah in the whale and of being completely off the radar for three days. My wife and children will be scared to death. But I found myself grinning as I thought of my son, John Williams, and his cavalry squad. He will have them armored up and scouring the earth to find me. They will come through, I was sure.

I turned back to John, waving my left hand in confidence and with a slight touch of defiance. "So you are telling me that *this* is the belly of the beast?"

"The belly of the beast is where Jesus meets us all."

Experience was written all over his face, and I could tell by his confidence that he knew what he was talking about, but his words also struck me as something of a personal challenge, a dare even, like I stood on the road to discovery if I really wanted it.

"Sir, I have searched for *life* from the day I exited my mother's womb; three more days—if this is real—I can handle, if my son doesn't find me first."

"We will see." He chuckled, his cheeks glowing. "We will see."

I had no idea what we were really talking about or what to expect next, but I knew somehow that I could trust this old man. He definitely didn't seem like the type to mislead me or anyone for that matter. Confident that my son would find me or I would find my way home in three days, I let my defenses down, and the theologian in me kicked into gear. I could not help but ask why he referred to the Holy Spirit as "she."

John smiled with satisfaction, as if he had accomplished a little mission of his own, and then his face shifted, like we were beginning an adventure. He drew in a breath. "Dear brother, the Holy Spirit is beyond 'he' *or* 'she'—or that horrible 'it' of the Greeks. But the Holy Spirit is spoken of in feminine terms throughout the Scriptures."

"Really?" I asked, settling into the security of my theological mind. "I have read the Scriptures many times," I replied, intrigued and, strange to me, warming to the subject, "and there is no 'she' or anything hinting at feminine identity with reference to the Holy Spirit, not in any English translation I've ever read."

The old man suddenly looked years younger as he paced around his room, like a coach on the sidelines before a big play. "Do you know the first part of Genesis?" He raised his arms and riveted me with his gaze.

"I think I do. 'In the beginning, God created the heavens and the earth. And the earth was formless and void, and the Spirit of God hovered over the abyss of the deep.'"

"Right you are," he declared, sounding uncannily like my old professor.

"But the word for 'Spirit' in Hebrew is feminine throughout the sacred Scripture. Why would someone leave that out of the translation?"

"Wait," I responded, though part of me felt like I should keep my mouth shut. "Are you saying that the word for 'Spirit' is feminine from the beginning of Genesis all the way through the Hebrew Scripture?"

"Of course." He struck a pose that made me think he was regarding me as his pupil, perhaps, and he had just led me to an important insight, although the significance of what I was supposedly seeing was a mystery to me.

As a theologian I had studied the ancient biblical languages, and while a long way from being an expert, I was shocked that I had never noticed or heard that the word *Spirit* was feminine in the Old Testament. I reckon I shouldn't have been too surprised, as even at the moment I could not recall the Hebrew word for it.

"'Spirit' is feminine in our Aramaic language, too," the old man added, interrupting my thoughts. "This is terrible. I must pray . . ."

With that he lifted his hands high and with open eyes started praying, "Blessed are you, Holy Spirit, Lord and giver of life, lover of our souls, keeper of our hearts, wonder of the cosmos." He had power in his words. I could feel it in the marrow of my bones. But then came strange words, at least to my ear, as the room seemed to swirl like a disco ball had descended and the light show had begun. Yet as bizarre as it was, I knew that *this* was more real than my own heartbeat—simple, good, utterly free, and beautiful.

I dropped like a stone to kneel, but John grabbed my arm and lifted me to stand beside him as he prayed, gazing upward. The hair on the back of my neck bristled, my heart stopped, and though my feet were on the ground I felt weightless—or maybe I was even floating. Fear, sadness, and every shred of my ever-present despair vanished. Pure wonder and more light filled the cave, passing in and out of us both. It felt like warm oil was being poured over my head, anointing me in authentic goodness yet flowing somehow from the inside.

Still in my body, but also beyond it, I felt connected to the One who is connected to all creation. I knew it was true.

Then I started seeing things, which unnerved me. At first I couldn't make them out, but as I focused I could tell that I was staring into a huge box of treble hooks, not neatly packaged but gnarled, entangled. "Your mind," I heard. It was not the old man's voice, and I did not understand. But I realized that I was seeing my own blindness—a terrifying confusion every bit as dark as my first hours in the cave. My mind was *broken*, which shocked my pride. My heart shuddered as I feared that my unworthiness would surely ruin my place in this moment. But *I* was in this moment, *all of me*, in the light. The light, the joy, was deeper than me—deeper in me than my own twisted eyes. *How can this be?*

I heard a hint of a song as I felt myself expanding, becoming more real perhaps, more open and ready for this life or this astounding Person. Then it all simply ended.

We stood still together in the center of the room. I didn't know what to say. It is rare that I have no words, but this episode made the rest of the day's weirdness seem tame by comparison. John was silent as if storing the joy. It dawned on me that he was simply enjoying her—the Spirit!—or maybe even enjoying her enjoying him, a thought as foreign to me as Pluto.

Some moments later, a bit overwhelmed and dazed but feeling greatly honored, I broke the silence. "Sir, is that what you mean by 'praying in the Spirit on the Lord's Day'?" It was a genuine question, but I also had ulterior motives, figuring that if by chance he was the Apostle John he would recognize his own words from the book of Revelation.

"Yes, young man," he replied with an odd wink, "but that was just getting on the chariot, if you know what I mean."

"I have no idea if I do, but I think I like *her*—that sounds so strange coming out of my mouth."

"Strange, perhaps," he responded, holding his arms toward me, "but it has the ring of truth about it, don't you think?"

"I definitely do. She is so real."

"The Holy Spirit is as deep as the ocean," he declared, smiling with satisfaction, "and as simple as air."

"I am not sure how much of this—or of her—I can take."

"She has plenty of time. This is about being loved. Give yourself to her. That is how life becomes more real to you."

"It's not a cave when she is here."

"She never leaves us. *Never.* We do not yet have wineskins stout enough to hold her presence."

HISTORY

"Oh, dear," John mumbled, offering me a seat, "I've forgotten my hospitality. What is your name? What is your country?"

"And I have forgotten mine. Tell me about yourself."

"I asked first." His look made it abundantly clear that I was to speak first, and I didn't argue.

"My name is Aidan Williams Macallan. Like I said, I'm from Brandon, Mississippi, which is a state in the United States of America on the other side of the world from Patmos. I mentioned that I'm married. My wife's name is Mary, and we have four children, mostly grown now. I travel and teach about God and history and some psychology, but to be honest, these days I do not know who I am and what my life is really about."

He gazed into my eyes with compassion without saying a word, which had the strange effect of opening my heart to hurt that I had long buried. To my surprise, I continued. "I have earnestly studied many things, but something critical is missing in my life. I feel empty and lost, and many days I have felt a great pain inside. I have searched and searched but found no answer. Well, that is not exactly true. I have always known that Jesus is the answer, but I do not know *how*. In fact"—I was totally shocked that the words were coming out of my mouth—"there were times when I wanted to end it all."

My words hung in the silence between us, as if they were waiting for my guts to come out with them.

The ancient man's beautiful gaze held fast in compassion, and I felt safer than I could ever remember. Never in my life have I seen eyes full of such understanding. I thought he was praying for me, and I am sure now that he was. He did not say a word, but I could feel the room becoming a sanctuary for me.

Then I suddenly saw myself as a little boy on our front porch swing where I grew up. I was standing across the porch watching myself, as weird as that may sound, but it was real to me at that moment. Little Aidan was swinging by himself. I smiled at him, or me as a young boy. But then I saw his eyes. He wasn't just swinging; he was trying to find comfort, trying to get away, to escape. *My God, what the hell happened to me?* I asked myself, starting to tremble.

John spread out his arms, and I sensed his heart, too, and it seemed to me that I was being embraced by the cosmos. "Welcome, Aidan from Missi—that is a hard word to say."

"Mississippi," I pronounced slowly, and the change of thought brought a little calm to my heart.

"What does it mean, this Mississippi? All names have meaning, except perhaps for your 'dude.'" He smiled.

"It's an Indian word. It means 'the Father of Waters.'"

"Mother of pearl," the old man erupted. "That would explain your thirst."

"I see you haven't lost your sense of humor in this desolate orange world," I said, deflecting the rather scary intimacy of the moment.

"The Lord's humor is everywhere, including here." He looked up and around as if seeing things that I did not.

"Now, tell me about yourself."

He drew in a breath as he sat reflecting, then said, "I am John, as I told you, born in Galilee. My father was Zebedee, my mother Salome. My brother, James, and I were fishermen with our father. I became a disciple of John, and then Jesus called me to follow him." He paused, I assumed

34

to gather his thoughts, but his face looked more like he was summoning a presence, or acknowledging one. Then I could tell that he was feeling honored, extraordinarily so, as he said proudly, "I am an eyewitness to Jesus's glory, young brother."

Like an idiot, I spoke before I thought. "So, we are back to John the Apostle of Jesus again?"

"You don't believe me, Aidan of Mississippi?" he asked in a way that disarmed me, and I suddenly felt foolish for doubting him.

"After what just happened, I am beginning to. And you've been very kind to help me. But to believe that you are *the* Apostle John is a bit of a stretch, to say the least. According to our history, the beloved disciple of Jesus died in Ephesus about sixty years after Jesus's ascension, following his exile on the isle of Patmos." As the words came out of my mouth, the volcano of emotions I had managed to calm down erupted again. "That was over two thousand years ago!"

"You mentioned that earlier. What do you mean, over two thousand years ago?" he asked, a little bewildered, although it seemed that he was far less surprised by this whole business than I was.

"Today is December 15 in the year 2013. We date the years from the birth of Jesus, and that was two thousand and thirteen years ago."

He crossed his right arm over his stomach and lifted his left hand to support his chin, thinking. "I *am* old, and my mind surely strays sometimes, but I am quite certain that I am not *two thousand years* old. Nor am I *dead*—yet. So, then, are you saying you are from the future?"

"Exactly. If you are John the Apostle, then there are over two millennia between your time and mine."

"Maybe you have your own spirits," he replied, enjoying himself.

This old codger doesn't miss much, I thought. "My dear friend, I don't know what to make of this; I'm as confused as a butter bean. But I do know this is the year 2013. Or was, where I came from."

"Butter bean?"

"Just another expression."

"What does it mean, young Aidan?"

I moaned to myself. "To be honest, I don't really know; it's just a phrase I've heard most of my life. I think it has to do with butter coming from milk and a bean growing from a vine, so a butter bean has to be confused about what it is."

"Mother of pearl," the old man erupted again, raising his hands. "That is the problem."

I almost asked him about his own bizarre little phrase, but I was more interested in what he was seeing. "The problem? What are we talking about?"

"The butter bean. You said it was confused about what it is."

"I did, but—"

"That is the problem," he interrupted, carefully enunciating his words.

"The problem with what?" I wasn't sure if he was speaking about me personally or in generalities.

"Adam's race." He waved his hand as if it were as obvious as sunshine.

"*What* is the problem with Adam's race?"

"Like your butter bean, we are confused! *We cannot see what is.*"

"Amen to that," I replied, feeling doubly lost.

"We don't know *who we are*," he continued.

"*I* certainly don't know who—or where—*I* am," I replied, half serious and half trying to find a little comic relief.

He mumbled for several seconds, rising to stretch, then stopped and spoke. "Aidan of Mississippi, I have no reason to doubt you, and I know *I* tell the truth, so perhaps we are both correct."

"Or both crazy." I lifted my hands and rose reflexively to pace the room myself.

"Strange travel happens to some people—Philip, for example. After he baptized the Ethiopian eunuch, he was snatched away in the Spirit and found himself in Azotus."

I walked around the room, letting out a sigh or two, eventually turning to face the old man as he now sat back down on his rock. "Yes, but did Philip ever travel into the past, the *remote* past, two thousand years into the past?"

John didn't seem terribly bothered by the thought. "If the Spirit can carry people across space in an instant, why can't she do the same with time?" Technically it was a question, but it surely seemed to me that John was stating what he regarded as simple fact.

"I believe you, Aidan; I believe you have been brought to me from the future in the wonder of the Holy Spirit."

"So, what do we do?"

"There is not much to do around here except pray and write, watch the birds and other creatures. Now that you are here we can talk. We have time. You must humor an old man and tell me everything that's taken place. Two thousand years! A lot can happen in that length of time."

You're telling me, I thought, as I noticed two bugs fighting just beyond my feet, or perhaps they were trying to mate. I laughed before I resumed. "*History*. You want me to tell *you* about history?"

"According to you, there has been over two thousand years of it, so what happened? Tell me about the churches."

"Whoa," I said. "Wait a minute! If by some psychedelic, scientifically impossible trick with prisms I have time traveled into the past and you are John the Apostle, we are not wasting time having me tell you about history. *I* have fifty thousand questions for *you*." My heart leapt at the thought, although in the back of my mind I was still thinking about seeing myself as a little boy and of what that could possibly mean.

"Well, young Aidan of Mississippi, I have wonderful visions and see beautiful and shocking things in the Holy Spirit and even meet unusual people from time to time, but you are my *first* visitor from the year 2013. So I have questions, too."

"I have it," I shouted, as a simple thought came to mind—one that I was sure would put to rest the question about the apostle's identity.

The old man's face lit up with sheer excitement.

"'In the beginning was the Word,'" I declared as solemnly as I knew how.

John jumped to his feet, stared a hole through my soul, and picked up without a hitch:

> . . . and the Word was face to face with God, and the
> Word was God. He was in the beginning face to face
> with God. All things came into being by him; and apart
> from him nothing came into being that has come into
> being. In him life was; and the life was the light of men.

His voice carried undiluted and unpretentious authority, and as he spoke the room brightened as if saluting. I had never heard a voice with such depth and passion and conviction—and *life*. I felt my heart give in, despite the questions in my mind, and take a step toward believing that this could actually be happening.

The ancient brother looked oddly at me and asked with a touch of incredulity, "So *you* know *my* gospel? I only wrote it a few months ago."

I was quiet for a while, collecting myself. Finally I answered, "Sir, you may have only finished your gospel a few months ago—assuming you are really John—but from where I come from that happened a long, long time ago. Your writings have been around for *ages*, and they have been translated into practically every language on earth. I have read your gospel and your letters—and those written by Paul and Peter—many times. Hundreds, if not thousands, of books have been written on your gospel! I can't count the sermons that I have heard preached from your work. Yours is the fourth gospel—*The Gospel according to Saint John.*"

John slowly took a seat. Tears streamed down his cheeks and disappeared into his beard. As thick as I am, even I knew instantly that such news, strange as it must have sounded to him, made his heart jump with hope.

Full of wonder, I sat beside the old man in silence. I was not about to interrupt it this time.

"The Gospel according to Saint John?" he repeated after a long, emotionally loaded pause.

I could feel his satisfaction. "Yes, sir. The New Testament is made up of four Gospels—those written by Matthew, Mark, and Luke, as well as your own—letters from you, Paul, and—"

"Slow down, young man. What is this New Testament?"

"Sorry. I forgot where I was or which time zone or millennium we're in." *Can this actually be real? How do I talk with a man in the first century?* I drew a slow breath and marshaled my thoughts. "Okay, here is the quick version. As you know, after the ascension of Jesus, the gospel spread across the Mediterranean basin and beyond. Peter and Paul had wide and very fruitful ministries, vindicated powerfully by the Holy Spirit, and then they were both martyred in Rome."

"Yes, I know," he whispered solemnly, and I realized that I had treated the deaths of those blessed brothers rather flippantly. "Peter and Paul were the best of all men, no stopping them. My heart was ripped open when I heard the news. But mark my words, the Holy Spirit never wastes a tear, and she is especially powerful with the witness of those slain for the Word and the testimony of Jesus." He reached for his satchel, opened it, and offered me some more of his bread, for which I was exceedingly grateful.

The toasted flat bread was not quite as light as New Orleans' French bread, but it had more flavors. I could taste garlic and olive oil and a fruitiness that was new to me, perhaps dates, I thought. "Thank you. This is wonderful. Is it from a new batch? It seems better than the bread you gave me before."

"Perhaps your tastes are awakening as you are, young brother." I was not sure what he meant.

"I hope you have enough. This is quite good."

John raised his left eyebrow, an expression laden with possibilities, which stirred my imagination. He motioned for me to continue talking.

"After the age of the apostles—at least that's what we call it in my day—letters about Jesus were everywhere. Some were clearly written by Jesus's close followers; others were not."

"Yes," the old man mused, "we have that problem now already. Diabolos is up to his usual tricks, but he is doomed; the Light wins in the end, you know." He paused abruptly. "Sorry. Please go on."

"But I want to hear more of what you have to say about Diabolos and everything else."

"He is not worth the time. Please continue."

"Okay, but you have to understand that I want to hear *you* talk, too—about your gospel and your letters."

"In time, brother, in time. Take a deep breath. I am an old man who wants to know, not envision, the future. You are a blessing to me. Do continue."

I felt my heart tear. *Who in their right mind wouldn't want to bless an old man, especially this one? On the other hand, who would dare miss an opportunity like this to listen?* "All right then," I finally responded, "but I want to hear the past, told by someone who actually was, or *is*, there."

"You told me you've been reading my gospel and my letters. They are the best I could say. Keep going, Aidan. Tell me the tale."

"Well, then," I said, standing up in order to move around like I do when teaching, still holding one last piece of bread, "most of the letters written by the apostles, including yours, were copied and passed around to other believers. In time the church found it necessary to make a statement about which ones it considered to be inspired by the Holy Spirit. It took several hundred years, but eventually, and not without politics and heated debate, it was decided that twenty-seven letters were from the Spirit. Your gospel and three letters and the *Apocalypse*—we will definitely have to talk about that book later—were among them. Together they formed the New Testament, which was added to the Hebrew Bible to compose the Christian Scriptures."

"I wrote many letters. Did only three make it into your New Testament?"

"Many? How many?"

"Well, seven, of course."

A chill ran down my spine. "What were they about?"

"Jesus and living in the light and other issues with the churches. Two of my favorites were on the Holy Spirit."

"Sir, you have to tell me what you wrote—or, better yet, what you think—about the Holy Spirit."

John sat pondering, as if sizing me up to get a read on how much of the Holy Spirit I could handle. "It is not wise to *tell* people *about* the Holy Spirit; it is best to help them *experience* the Holy Spirit for themselves."

With his words I suddenly felt like I had been fighting my way through a thick jungle all my life, but now I stood at last on a beach with a warm breeze hitting my face and the wide ocean in front of me. I repeated his words to myself as my face flushed like I was mistakenly given an extraordinary gift intended for someone else. But something inside cheered me on, and I found my embarrassment turning into hope. I ventured forward shyly but wide-eyed with possibility. "So how can I experience more of the Holy Spirit?"

"She is already in you, my brother," he said simply yet definitively. "*Ask her to make herself known.*"

"Whoa. That's daunting. I need a little space on that one. Like I told you, until I arrived here I have been afraid of the Holy Ghost."

"Do you like parties?" John asked, which I thought odd, yet at the same time I felt that he was trying to help me take another step on the road of discovery.

"Of course. Most everyone likes parties. But we were talking about the Holy Spirit."

He looked around the room slowly and then into my eyes, his own bright with marvel. He seemed to be trying to communicate with me without words. "Young Aidan," he finally said, "the Holy Spirit is the *life* of the party."

"That's a little too off the wall for me," I said, and then, thinking I might have used yet another impenetrable idiom, added, "It's hard for me to think of the Spirit that way."

"Joy, young brother, the Holy Spirit is joy in person," he replied.

"But, sir," I said, pacing again, "most folks in my time, including me, think of the Holy Spirit as an impersonal force or some kind of invisible power."

"The Holy Spirit certainly has power." He chuckled, waving his left hand. "But she is about fellowship." I could tell he was speaking out of his own journey and experience and not merely spouting off theological axioms as I often do. "In fellowship life and joy come to be."

His ideas about the Spirit struck me as too simple, but my heart was having another conversation. Then a question came: "Did you not write in your gospel that the Holy Spirit would convict the world of sin? That doesn't sound like joy; it sounds scary like judgment."

"'Convict' is not a good translation. 'Expose' is better. The Holy Spirit exposes our darkness and unbelief to give us eyes with which to behold Jesus."

THE PATMOS SHUFFLE

The tone of his voice told me that John figured I'd had all I could handle of the Holy Spirit at the moment and he wanted to return to an earlier part of our conversation. No sooner had the thought crossed my mind than he asked, "Young Aidan, you mentioned the church, as if there was only one. Is there only *one* church left in your time?"

"Now *that*," I said, "is a long, long story."

He chuckled. "We are in a cave, brother, in the side of a cliff on the isle of Patmos. I think we have time."

"I know, but history is complicated." I sighed, then took another deep breath, thinking of my friend's road lizard.

"Why don't you start with the churches? What happened?"

He seemed remarkably at ease with this whole situation, which I found rather incomprehensible. Out of nowhere I had appeared from the future, and he was quite content to accept it as a simple fact. He genuinely wanted to talk, eager to hear about history. At the same time, I had a sense that he had been sent on a mission, and the mission might well be me. I was out of my comfort zone, with no control, yet I felt like I was being led into an unknown good. I couldn't help but wonder how all this related to my seeing little Aidan.

"Okay, then," I said, not exactly sure how to proceed. "As *you* well know, as the gospel spread, it came into conflict with entrenched belief systems. Jesus stirred up a rather large hornet's nest."

"A *cosmic* one," the old man erupted, full of life. "John used to say, 'The cat's out of the bag, and the cat is the Lion of the tribe of Judah.'"

"That's a great line. It sounds like something John the Baptist would have said."

He picked up quickly. "As sharp as a briar he was and tough as an ox tongue. We had never met a man with such conviction."

"Was he a big man?" I asked quickly. "I imagine John the Baptist as tall and strong, with a bushy beard." I noticed the shadows on the wall as I formed a beard shape with my hands.

"You are a big man, tall *and* wide. 'The Baptist,' as you call him, was not as big as you but larger than life to us and strong in heart. He knew the *Lord* had called him." The apostle's words carried force, a depth and reality that I was not used to.

"You said in your gospel that he was called to prepare the way of the Lord."

"I saw it all firsthand. I was there. John stood down the whole delegation."

"Delegation? I didn't know there was a delegation."

Church history would have to wait; I could see fire in John's eyes as he leaned forward in excitement. "Indeed, must have been twenty of them, the robed religious elite, sent like spies by the Pharisees. They shook their finger at John, demanding, 'Who are you?' The accuser of the brethren tried to have his moment, but John stood strong as a terebinth, staring them down. 'Among you stands,' he shouted, pointing at them and sweeping his arm from one side to another, '*one* whom *you* do not *know*.' In one statement, I tell you, he knocked their self-righteous smirks right off their faces. He shamed them to silence just by the sheer confidence of knowing that he had heard from God. They snatched up their robes and stalked off, muttering to themselves. We cheered."

He paused, obviously reliving the scene and feeling its emotion all over again. Then he shook his head and looked at me. "From that moment the game was afoot." He sounded almost like Sherlock Holmes.

"Sir," I responded, amazed that this conversation was happening, "there are several famous paintings of John the Baptist that people have made over the centuries. Your description reminds me of one by a medieval artist named Matthias Grünewald. It's called *The Crucifixion*. It's a haunting picture, with Jesus hanging on the cross and the Baptist standing beside him, pointing at him with an overexaggerated, bony finger."

"I remember the day and the very moment I first saw it," he said.

"Saw what?" I asked, not at all sure that the old man wasn't talking about Grünewald's painting.

"Jesus's *glory*, of course," he answered, with an odd wink, which I found puzzling, but before I could say anything he went on. "We were in Cana at the wedding, and Jesus turned the water into wine—*good* wine. Never had better since . . ." His voice trailed off as he spoke, remembering. "I always wondered why the headwaiter did not bother to talk to Jesus or to us. He tasted the wine, even commented on its quality, but then went on about his tasks."

As he spoke of the headwaiter's apparent indifference, I thought of my own people-pleasing and how I get so caught up in making sure that everything is just so that I too often miss what is right in front of me.

"When Jesus transformed that water, it was like a glimpse of the transfiguration to me. I saw who he really was or is: the Father's Son, in person, full of the Holy Spirit, with us, with *me*, with *the whole world*. I will never forget that moment. Such astounding humility! The Baptist was the first to see."

"Is it that simple?" I asked. For the moment the truth seemed so palpable I could taste it.

He motioned for me to sit beside him. "Simple? Yes, it is. But we humans are a blind lot, are we not? We have been terribly deceived, but the Holy Spirit is here. She has no quit in her. You can see the Spirit's work best when you look back."

"If you want to know about history, that pretty much sums up the last two thousand years. Both the blindness of humanity and the relentlessness of the Spirit."

"How is that?" he asked, glancing around the room as if listening for the voices of others.

"Looking back, it is clear that there have been times of great awakening, like your time, and then upheaval and confusion and fighting, and things got blurry, and then the truth was recovered again and another awakening, and then we lost the point—"

"Sounds like the sea to me," he interrupted.

"The sea?"

"When the tide is rising, a wave comes in, then falls back over and over, but each time the wave comes in a little farther."

"I'm seriously glad to know that the Holy Spirit won't give up on us until we know the truth. I have searched my—"

"And the truth shall set you free," the old brother cried out, raising both hands.

"Brother John, we need to pass the plate and get you to do the 'lip quiver.'" I snickered. "We could call it 'The Patmos Shuffle.'"

The apostle looked mystified.

"In our day we have TV preachers who are always wanting money, so they get all emotional talking about *Jeeee-Zus* to stir people up. Then they make their lips quiver like they're on the verge of crying and pass a plate around so people can give for the *glowree-o'-Gawd*."

The apostle shook his head and laughed to himself. "What is a TV preacher, and what is this *glowree-o'-Gawd*?"

"You could never imagine," I answered, smiling at the thought. "Well, come to think of it, with your rather wild imagination you might well understand. But let's not waste time on that now. Where were we?"

"We were talking about history, Aidan, the Holy Spirit, John the Baptist, and the first time I saw Jesus as he really is."

"Jesus and his disciples—and I suppose that means you, sir—changed the world. That much is clear. And then things went in a hundred different directions. It seems that the truth in Jesus—"

"Also creates conflict," John interrupted, with not a little sorrow in his voice. "I have no desire to hurt anyone, but look what happened to me— an old man rejected by the ancient people of God, poisoned, and exiled by the false empire. It took me a while, but finally I began to understand." His gaze made me think of a fine tea, subtle with a variety of flavors, in this case sorrow and joy, strength and compassion all fused together into one look, radiating depth and character and *life*. "Jesus told us it would happen."

His eyes now had that veteran warrior look. I knew that hard-won wisdom was on the tip of his tongue.

"The testimony of Jesus always exposes darkness *as* darkness," he said, obviously remembering his adventures and triumphs and losses. "When the light dawns, the darkness reacts—and all the more intensely when the darkness is religious. That, my friend, is the way the kingdom *comes* in this age. We reign with the *Lamb*."

In his presence I now felt as shallow as a thimble, which was embarrassing as I prided myself on being something of a deep thinker. But this brother was a deep *man*. I spoke again when silence would have been wiser.

"I do believe I read somewhere, 'And the light shines in the darkness, and the darkness did not comprehend it.'"

"'Conquer,'" he corrected quickly but with no hint of superiority.

"What do you mean?"

"The word I wrote means 'to conquer or master by comprehension.'"

Shaking my head, I muttered, "I don't understand."

"That's what I call ironic," he joked, sounding like Foghorn Leghorn again. "The darkness," he said, becoming serious, "did not comprehend the light so as to become its master. Ideas, especially dark ones, are no match for the light of Jesus. It takes time."

"Yeah, like over two thousand years," I blurted out, somewhat too sarcastically and certainly too quickly. "And the battle still rages."

"We must stand firm," he declared, looking straight into my eyes. After a pause during which he seemed to be deciding whether to divulge something, he said, "I have seen the end in the Spirit."

My eyes widened; my mind locked in focus. It seemed like I was suddenly in a tunnel of some kind, perhaps a surfer's tube. All I could see was the old man's face. "You have seen the end, the end of the world, of history?"

"I have indeed," he said confidently, smiling like the cat who did in fact eat the canary.

"You have to tell me what you saw," I pleaded.

"Aidan of Mississippi," he replied, with a touch of what I could only take for apostolic swagger, "I saw the appearing of the bright Morning Star." His face flooded with delight. "As I beheld in wonder, the star became the Lamb—" He lifted his arms in adoration, apparently seeing it all again. "The *Lamb*," he exclaimed, turning to me, his brown eyes flashing hope, "upon the Throne of thrones. His light permeating the cosmos, like a vast burning bush—no shadows!"

The profound veneration in the apostle's voice and the image of the Lamb upon the throne filling all with light completely captivated my imagination, stirring the longing in my heart that I had known all my life. I wasn't sure what to say or how to react. I had never met an apostle before, especially one who had such visions and such a huge heart. I sat quietly trying to imagine what he saw. "That must have been breathtaking and inspiring. What did you do?"

"I fell on my knees in joy, of course."

"I wish I could see that. When does the end come?"

"The time is near," John said, not in warning but in compelling hope. I thought of the book of Revelation as he drew in a breath, his face beaming. "We will *all* see Jesus as he is. This I know. Our joy is proclaiming the truth and persevering the tribulation of enlightenment."

After a moment he looked into my eyes. "Aidan, listen," he said, then paused. I could feel his mind working as he looked away for a split second to form his thought, then turned back to me. "Intercession often means bearing the scorn of another's enlightenment. It is the way of the *Lamb*."

"What *all* do you mean by that?" I asked, my mind reeling.

"We will have time to talk some more, but for now you must rest. You have had a long journey, and I have a hunch that you will need strength."

"Is that a good thing?" I asked, not exactly sure I wanted to know.

John walked over, grabbed his pile of rags, and shook the dust out of them, then folded them one by one to make a bed. "You can rest here; it's not much of a bed, but it has served me well. I have had many visions sleeping here." His tone was full of suggestion.

"You are very kind to me. Thank you," I said, unsure of what to expect, but certainly aware of the fact that I was about to have a nap on the pile of rags where John the Apostle himself had slept—on the isle of Patmos.

As I started for the bed of rags, he took a seat again on one of his rocks.

His face was vibrant in the flickering light. "Many, many years ago, when I was a boy," he said in a subdued but weighty tone that commanded my full attention. He had apparently changed his mind about my need for rest. *Or perhaps this is a bedtime story.* Either way, at age fifty-three I had learned that when an old veteran quiets down and picks a story from his youth, it is wise to listen carefully. So I sat eagerly with my heart open.

"I once saw a great eagle that had been caged for many years. So long, in fact, that the bird came to believe it could not fly at all. When it was set free, it merely walked away a few feet and pecked the ground like a yard bird. A man swatted at the eagle with a broom, but it only hopped away. Again and again the man swatted at the great bird, shouting. But each time the bird jumped only a few feet." A fondness became apparent on John's face, which I supposed was from remembering how weird the scene must have been to a boy. I am not so sure now that he wasn't smiling at what he knew was coming my way.

"So finally the man calmly caught the bird and began to walk. We boys followed him, curious to see what he would do. With the eagle in his arms, he walked for several miles until he came to a cliff, and before we could understand what he was up to, the man threw the bird off the cliff." He motioned with his hands, all but horror in his eyes. "We yelled as we ran to the edge of the cliff to see."

I was so captivated that I almost screamed, too. "What happened? Did the bird die?"

"Young Aidan, the bird fell like a stone, as sorrow filled our hearts."

I found myself standing next to him at the edge of a cliff in my mind, leaning over to look at the rocks below to see the disaster unfold. Suddenly, like a monster trout rising to take a fly, my despair rose with a vengeance within me. I could hardly breathe.

The apostle continued his story. "But only feet from certain death on the rocky ground, the bird's wings unfolded, and he began to soar. We boys *shouted* for joy," he said, smiling and spreading his arms wide like an eagle's wings, "and we watched as the bird flew higher and higher." He swirled his left hand, with his face upturned, and whispered, "I can see the eagle sailing in the sky above us in my memory even now."

THE GROVE

When I awoke from my nap, St. John was standing in prayer, as another refreshing breeze swept through the room. He glanced at me with one eye and pointed with his chin at some bread on his rock and the pitcher of water beside it.

"Did you dream?" he asked, a note of anticipation in his voice.

"Dream? I don't think so, or at least I don't remember."

My response obviously surprised him, but he seemed content to shift the subject, like he was changing channels on TV. "Tell me about your world, this Mississippi." Then he stooped over and wrote *The Grove* in the dirt with his left index finger. "What do these words mean?"

"What? How in the wide world do *you* know about The Grove?"

"Oh, I see things," the apostle replied a little facetiously, closing his eyes and striking what I assumed was a visionary pose. "Visions in the Spirit, like I told you." But a moment later his cheeks flushed as he laughed and pointed to my shirt.

I had forgotten my T-shirt. "The Grove" was printed on the front.

"You had me there, for a minute at least."

"Well?"

An idea popped into my head. "I'll make a deal with you. I'll tell you all about The Grove if you tell me what Jesus wrote in the dirt with his finger."

"Jesus was always writing in the dirt, but I suspect you are thinking specifically of the scene with the woman in my gospel?"

"Of course, you left the world hanging on that one. I have had many discussions about what Jesus may have written. My teacher loved that story. I can see his face beaming now, his hand in the air. 'Here is a woman caught in the very act of adultery; how did Jesus respond? He embraced her in forgiveness before she even believed.'"

A smile of great satisfaction swept across the apostle's face. "You have a deal, young Aidan from Mississippi," he declared, reaching out his hand to help me up and leading me to the mouth of the cave and to some fresh air.

We stood quietly for a moment, enjoying the sunshine and the blue sky, and I could feel excitement in his heart. Patmos was starting to seem less orange to me.

"Now, tell me of this Grove."

"Okay, then. The Grove is a stand of beautiful hardwood trees covering about fifteen acres in the middle of the campus of Ole Miss, where I went to college. But The Grove is not only a place; it's people and tents and parties, the best tailgating in the country." I found myself struck dumb by the impossibility of communicating across so many centuries. *How on earth do I communicate The Grove to a man in the first century?*

The apostle folded his arms and leaned against the rock wall in expectation.

Then it hit me. I took a deep breath and let it go. "The Grove is a Mississippi version of the Feast of Tabernacles in a forest like the Cedars of Lebanon, surrounded by fifty buildings about half the size of Solomon's Temple, with an arena twice the size of the Roman Coliseum, with gladiators who don't die but play a game with a ball, with a hundred thousand people watching and laughing, sharing food and drink, and having an altogether *large* time."

He looked out over the expanse of Patmos, I assumed trying to imagine the Grove, then he roared, "That must be a sight to see." He clapped. "I must hear more about this Grove and this large time."

"One day, dear friend, I will cook crawfish for you and take you to The Grove so you can see it with your own eyes." I smiled, knowing this was impossible and that he had no clue what a crawfish was and certainly no way of knowing how we cook them—all of which made me exceedingly hungry for some real food. "But first let me tell you that there are now seven billion people on this planet. Since your day, so to speak, or maybe I should say *this* day, we have discovered that the earth is not the center of the universe and that it is not flat but round—"

"I know," John interrupted, cocking his head. "I have seen our world— from the moon—hanging in the cosmos by the grace of Jesus and Abba, as blue as the Mediterranean Sea, round and beautiful. And I have seen another moon with rings around it, quite breathtaking . . . In a vision, of course," he added quickly, reading my shocked face.

"So you have been to the rings of Saturn in a vision?"

"Is that what they call it?" he asked, still staring over Patmos. "Someone named that amazing place after a pagan god?"

"That they did," I said.

"You have to get that changed in your 2013," he declared, turning toward me, his eyes fully aflame. "This is *Jesus's* cosmos."

"I'm beginning to think that you want me to change the world."

"Jesus has already done that. We are his witnesses. The light must shine in the darkness until the darkness is no more. Now, on with your story." He sat down, propping both arms on his raised knees.

"Well, then, John the Apostle, here it is. We have seven billion people on earth in 2013, in nearly two hundred different countries, each country populated by people of many diverse cultures, and each culture having hundreds of different kinds of food, music, and language. It is quite amazing. And, I might add, there are too many religions to count. The Christian faith alone, I am ashamed to say, has thousands of different factions. Then there is the ever-present Jewish faith, as well as Buddhism, Hinduism, Islam, good old-fashioned pagan earth religions, and hundreds of other philosophies and worldviews."

The apostle listened carefully, as if taking mental notes.

"We have electricity, which is something like lightning that runs through wires into our homes and gives us indoor lighting and a way to heat and cool the inside of our houses. We have covered chariots that we call automobiles; they work by means of thousands of little controlled explosions and don't need any horses to pull them—in fact, they can outrun a hundred horses. We have television, by which we can see ourselves and others and events from around the world as they happen. I suppose it is a bit like the way you see in your visions," I said, as I turned to form the shape of a big-screen TV beside the mouth of the cave, "except these visions appear on screens on the walls, and we can all see them.

"And we have cell phones," I continued, forming a small rectangle with my hands, "through which we can speak and others can hear us across vast distances, even around the whole world. And there's the Internet, YouTube, and Facebook." I threw up my hands, realizing the impossibility of what I was attempting to do, and let my stream of consciousness loose on the apostle. "In my day, we have pocketknives, fishing rods, reels and lures, huge cities much larger than Rome, Black Angus beef, wooden floors, dishwashers and refrigerators, universities, museums, to name a few random things. We have huge iron ships that sail the seven seas, and we can fly in the air in machines. We have even sent men to the moon and back in spacecraft—"

"Mother of pearl," the old brother interrupted. "I have seen those! They look like Egyptian obelisks with fire. You call them spacecraft?"

"We do, and there are people sitting inside the obelisks as they fly into space. We call them astronauts. And we have terrible weapons of war, nuclear weapons."

"I've seen those, too," he replied, his expression changing instantly, now troubled and sad. "They make a great wind and fire and flashing light and noise like quaking mountains, melting people and the earth like wax before a flame of horror."

"Sir, there is so much beauty in our world and so much goodness." As I spoke I became aware of the serenity of Patmos and the peace of its silence, which gave me hope. "In my world, there are mountains and flowers, rivers and waterfalls, and a million colors, music and exquisite art that will move you to weep, people everywhere loving and being loved, brilliant men and women. Yet there is so much sadness and brutality, bitter prejudice, wars and beatings and rapes, abuse and pain, lust, greed, and envy. It is crazy and gut-wrenching."

"The Greeks," John said as he turned to his left and watched a small spider making a web in a crack, then looked up as if surveying the rock formation above us, "always worried about the tragedy in the world, fearful of change as they were. And believe me, I know tragedy firsthand, but tragedy is not the deepest question."

"And what *would* be the deepest question?"

"What is tragedy but missing the good? Yet who said there should be any good? Why is there good in the world, any good at all? That," he declared, lifting his left arm, "is the real question."

"And it is a great one, and I am not going anywhere until I get your answer."

"Jesus." He stood up slowly and headed back into his room.

I followed. It took me a second to recognize that this was his one-word answer to the question. "Sir, I don't want to be argumentative, but what do you mean?"

He took a seat on his rock in no particular hurry, then said, "Jesus shares his goodness with us all, everywhere, my young brother, and the life he enjoys with his Father."

"That is a beautiful thought but way too simple—at least in my world. It's scarcely believable in our day," I responded mostly to myself, my heart yearning to understand.

"Perhaps that is why history has lasted so long?" he replied wide-eyed, seeing the possible answer to what was apparently a long-standing question for him. And I suddenly realized that the apostle knew far more than he was saying at the moment. I could tell that an idea was crossing his mind that he was enjoying. He sat still for a good while, smiling to himself.

"Perhaps," John said seriously yet raising both hands with a flair and tilting his head, "we are all in your Grove but are too blind to have a large time together."

"But," I blurted out, before I could even enjoy the old man's wit, "there are thousands and thousands of Christian factions alone, and we can't even get along with each other. I don't see any way that we can all come together."

"Young Aidan," he said, affection rising in his eyes, and I should say an unbridled confidence in his voice, "we already are."

"Already are what?"

"Together, of course. Jesus did that."

The thought shocked me, and I glanced at the brown wall. Then I looked down at my tennis shoes, which were now virtually orange, or at least orange and brown, and at one of the lamps, which was dying.

The old brother rose and found a black wineskin, which I assumed was full of oil. Just before the lamp died out completely he filled it with oil, and it revived. Somehow I knew that this moment was a parable of sorts, but I couldn't understand. The apostle sat on his pile of rags.

"Sir, even if we were all together in Jesus, in some kind of eschatological way, we are largely clueless about it. How will we ever come to know such togetherness?"

"Time," he replied, with just a hint of self-satisfaction.

"Time? We've *had* over two thousand years," I said, again a little too sarcastically. I was afraid I had offended him.

He lay back unfazed, in a confidence unknown to me. "The Holy Spirit," he whispered with the patience of a sage, "gives us time to make fools of ourselves, so we will long to see with Jesus's eyes." He imitated a blind person suddenly seeing. His words reminded me of George MacDonald's. "This is how we learn. As we do, we see people, even the Romans, with new eyes."

"But we are destroying one another and the planet," I protested, surprised at the grief I was feeling.

The old man lay still, staring silently into space. After a few moments, he blinked and shook his head as if he was waking up. Leaning over and peering straight into my heart, he said, "Young Aidan from Mississippi, freedom . . ."

I took a step toward him to hear.

"Freedom is necessary to our glory in Jesus."

PROLOGUE?

"Sir," I pressed, troubled, "words like *freedom* and *glory* are noble, but I'm afraid that in our day they have become largely empty. Would you tell me what you mean by 'Freedom is necessary to our glory in Jesus'?"

"Now *that*," John said, patting his chest, "is a long story."

"Well," I replied, somewhat disappointed to find the conversation at an end, "to quote an old man I know, 'We are in a cave in the side of a cliff on the isle of Patmos. I think we have time.'"

"That we do, but now I am having a wee rest."

As the apostle napped I made my way outside, although I was so absorbed in my thoughts that I was oblivious to my surroundings. "Freedom is necessary to our glory in Jesus," I mumbled. *What on earth does he mean? What glory? How are freedom and glory related? What is glory?*

Pacing and thinking to the very edges of my imagination, and perhaps beyond, I worked myself into a frenzy, but at last I settled on supposing that the prologue to his gospel was the obvious place to continue our conversation, as if I had a clue what our conversation was actually about.

As I sat down outside, right where the apostle had sat earlier, I could suddenly see myself as a little boy again—this time not in the swing but on the concrete steps by the garage. He or I was gazing at the gigantic magnolia tree in our backyard. That tree was the home of our beloved tree house and the place of many mock battles. It's a wonder we all survived as many times as we fell from its limbs. I stood between little Aidan and the magnolia, facing him. I smiled at his haircut and his tan cowboy shirt with embroidery. I knew that he could not see me, but I looked straight into his face. I almost threw up as I noticed his eyes so full of sorrow. I could hear his thoughts but could not make them out. Feeling his sadness, I mumbled a prayer as to what this could be about.

Out of thin air my grandmother appeared, standing beside the steps, staring down on little Aidan. She wore a green dress, a pearl necklace, and her crazy glasses that always reminded me of a cat. Her graying hair was perfect as usual. I grinned, remembering that we called her Napoleon behind her back—there was no doubt who was in charge of the family. Her lips were moving, but I couldn't hear what she was saying. As she turned to walk away, little Aidan looked down. I could feel him burying something deep in his heart. I wanted to give him a hug, hold him tight, and tell him that he would be fine, that he would marry a beautiful woman, have four children of his own, and travel around the world. He just sat there on the steps looking down. I realized that I was doing exactly the same thing.

I thought of my therapist's first words to me, "Aidan, you are a good man, but I sense a great frustration, a despair in you." I remembered thinking, *Duh. And I'm paying you to tell me this?* But she was actually good, helping in many ways, especially to stop blaming others for my flare-ups of intolerable angst and to pay attention to my pattern of personal disappearance. We even laughed together the day it dawned on me that I had more issues than *Reader's Digest.* She alone encouraged me to face the fact that a part of my despair, or at least a layer of it, was related to Jesus.

I was shocked when she first made the suggestion, but she wasn't saying that Jesus was the source of my depression, only that I was in fact angry with Jesus for not answering me. I had never doubted for a moment in my life that Jesus was the answer to our ills, mine included, but the unanswered question that dogged me was: *How* was he the answer? In over fifty years it hadn't crossed my mind that there was a difference between my Jesus and the real one.

A groan from inside the cave startled me out of my thoughts. *The apostle must be rising from his nap.* He was stretching as I walked in. "Did you sleep well?" I asked, conveniently placing my encounter with little Aidan on a shelf in the corner of my soul, as if such things were inconsequential. *Detached* was my therapist's word. "Sir, I think it would be great if we talked about your prologue." It amazed me that I could shift gears so quickly.

John's look let me know that it was impolite to press an old brother before he had time to get on his feet and to loosen his load. He disappeared for a few minutes, and I did not badger him.

When he returned, he was obviously agitated. "What do you mean, *prologue*?" His voice rose slightly, and he folded his arms, widening his stance.

"*Pro* means 'before,' and *logos* means 'word.' So it would mean 'before word' or 'word before.' You know, the first—"

"I know what the word means," he exclaimed, indignation rising in his eyes.

I was completely embarrassed. Of course he knew; he wrote in Greek after all.

"There is no prologue, no before word in my gospel. I thought you said you had read The Gospel According to Saint John, as you called it?" It struck me that perhaps he needed to go back to sleep. He certainly seemed to have gotten up on the wrong side of his rags.

"Yes, I have read your gospel many times. It is my favorite book in the Scriptures, and I have memorized a lot of it, including the prologue, which is one of the most famous parts."

"Well, then, perhaps you need to read it *again*," he replied, shifting his weight to his left side and moving his right foot forward like he was getting ready to deliver a punch, "because there can be no before word. That is the point of the first sentence of my gospel! If you missed that, you were not paying attention."

"I'm not following you."

"You quoted that first sentence earlier, did you not? And now you are talking about a before word?"

"Yes, I did. 'In the beginning was the Word, and the Word was with

God, and the Word was God.'"

"Exactly!" John nodded, lifting his bushy eyebrows and looking at me like I had a third eye. "What could be *before* the Word? Young man, the Word is Jesus, and he was there in the beginning, the eternal Word, the first Word, the Word *before everything else.* There is no word before Jesus! Has someone in your world put a word *before* Jesus in my gospel?" he demanded, and I realized why Jesus called him a "son of thunder."

"No, no, heaven forbid," I said, feeling horrible that I was frustrating and offending the ancient apostle. "No one put a prologue into your gospel. It begins just as you quoted. But the first part of your gospel people consider your introduction, and some call it the prologue."

"They should call it an introduction then."

"I believe a cup of coffee would be pretty good about now," I mumbled, "or some chocolate."

"What's that?"

"Nothing of note, sir. I was just talking to myself. My favorite line in your gospel says, 'In that day you will know that I am in My Father, you in Me, and I in you.'"

"*That* is the truth of all truths, the heart of the cosmos," the apostle said. Then he raised both hands and cried out, "The light of life, the river, the secret, the mystery, and the glory of it all!" He jumped around, dancing. "Now you are making sense, my young brother." As if I were the one who had written the line and not he himself!

"Please tell me what you were thinking in the first part of your gospel. Your words have astounded the greatest minds through the ages."

"Do you have memory problems?" He chuckled. "You just quoted one of the most important statements in my gospel, the very heart of it. Now you're asking me about the *Word*, as if the two were unrelated."

My heart sank. "I'm beginning to feel as low as a snake in a wagon rut and as confused as a whole garden of butter beans." I snickered, glad the "thunder" was settling down.

John took a seat, ignoring my weak attempt at humor, then looked up and said softly, "Ophis, be gone."

"Ophis?"

"Greek for 'serpent.' This confusion is his *skubala.* He hates *the Word.*"

Surprised, I looked the old apostle in the face but said nothing.

Compassion filled his eyes as he gazed back at me. "Ophis, the serpent of old. Jesus called him 'the father of lies,' 'the author of confusion,' and 'a murderer from the beginning.' That slimy deceiver just tried to slither his way into our fellowship. He tried to arouse my impatience. And he's trying to confuse you about the Word. That's what he does, you know."

Then he calmly but resolutely raised his hands. "Lord Jesus, living Word of God, beloved Son of the Father, in your name we bind Ophis and cast him from our fellowship. No voice, no word shall be uttered in this cave and in our time together except that which proceeds forth from you in your communion with your Father in the song of the Holy Spirit."

I listened in simple awe as John's prayer calmed the troubled seas of my soul. I took my seat beside him.

"Ophis was trying to poison our joy," he said. "I should have noticed more quickly. He smells like rotten cucumbers."

"I smelled that when I first came to the cave."

"Indeed, you did, but he is gone now," he waved his hand. "So, *the Word*," he resumed, with his lively good cheer fully restored. "Jesus is the first, the last, and the only Word of God, the way to turn toward the Father, the truth, the life, the light of the cosmos. I thought you understood that when you quoted, 'In that day you will know that I am in My Father, you in Me, and I in you.' But these are deep truths, and it takes time for them to rise from our hearts. After the Cana revelation, it still took me *years* to understand. Jesus did miracles, drove out demons, healed the sick—because he is the *Creator of all things*. It finally dawned on me that *he* is the *arche*, the source and the meaning of our existence."

"Arche? That means the source, the thing that gives meaning?"

He nodded. "Like in your word *archetype*, I believe."

His ideas were simple but startling. They weren't new, and yet they were. My heart fixated on the way he saw Jesus as the Creator. "It's quite amazing. In all my years of church I have heard plenty of sermons on God as Creator, but I don't know if I have ever heard a single sermon on Jesus as the Creator. Yet you put it first."

"Not *first*," he corrected, "Jesus as Creator comes *second*, if you are paying attention. 'In the beginning was the Word, and the Word was face to face with God.' Relationship is first—relationship between the Word (that is, the Lord Jesus) and his Father.

"Moses teaches, 'In the beginning God created the heavens and the earth.' The heavens and the earth, that is Jewish code for *all things*, everything," he declared, rising.

"*Not one thing*, Aidan, *not one thing* was created apart from God. Are you listening? This is important."

I do believe the old man is getting on his chariot again. "I think I am, but you are full of surprises," I replied, keenly aware that his thoughts were quite different from my own and having no idea what I should expect to hear next.

"Listen carefully," the ancient apostle commanded, his intense eyes staring into the quick of my very being. "God, to us boys—that's what we were in those days, just boys, lost in the fog—*God* to us was a powerful and good being but distant. We knew we were part of the chosen people, but he was so far removed from us, not as removed as the abstracts think and not impersonal like they say, but far away."

"The abstracts?"

"The Greeks. Always in their heads."

"I like that, 'the abstracts.' Can I quote you?"

"John started stirring the pot with his baptizing and preaching," he replied, steering around my facetious remark. "He saw the Lord coming; he was the first to see. The people loved the Baptist, and some even thought he was the Lord himself. And the Pharisees feared him, as I told you.

"I will never forget that day. 'Behold!' he declared, and he had a way of speaking that made even the camels stop to listen. 'Behold the Lamb of God, who takes away the sin of the world.' John guided us to Jesus, and that was his great joy—being the *witness* to Jesus. That is the purpose of my gospel—helping people *behold* Jesus." The apostle, too, had a way of saying "behold" that seemed to make the world stop.

"You said you were a disciple of John the Baptist. Is that—?"

"I was indeed," he interrupted with pride. "Andrew and me, and others. But we followed Jesus after John directed us to him. We knew something amazing was stirring, but we were a little scared. Nothing much had happened in our world for many years, centuries in fact. We knew the ancient stories, but before John not even my grandfather had seen the *Lord* act in Israel—or even heard a word spoken by him through a prophet."

The dust particles floating in the air caught my attention as I thought of how exciting it must have been when the Baptist started his preaching after so many centuries of divine silence. Then Jesus appeared on the scene and the Baptist pointing to him as the Lord, the Lamb of God, and the one who baptizes in the Holy Spirit.

"Were you one of John's disciples following Jesus when he turned and asked them, 'What do you seek?'"

"Yes, and let me tell you, hearing Jesus's question was like swallowing lightning."

"That must have been breathtaking. What happened next?"

"How long is next?" He smiled, his eyes full of adventure. "It is still happening, my brother, and will be forever. But that day a light dawned in my soul that keeps shining and summons all that I am. We began to see the truth, and the Holy Spirit has been expanding my thoughts ever since until they are worthy of their theme."

"So, what *exactly* did you see?" I asked, wishing that I could climb inside his mind and witness the world through his eyes.

"Jesus and his Father, as I keep telling you. We had never heard anyone call God 'Father,' and Jesus always addressed him as 'my Father,' as if they had a long, intimate history together. In time it became clear to me in the Spirit that Jesus and his relationship with his Father stretch back before creation. That is the reason I started my gospel before the creation, with the Father and the Son face-to-face."

If this brother played baseball, he would definitely be a pitcher. He had just thrown me a second curveball. First, Jesus as Creator. Now Jesus and the Father face-to-face before creation. As I reflected I noticed that the room, though not large, was actually the perfect size for us both to pace at the same time without feeling we were on top of one another.

The apostle, standing now at the entrance, spun around toward me as if *he* was inside *my* head listening to my thoughts. "Yes, *pros*, 'turned toward,' 'face to face.' It is a Greek word but filled with Hebrew meaning. The Word, who was God, was *pros*, face-to-face with God."

The apostle's simplicity was astonishing, but I could see something of what he meant. I thought of Matthew and the other Gospels and how each placed the coming of Jesus into specific historical contexts, and it dawned on me that John had reversed the order. He had placed John the Baptist, Abraham and Israel and Adam, and indeed all of creation in the context of Jesus. "I think a big kaleidoscope just turned in my mind," I said, shaking my head. "I will need some time to process this."

"Kaleidoscope? That sounds dangerous," he muttered, grinning.

"Think of a tube, with pieces of colored glass . . . prisms," I said, then shook my head in frustration, partly because I could find no way of explaining a kaleidoscope and partly because something very much like one actually did turn in my mind. What I had thought was clear was now in disarray. "I feel like I have been studying the same vision for many years, even memorizing the details, and now suddenly the things in the vision have moved, the vision itself has transformed, and the change is rather large."

He took a seat on his rock beside me, listening intently, waiting for me to go on.

But I wasn't sure how. "Sir," I finally said, "are you saying that before there was anything, any creation at all, when there was only God, *that God was the Father and Son, in relationship, face-to-face*? That's what you're saying, right? And out of this relationship comes creation?"

He nodded slowly, with his detective look. Then a beautiful smile broke over his face. "Flesh and blood did not reveal this to you. That would be *Ruach HaKodesh*!"

I, too, grinned as I remembered that *ruach* is the Hebrew word for "spirit," sometimes translated as "wind" or "breath."

Then out of the blue three chairs appeared in the room. Well, *appeared* is not exactly the right word. I could see them in the room, yet I knew that they were not actually there, but then they weren't only in my imagination, either. I was having a vision. The chairs, side by side in perfect alignment, were overstuffed and inviting, and identical in size, but each was unique, one red, one purple, and one had many colors. I thought of home, of Mary and our children, and as I did, the three chairs started moving in and around each other like someone was playing a shell game. When they stopped they formed a circle, each one facing toward the other two.

The apostle must have seen the chairs as well, although he did not say anything about them directly. He opened his arms and whispered, "That *relationship* between the Father and the Son is the heart of *everything*."

8

KARLI

A great calm enveloped me as I repeated John's words. I had heard a similar statement before many times. "Sir, you sound like my old professor. He would often tell us that the Father-Son relationship is the heart of the New Testament, the universe, in fact. And he loved to quote Karl Barth, his own teacher. His favorite quote from Barth was, 'Not God alone, but God and humanity together, constitute the meaning of the Word of God.' I have wrestled with these ideas for many years and thought I understood, but I see now that I have missed the boat entirely."

The apostle's countenance changed, and I thought it was because I had used another expression, but I noticed surprise and curiosity in his eyes, even marvel. He glanced away for a second, then turned, extending his left hand toward me. "Have you studied Karli's writings?"

Stunned and more than a little afraid, to say the least, I didn't know what to say.

"I met him once," John declared casually, responding to my shocked face.

"Karl Barth? You have *met* Karl Barth?" I asked incredulously, and I swear the smell of pipe tobacco wafted through the room. I felt faint.

"Yes," he answered, as if such things were ordinary—and for all I knew, to him they were. "Karli was dreaming in his room, asleep while sitting in a big chair with his right cheek resting on a book, surrounded by many books on a long and wide table, with strange music playing. Your painting of the Baptist with his bony finger—who did you say it was by? Grünewald?—hung on the wall behind him."

I could hardly speak. "You are well and truly trippin' me out now."

"We talked about the Word," he replied, ignoring me for the moment. "Karli was in a house beneath a great mountain covered in snow."

"How can this be?" I murmured, shaking my head. I suddenly felt like I had spent my life playing checkers at a three-dimensional chess match.

The apostle continued, "Jesus told Nathaniel that we would all see the angels of God ascending and descending upon *him*. Heaven's Gate, my dear brother—the great High Priest, Jesus—has united heaven and earth, the life of God and human life, *in himself*. Just as it was planned before the time of the ages."

"I feel like a mosquito that just ran into a bug zapper." I was still reeling from his matter-of-fact account of meeting Karl Barth and had barely heard what he'd said next. This brother was too much!

"Bug zapper?" His face was priceless: eyebrows dancing, eyes almost crossed in his befuddlement, as I am sure were mine.

"What I mean to say is that you are hurting my head with your ideas—and your *meetings*."

"Forgive me, but I thought you had read my gospel and Paul's letters. Is this new to you? Why should my meetings seem strange to you? Have you forgotten where *you* are?"

"Sir, water is not new, but it is different when you drink it from a fire hydrant." I knew the moment I said it, of course, that I had done it again. But I was buying a little time while I tried to understand what I was hearing. No use. It was overwhelming. "Would you excuse me?" I asked, rising. "I need a moment to think about all of this."

This brother walks in the Holy Spirit in ways beyond my wildest imagination. Completely bewildered, I looked out at Patmos, the long shadows that had formed in the afternoon sun somehow helping me relax. *But who am I to think that the apostle could not have spoken about the Word to*

Karl Barth in a dream? It does explain a lot. Barth is known as the theologian of the Word . . .

My mind raced as I walked the path back and forth, wondering how such things could be. *Whatever may or may not have happened with Barth, I'm here now on Patmos with St. John in person. Stay focused on the prologue and on this relationship.* I sat down on the path, dangling my feet over the edge, lost in questions, yet determined.

I noticed a black-tailed lizard moving to my left, about a yard away, easing his way toward me. Sorely needing the amusement, I watched him until he stopped inches from me. The markings on his dark back were not familiar to me. He crawled up my left thigh and stopped, then looked right at my face with his curiously oversized red eyes. It was almost like he knew what was going on in my mind, and I half expected him to speak. I laughed so loud it scared him, and he dashed into a crack and disappeared. *Who knows? The lizard is probably a message.*

The apostle gave me plenty of time, eventually coming outside to sit beside me. "Are you all right?" he asked, eyes full of compassion. "Believe me, I understand how you feel, my young brother."

"Sir, you have blown me away." I caught myself. "I mean, you've astonished me on two different fronts that I can recognize, not to mention my journey to Patmos itself."

"You are troubled about my meeting Karli in his dream?" he asked, reading me like a book and handing me some of his tasty bread.

"The fact that you know him at all is perplexing, but only his close friends knew him as Karli. You said that I am your first visitor from 2013. Have others been brought to you from other times? Have you met many people in their dreams, people all through history?"

"The Holy Spirit was poured out on all flesh," he replied, with a hint of risk in his voice, as if aware of inviting me into what might be dangerous territory to me. "She is everywhere, and in everyone, sharing herself with us all. She is a mystery like the wind, as you might recall from my gospel, but as you trust her you will find yourself involved in *her life*, and believe me *amazing* things will happen. She is full of surprises—an *impossible possibility.*" He grinned and winked as if that was supposed to relieve me.

"That is the most remarkable thing I have ever heard, even after this day and all that you have said in the last hour or so. It makes sense in an astounding and exciting and scary kind of way, but these things are way above my pay grade. Do you know everything 'in the Spirit'? I mean no disrespect, but if you do know all, are you humoring me with your questions?" I grabbed some rocks and started throwing them over the edge, watching in my uneasiness as they ricocheted like a pinball off the boulders below us.

"The Holy Spirit does not disclose everything to me, only what she thinks best. I do see visions, even as you have this hour, and I have met several people in their dreams, and a few have even come here to Patmos. As the Holy Spirit leads, I will share all that I know with you."

"You must tell me of your other visitors, and of those you have met in their dreams. I want to hear about it all."

"As the Holy Spirit leads," he admonished, leaning toward me and patting the hard earth between us for emphasis.

The lizard reappeared, as if to let us know that it was listening, and then darted away. We both smiled watching, then sat quietly for a while enjoying the moment.

John cleared his throat and rubbed his beard. "We were talking about your teacher quoting Karli, who preached that the relationship between the Father and the Son is the heart of the universe—"

"Oh yes, I remember my question now," I interrupted, aware of the apostle's gentle patience. "In your gospel, when you start off, 'In the beginning,' are you purposely harking back to Genesis so you can fill in the idea of God from Moses with the relationship of the Father and Son?"

"That surprised me, too," he answered, making clear that he was neither omniscient nor unsympathetic to my bewilderment. "But it is there in Genesis, even in the Shema, and"—his voice rose in excitement—"in the *Blessing!*"

"Slow down. I am seriously struggling to keep one train of thought. There are so many layers! What is *there*, exactly?"

"Relationship."

"In *Moses?*" I asked, astonished again, becoming more focused.

"Indeed. I had not seen it at all."

"And who on earth has seen that, sir? That, too, is utterly remarkable.

My heart is soaring, but I feel like I'm trying to count the waves of the ocean. It is too much."

"I surely know what you mean." He laughed as he stood up and headed inside, and I followed.

The apostle stopped in the mouth of the cave and turned around toward Patmos, lifting his hands. "Everything was created by the Father and the Son, who is the Word. The love of the Father and Son is at the center of the entire cosmos, the *cosmos*!" He faced me. "Including you and your life. And the Son, who is face-to-face with the Father became flesh, so that we, too, could know his Father. And—"

"Whoa! Sir, can we punch the pause button? There is so much in what you just said, and I can now see it all crammed into the very beginning of your gospel. I love your vision, what I can understand of it, and I'm embarrassed to say that I used to pride myself on being a theologian, but now I feel like an ant before a mountain. I need to take smaller steps."

As a gesture of kindness, he put his right arm around my shoulder and led me back into his room. "We will move at your pace," he replied with more respect than I thought I deserved. "I do get excited about Jesus."

"Can we back up?" I asked.

John nodded and began to recite again.

> In the beginning was the Word, and the Word was face
> to face with God, and the Word was God. He was in the
> beginning face to face with God. All things came into being
> by him; and apart from him nothing came into being that
> has come into being.

"There's so much going on in my mind right now that I hardly know what to say."

I noticed his eyes shining as they started to well up, and he closed them. "At times when I was writing, the revelations from the Holy Spirit were too much, and I had to stop."

"Believe me, I understand."

"Jesus is far greater than we can imagine and as good as he is great! No one can overestimate him. And his Father . . ." He paused to take in a deep breath. "The wonder of their relationship I am only beginning to know, but I see it, beautiful beyond thought. *Everything, everything is about their relationship*. It is the womb of the cosmos. Jesus is the center of it all."

We were both startled by a wind that found the cave. The old apostle looked up as if he had seen a dear friend, smiled, and then sat still for a long while. Even now I have no idea what he was thinking or where he might have gone, but he was at the other end of the universe from sad, and I was full of hope, even though I felt like everything I thought I knew was being thrown into the air.

A MATTRESS FOR AN OLD SAINT

"What time is it? I am so hungry I could eat a horse."

"Do you *eat* horses in your country?" John asked, looking askance at me as if suspecting it was just another of my expressions.

"Hungry, sir, really hungry," I moaned.

"You have a lot of expressions." He lifted his hands and his white beard in mock surrender and also in a tender gesture of identification with me.

"I guess I do, but I'm as Southern as sweet tea." I grinned. "Have you read The Gospel of St. John lately or the book of Revelation?"

The old apostle groaned, letting me win one. "I will see if I can find some more bread and fish."

"You have fish?"

"I *am* a fisherman, you know," he replied, eyes twinkling.

"I am, too, but I didn't happen to bring any fish with me."

"I have friends. They look after me."

The news warmed my heart, but I wasn't sure if the dear brother wasn't half expecting Jesus himself to show up and make something happen with fish—again—or if people simply appeared from around the world "in the Spirit" every other day or so with supplies.

"My mind is reeling, and I need a break. We have not talked about the Romans; I'm guessing they are soldiers, and I know from history that they were cruel and heartless. Is there anytime when it would be safe to go outside beyond the mouth of the cave?"

John drew in a quick breath, and his expression changed. "Ruthless they are; they show no mercy at all." He wasn't afraid, but his tone and his tight lips made it plain that he was deadly serious. Then he cocked his head. "They have one weakness. They are predictable. Every day they patrol at first light and an hour after midday. Only once have I seen them deviate from this routine. I always take care. 'Never be seen' is my rule around here. Today they have come and gone while you were sleeping. Why?"

"So it's safe to wander around outside now?"

"*Safe* is not the right word, but the air should be clear of the Romans. Keep your eye to the north. They always come through the pass between the big cliffs. You will hear them marching first. What are you thinking, Aidan?"

"So there is actually something that you do not know or have not seen in one of your visions?" I asked, enjoying myself.

"I have seen the Romans glowing like Moses's face, whatever else you may be talking about."

It was an odd statement. Of all people why would the apostle think of the Romans glowing with the glory of God like Moses? Then I realized he meant that like Moses their "glory" was fading.

"Well, I think I have something to share with you about the fading of the Romans, but that will have to wait."

"Why wait? When does Rome die?" he asked excitedly. "You must tell me all that you know."

"Rome dies a few centuries from today, but we will talk about that after we talk about why you spoke of the Word instead of the Son in the first lines of your gospel. Meantime, can I have a few of your rags?"

"My rags?"

"I need the two largest ones."

"Well, of course, but why do you need my rags, as you call them?" he asked.

"I know I'm out of my league, but you're not the only one who can get

74

an idea from the Holy Spirit."

"As you wish. Take what you need. Now, what do you mean, the Word instead of the Son?"

"After what you've been telling me, there is no way that you don't know what I mean by that, but I will leave you hanging on that one," I answered, half afraid to say it too loudly but proud that I managed to ask a great question. *Imagine that, leaving the Apostle John hanging with a theological question. I wonder how many times that has happened.* "I can't wait to hear what you have to say, but I need to do something with my hands, focus on something else, be creative, so my exploding mind can settle."

"Not much to do around here, except mining. And believe me, you don't want to do that."

"Your world may be mostly rock, physically speaking, of course, but there has to be some grass and leaves somewhere. Do trees grow in this place?"

"There are a few scattered down the path and more near the sea. But they are not cedars of Lebanon. I'm afraid there is nothing of your Grove around here."

"The Grove, my friend, is a state of mind as much as a real place." I laughed. "There may not be any large trees around, but there is definitely a lot of the Grove here and more! Let me see what I can find. If I don't return, you will know that the Romans got their first Southern gentleman. They will probably keep me alive just to hear me talk." I smiled as I headed out of the cave and down the narrow path. I knew the apostle would be praying for my safety.

The dear old brother's sleeping arrangements had broken my heart the minute I saw them, so I figured to find some leaves, or at the very least, some grass, and find a way to make him a mattress. *We will see.*

For a while I saw nothing green, but as I moved on toward the sea and out of sight of the cave, I spotted a few sprigs of life here and there. So I made two bags out of the long rags and gathered everything that was green and soft, always alert for any hint of the Roman soldiers. At last I found a few trees, which were more like stunted broccoli, but they were alive and had fairly soft leaves.

Then a smile spread across my face as I came upon what looked like a miniature Christmas tree—a stubby little cedar! There was a patch of them, maybe a hundred or more, with straw underneath their limbs. I stuffed both makeshift sacks with straw and more leaves until I could barely carry them.

As I turned back toward the cave, I thought of home and my family, which made me laugh and tear up. *Mary has had to pick up the tab on my despair more times than I can count, and she has had to learn to swim in the sorrow of my absence even when I was present—my "absent presence," as my counselor would say.* A wave of guilt flooded my heart. I felt regret sneaking around inside me. Then I dropped the bags and sat down, shaking as a new thought rolled in. *Could it be that I am here to be healed?* Is that what John meant by my finding home? I grabbed the bags and jumped up, not at all ready to allow such a hope to get a toehold in me. *There is no pain greater than disappointed hope.*

Then the present moment captured me. *Now that I have the stuffing, how can I make a mattress? What can I use for thread?* My mind wandered in a prayer of sorts. "Aha!" I laughed when it came to me. No man in Mississippi would be caught dead without a pocketknife, and I was no different. Years ago I was upgraded by a gift of a Leatherman Micra. I have been through a dozen, but never a day passes without me carrying one in my left pants pocket.

So, I have on long pants, which I don't need in this dry world. I can make shorts and cut the legs into fine strips for thread. It dawned on me that I had on a pair of tennis shoes with shoestrings. *That's it! Surely I can find a way with these rags and these leaves and straw to make a mattress. The old man will have a good night's sleep if it's the last thing I do.*

When I finally made the arduous climb to the cave, the apostle stood staring at me like I was Santa Claus caught in the act. He was certainly pleased with my safe return, but he had no idea what I was up to, which surprised me and made me smile.

I sat down on one of his rocks, pulled out my shoestrings, took off my shoes, then my pants, and started cutting strips.

"What, brother Aidan, in the name of Patmos are you doing?"

"I will remember that one: 'in the name of Patmos'!"

"Well?"

"After these last few hours it is hard for me to believe that you don't already know, but you, dear sir, need an adjustment to your lodgings."

"We have been talking so much I have not taken the time to clean up since I returned." But looking around, he obviously realized that there really wasn't much to be done in a cave.

"I mean that you need a better place to sleep, and I intend to make you a mattress."

I noticed a strange feeling in the room, one that had not been present before—a heaviness, perhaps sorrow. The room had definitely changed from the intense, mind-boggling discussion we had been having to an air of somberness.

"Sir, is everything all right?" I asked. "The room has changed somehow."

"I am alive, upright, and still in the battle."

"That you are, still having visions and writing, and changing the world ✳ beyond your time. And I intend to use a little Southern ingenuity to make you more comfortable."

"Thank you," he replied, with a funny look on his face. "But do not try to rescue me from the Holy Spirit."

My hands rose instantly in front of me, as if to give myself space to register his comment. "Hang on," I exclaimed. "I have never thought of rescuing anyone from the Holy Spirit. What 'in the name of Patmos' do you mean by that?" I asked, proud of myself, yet dead serious.

He moaned under his breath. "I have been guilty of that a time or two in my own life. Some years ago I realized that there are occasions when the Holy Spirit has no intention of delivering us from our pain, at least not at the moment. Without care," he said with emphasis, "we can find ourselves trying to save someone from the very sorrow that in the Spirit's grace may give them eyes to *behold* Jesus and find real healing."

"Surely you are not suggesting that the Holy Spirit authors pain in our lives?"

"Of course not. In the madness of Ophis we create enough pain to make a mess of things. And then, of course, there are the wounds of war."

The phrase flung open a door to my encounter with little Aidan, but I slammed it shut quickly.

"But the Holy Spirit is a redeeming genius; she specializes in using our sorrow to give us Jesus's eyes. Do not ask me *how* she does that."

"No way you're getting off the hook on that one."

"Getting off the hook?"

"Sir, you're a fisherman. Surely you know that metaphor."

"That I do, Aidan. I suppose I am avoiding an old sorrow myself."

"You?" Shocked, I looked away in a vain attempt to turn from the weirdness of the moment and from the obvious fact that he could see right through me. I had not said a word about avoiding sorrow, yet he clearly thought I was.

The old man lowered his gaze as if he were about to confess a mortal sin, which made me as nervous as a cat in a room full of rocking chairs. He sighed, folding his arms. "Aidan, I have enjoyed your brief time here with me. But I have an ache that has been stirred up by your presence, by your coming from the future."

"Sir, you are starting to scare me. How could anyone, let alone me, disturb the Apostle John?"

"I am overseer of several churches on the mainland. I have seen visions of what could take place in the times ahead. A few years ago I sent out a letter to focus them on Jesus again, to give them hope to stand firm, and to warn them of what would happen if they gave in to the darkness. I'm not sure I want to know what became of the churches. I suppose I am afraid of what you might tell me."

I had no idea how to respond. *This dear brother has seen the end of history, visited people in their dreams, had visitors come here, and sees visions in the Spirit. How could he not know what happened to the churches?* As I pondered, it dawned on me that even the Apostle John—who, after all, did not know everything—might need to be encouraged.

"Sir, one of my favorite things about the New Testament is that it is so real. No writer pretends. Jesus clearly knows something that the rest of you don't, and it strikes me that no author of any part of the New Testament tries to make you men appear other than regular people who have seen something in Jesus that they cannot quite understand but long to share. You trusted in him enough to commit everything to him and wanted to show the rest of us why. And the best part is that y'all would not give up— and not a one of you would take religion as the answer."

"Y'all." He smiled. "I like that. The real Aidan of Mississippi talking."

"As Southern as turnip greens and fried chicken, 'y'all' combines 'you' and 'all' into one word."

"It speaks of oneness," he replied with honor in his voice. "It would be humorous if I used that in one of my letters, would it not?"

I shook my head at the thought. "Better not confuse the scholars by throwing colloquial Southern American English in with the Greek. They'd never get that one. But then again, why not? Anyway, John the Baptist was a fiery brother, passionate and true, as you know far better than I, but in prison he struggled, didn't he? He had to be thinking that he may well be as crazy as a water bug, perhaps even wrong about Jesus, and thus that his own life was misspent . . . Have you ever had doubts?"

"No," he answered quickly and with obvious integrity, "not since I met Jesus after his resurrection and ever since. I walk with him and he in me, and I have seen the end, as I told you. But before the end comes we have very dark waters to go through. This age is the age of the Ophis wars. We must all learn to stand in Jesus's 'I Am' for ourselves and fight the darkness—in the way of the Lamb, of course. We are mere men. I, a fisherman."

"A fisherman who 'beheld the glory of Jesus' and has the courage to talk about it," I said, passion rising in my heart. "And to suffer exile on this lonely orange rock. *And* to write in his exile in order to encourage others in their struggle," I exclaimed rather too loudly. I was suddenly alarmed that I might be climbing onto Saint John's chariot myself. "Brother John," I resumed more quietly, "perhaps I have been sent to you from the future to encourage you."

"That you have done, and I am grateful."

"I'm not trying to be kind, and forgive me if I *way* overstep my bounds," I replied, as more fire rose within me, "but I feel compelled to say that *you, your work, your writings*—some of which were written in this cave on the isle of Patmos—have been used by the Holy Spirit to impact millions upon millions of people, for century after century, shaping *history* itself! I have not seen this in a vision; it is not the truth of what will be but of what already *is*. I have seen it. Read it. Studied it. And I feel equally compelled to make the best mattress in all of Patmos, perhaps as a *sign*," I said, lifting my right eyebrow meaningfully, "of the love of the Father, Son, and Spirit for a dear son who deserves a place to rest his head."

The old saint sat still, taking in my blitzkrieg. He had no words, and I wasn't sure if he was stunned by what I was saying or by my spirited way of saying it, which surprised me as well.

"Thank you," he finally responded gently. "It strikes *me* that you know more of the Holy Spirit than you realize. I look forward to this mattress of yours, my friend." He was quiet for a few seconds, then chuckled softly.

Silence fell in the room, for which I was thankful, and we sat together as I worked on John's mattress under his pensive gaze.

Then a flash of light went off in my mind the likes of which I have never experienced. My thoughts stopped. Every chamber of my inner world was as quiet as a toad while a single question found words and eased its way into my mind: *What if history lasts another fifty thousand years?* At first I was dumbfounded, thinking this was more proof that I was losing my mind. After all, we were in the end times, the last days, weren't we? But then the question came out of my mouth, without me trying to ask it.

The old apostle listened as if the Lord Jesus were speaking in person, which scared me even more. After a brief silence he beamed, calling out, "*That* would mean that y'all"—he winked—"are still *in the beginning!*"

"Yes, sir, even in the year 2013, we would still be—or are—in the *early* church!"

TRAGEDY

"When was the last time you had a decent meal?" I asked, fiddling with the strips of my khakis that I had cut and starting to give form to Saint John's mattress.

"That depends on what you mean by decent. I like bread and water and fish, as long as the Lord is with me."

"I'm sure that is true, but a little 'back strap' on an open fire would be awesome about now—properly marinated and not overcooked, of course. I will find us some real meat."

"Lizard is about the only meat you will find around here."

I mumbled under my breath, "Please tell me it's not *road* lizard."

John looked up, slight confusion on his face.

"I was just being a little *cheeky* . . . That's a Scottish word, by the way."

"Scottish?" he asked, with just a trace, I thought, of a lilt.

"Scotland is the beautiful land just north of what the Romans call Britannia. The Romans never conquered the Scots, or the Picts as they were called in your day. Their land is cold and wet even in summer, but it's beautiful," I said, my mind flooding with memories. "A land of green mountains and valleys, with lochs—that is, lakes—and heather, a wild shrub with purple flowers that grows everywhere. It is the home of my ancestors, a fiery lot—and the home of golf," I added proudly, "as well as single malt scotch and, sadly, Scottish Calvinism."

Before he could ask, I continued. "Golf is the greatest game ever invented. It is played with a little white ball that you hit with special clubs to make it fall into a shallow hole in the ground in the distance. If we can find the right kind of stick and make a ball somehow, I can teach you to play. Golf is wonderfully maddening, which is probably why the Scots invented single malt whiskey, the best drink in the world. And Calvinism is a way of thinking about God and his eternal plan, a brilliant example of selective reading and pretzel logic. You would not like Calvinism."

"Why not?"

"Calvinism was founded, I suppose you could say by accident, by John Calvin—actually, by his followers in the wake of the great Reformation in the 1500s. The church in the West had been dying for centuries when a serious protest began to emerge. Martin Luther is credited for its beginning, but there were others before Luther. Calvin distinguished himself as a fine theologian and biblical scholar. He found himself trying to sort through two streams of thought—or bring them together."

As the apostle listened intently, I noticed a quaint look on his face that I was at a loss to interpret. Before I could ask, he motioned for me to continue.

"The first stream, we might call the stream from Patmos," I said with pride, "meandering through Paul, Polycarp, Irenaeus, and Athanasius and the Nicene Creed—"

"Polycarp!" the ancient brother interrupted, his eyes alight. "Polycarp is one of my disciples, a true brother. The very best." I could tell by the fondness forming on his face that Polycarp was more than a disciple to the apostle. He was a deeply loved and respected friend. *Brother* was not too strong a word. In that moment history ceased to be a subject of distant names and facts, dates and time lines and became strikingly personal to me.

"You would be proud of Polycarp, the Bishop of Smyrna," I said. Then mourning swelled in my heart on John's behalf when I realized that he had no idea what would happen to Polycarp. I wasn't sure how to continue but decided to be straightforward. "Sir, it grieves me to say that your Polycarp is one of the most famous martyrs in history. He heeded your call and was faithful until death."

"Oh! Dear Lord Jesus," he responded, his countenance ashen.

"Polycarp lived a long time and served the Lord and the church well. He was arrested because of his faith and was brought, if memory serves me, before a Roman proconsul who demanded that he deny Jesus and declare 'Caesar is Lord' or die. As the story is told, Polycarp stood firm for the faith. He rose, faced the proconsul, and with an angry mob of heathens shouting at him, proclaimed, 'Eighty-six years I have served Christ, and he never did me any wrong. How can I blaspheme my King who saved me?' He was," I finished gently, "burned at the stake."

John sat quietly, his eyes downcast. I could feel his pain, yet I could also feel pride rising within him as he thought of Polycarp's stand.

"I read a story about Polycarp's death that said the flames did not burn him at all, and the barbarians had to stab him with a knife. His death and final words have been a strong encouragement to a lot of brothers and sisters through the ages."

The ancient apostle looked away, no doubt grieving.

"Polycarp is celebrated as one of the apostolic fathers," I added, still looking for a way to console my friend. "He had a major influence on Irenaeus—your grandson in the faith."

It took a good while for his emotions to settle and for him to reengage our conversation. When he did he seemed quickened with genuine interest. "Who are Irenaeus and these other men you mentioned? What is this creed you were talking about?" I could see in his demeanor that history, in his case unknown future history, had quickly become personal to him as well. For some reason I thought of the DiSC personality profile system and realized that the apostle, like me, was probably an *i*. He was wired to *influence*, and I truly was in a unique position to encourage him.

"I will be quiet." He chuckled. "Please tell me of this second stream and this Nicene Creed."

"I will share with you what I understand, but first I have a question." I realized that this was not the time to ask the question I had in mind so I looked down, fiddling with the mattress.

"Your mind is burdened," he prompted, motioning with his left hand for me to speak.

I suddenly caught the faint sound of singing, like a choir in the far distance. I looked at John. His face was without expression as he waited. "On second thought, I think it best now to talk about the creed, as you asked. I'll let my question go for the moment."

"You're concerned about Polycarp?" It was both a question and a statement.

"Not Polycarp specifically, though I can see how much he means to you, and he has now become something more than a figure of ancient history to me, but my question is more about tragedy in general."

The apostle said nothing but simply gestured again for me to continue.

"I shudder to ask at this moment, but where is Jesus when these tragedies strike us? I cannot imagine Jesus standing by while great men, or *anyone*, suffer such horror."

He moaned, no doubt remembering the tragedies in his own life. "When my brother, James, was murdered, a great anger rose within me and the same when they cut down Paul and Peter," he replied, pounding his knee with a fist. "I was proud, of course, that my brothers stood so beautifully for the truth of all truths, but I was cut to the heart by their suffering and cried out to the Lord. Jesus, too, cried out in his hour to his Father. The Father was with him, and Jesus is with us all."

"But why does he allow such terrible suffering? Great men and women and innocent children are tortured, grotesquely beaten, and brutally murdered. Your beloved Polycarp was burned *alive*! And Jesus was beaten and *crucified*!"

"We are not orphans, my young Aidan," he declared simply, calming me down and calling to my memory Jesus's statement in his gospel. But I was not sure of the significance of his point. "This is Jesus's promise to us and to all. He will never forsake us and is always with us—*in* us, in fact. Death is but a transition."

"I love that thought, but death can be so utterly horrible. To be honest, it doesn't seem like Jesus is with many of us, certainly not with me." I was surprised at my intensity, not really conscious yet of how important the question was to me personally.

John put both hands on his knees and leaned back a little. "These are difficult questions, but *this I know*: When the Romans beat me and poisoned me, Jesus held me. He was with me, as he was in old times with Hananiah, Mishael, and Azariah, and I am sure with James and Paul and Peter—and everyone."

"And Daniel and many others, sir, but those were *miracles*. Hundreds of thousands have not been so lucky or so blessed. They died in merciless *torment*." I thought again of little Aidan. I could see his face—tormented with anguish. *My God, what happened to me?*

"Have you faced such a death, young Aidan?"

His question was terribly ironic, and I answered quickly in an attempt to protect myself. "I have not, at least not at the hands of others. I only know what appears to be obvious from the outside and from my own suffering."

He was calm and deliberate as he said, "Things are not always what they appear, young brother. From the outside no one saw Jesus standing in honor, out of the Father's right hand, as Stephen was stoned to death. But Stephen did. His vision was inside his heart." He winked, like he was giving me a heads-up of some kind, but it was incomprehensible to me at the moment.

"I have never considered that." I tried to be detached, even as anger rose within me. *I called out to Jesus in my torment and never saw or felt him,* I thought.

John must have seen it in my face. "Let me tell you, the poison made my body writhe as though it would shed my skin, but inside I had no fear, only peace." He raised his hand as if blessing me, and though he said no words, I read the thought in his eyes: *I, John, your brother and fellow partaker in the tribulation and kingdom and perseverance in Jesus . . .*

I knew he spoke the truth about his own experience, even though what he had experienced was way beyond anything I had ever known in my life. No one—not even an abstract philosopher sitting where I was and looking into the apostle's eyes as he shared his own trauma and Jesus's presence—could have doubted him. Yet I had very real questions, such as: Where was Jesus when I needed him, when I cried out overwhelmed? I wasn't ready to face these questions for real and settled on a less personal line of thought, though one that was critical.

"I'm pretty sure that by now you know that I mean no disrespect, but I must ask, why doesn't the Lord stop these horrors before they happen?"

The apostle was in no hurry, again reflecting deeply and choosing his words deliberately as he tried to help me understand. "Men are not trees or rocks," he finally answered, both eyebrows raised.

"And?" I shrugged, not sure how that had anything to do with tragedy, horror, and death.

"As I told you," he said, his voice settled and sure, "freedom is necessary to our glory in Jesus."

There was that noble-sounding statement again, and I was not an inch closer to understanding what he meant.

"Moses teaches that trees and animals were created after their kind. But we, dear friend"—he smiled slightly—"were created after *God's* kind—in the image and likeness of God."

Anticipation rose within me, and my fingers tingled like I was about to hear the combination to a locked safe.

"Our glory," he whispered, "is that we share in the life of Jesus with his Father. This we cannot do if we are trees."

I could feel the tumblers turning in my mind, trying to fall into place, and I knew that freedom was the key. "So freedom is what makes us like God?"

"Yes," he answered with satisfaction, raising his left palm and pausing to make sure I was following him. "Yet freedom," his fingers closed around his palm leaving his index finger raised and bouncing, "is the crack in the door that lets in Ophis. In his madness, terrible, terrible things happen."

"But, sir, is the Lord not able to stop the horrific injustices?" The question seemed obvious, but once I asked it, it suddenly became as complicated as silence. I was torn. The apostle seemed so settled in his experience, so simple and whole, but I felt ripped apart like my emotions and my mind were two railroad tracks running side by side but never connecting.

"Of course he is able. Able to *submit himself* to be *crucified* by men." He stopped as if he could feel the canyon between my mind and my heart. He had a wonderful way about him. Never in a hurry, always, I see now,

86

aware of the different pace of my mind and my emotions. Rubbing his beard with his left hand, he lifted his hand. "Our Lord Jesus was able to unite himself with us in our darkness. The Lord does not remove our freedom; that would make us trees. The Lord"—his vivid eyes could hardly contain his wonder—"has instead taken responsibility for what we have done and do in our freedom. He meets us in Ophis's madness, in the belly of the beast, as you called it. Do you understand what I am saying?"

The apostle's words struck a chord at depths I have rarely known. I didn't know what to say, so I sat still, trying to take it all in.

A few moments had passed in silence when John began a story. "Many years ago in Galilee, I saw a young girl running home crying. I did not know what had happened to her, but her heart was obviously overflowing with sorrow. Her grandmother ran to embrace her. I watched the old woman hold her child." He paused to make sure he had my attention—needlessly, as I was hanging on every word he uttered.

"The grandmother *felt* her granddaughter's pain, shared it personally," he continued, watching my eyes and reading my heart, "yet as one who knew that the world was not at an end, even though it certainly seemed so to the little girl. The little girl found comfort in her grandmother's arms. She *felt* her peace."

I could see the little girl in my mind's eye as I pondered the apostle's words, fascinated by the apparent exchange of pain and hope as the grandmother held the girl. I enjoyed the moment of revelation. I knew that this was an important story, one that resonated with serious hope.

John held his breath for a moment, seemingly aware that his light was shining in my darkness. "Jesus found his way into *our darkness*."

For a second I could see clearly, and I knew that I had read the Bible the wrong way my whole life.

"The Lord himself holds us—from the inside—shares our sorrow, feels it, endures it with us right to the end, yet as one who *knows the Father*." He reached out with both hands as if gathering the air, then drew his hands to his heart. "We feel *his* peace. Jesus brings us through to resurrection and victory. Not a hair on our heads will perish."

I sat quietly, astonished and moved in the realization that what I had just heard was distilled apostolic wisdom. I repeated his words with great care to myself, memorizing them all, even the way he'd said them. Never had I heard words filled with such hope. I could see the answer right in front of me, but I could not feel it. I suddenly realized that the rest of this journey would require my heart.

SEPARATION

"What is a creed?" John asked, startling me. I was still mesmerized by what I had just heard.

"Sorry, sir. I did not hear you."

"A creed," he asked again, motioning with his hand. "What is it?"

"A creed is a statement of faith, like the Shema, only expanded, usually in the context of condemnation and confusion. The conflict in the church got worse after you graduated to the cloud of witnesses."

"I know the cloud. I have seen them many times and *heard* them. They pray with good eyes." A look of joyous fascination crossed his face, and he asked, "Do you think Polycarp had anything to do with your creed?"

It was more than a question, at least more than a query about the influence of Polycarp's ideas through history. It dawned on me that he actually believed in the resurrection and that Polycarp was alive and could very well be involved in history. The apostle had taken my reference to the cloud of witnesses to another level. But then I remembered that years ago I had actually seen the cloud in a vision.

As I told the apostle, he chuckled with his winsome half smile. "*You* had a vision?"

"It caught me by surprise, too," I replied, not sure if John was expressing real doubt or just having a little fun. "It happened when I was teaching in Adelaide, Australia. I was only beginning to escape the twin clutches of fundamentalism and modernism in those days."

"You are speaking in tongues." He laughed.

"And you," I said, pointing at him and smiling, "are sounding like a Presbyterian! They're skeptical of visions and miracles and tongues."

"Presbyterian. That sounds like a foot fungus," the ancient apostle replied with a broad grin.

"'Presbyterian' comes from *presbuteros*. Surely you know—"

"I know," he interrupted, patting the air with his palms toward the ground, calming my intensity. "I was being *cheeky*."

Quick on the uptake, I thought once again.

"The Holy Spirit is cheeky, too," he said seriously but nodding. "That may strike you as strange, but look for it and you will do well."

"I believe you. It's dawning on me that the Holy Spirit has been having a deep conversation with me my entire life, but I have scarcely noticed."

"The Holy Spirit shares thoughts unspeakable with us all, giving us new ears and eyes little by little. It takes time." The apostle sat there just the least bit self-satisfied, it seemed to me, with an I-told-you-so look on his face. "Now, tell me about this second stream and these brothers. What happened? And this creed? I won't interrupt."

"I will tell you what I know in the hopes that, at the very least, you can see what you have done. But first let's have some water and bread and fish."

As we sat eating, I ventured a resumption of my patchy narrative. "After your time things got seriously confused, but the worship of the church continued. My professor told us that the worship set a *standard* in the soul of the church. The brothers and sisters loved Jesus, and he had one he loved called 'Father.' And then there was the Holy Spirit, as you know well. Baptisms, according to Jesus's instruction, were in the name of the Father, the Son, and the Holy Spirit. Actually, that took a little time, but eventually it was the way all baptisms were performed.

"Irenaeus wrote an amazing book against the heretics. He was the best in the early days; there were others, Origen and Tertullian chief among them, but Irenaeus had that deep sense about him. Like I said, there was a mind of sorts"—the word *logos* popped into my head—"that was given to the church in its worship. Irenaeus wrote with passion out of this mind against the Gnostics."

St. John straightened, with more than a hint of pride in his eyes, and raised his hands like a warrior receiving good news from the field. "So, the battle continued!"

"There was certainly a battle, but I get the sense that you are referring to something very specific."

"There is only *one* battle."

"One?" I asked, curious.

His eyes flashed, and he looked straight at me. "Union or separation," he said definitively.

"Once again, sir, you have my undivided attention."

"Indeed," John boomed, as if he had been given permission to hold forth. "The Greeks and the Pharisees make the same mistake, though in different ways—a *large* mistake," he exclaimed, with a sigh of lament, "and apparently these Gnostics are their children."

I knew to the core of my soul that we had arrived at the heart of everything. I could see it in his face and in the way he held his head. I was not sure what he meant by union or separation, but it was clear that to him this was the crosshairs of the cosmos. "I think I could come up with some reasonable ideas about the connections between the Greeks and the Gnostics, but how could the Pharisees be connected?"

"The truth of all truths: *Jesus*. Jesus in his Father and us in him. Without Jesus, what do you have?"

"Not much, I reckon. Just ourselves."

"Ourselves and ideas of *separation* from God," St. John declared in his most authoritative apostolic tone. "Listen, young Aidan."

And as I did, I felt that my world was about to be shattered.

"The assumption of separation is the great darkness."

His words hit me like a blow to my gut, but before I could recover he continued on. "Then, you see, we have to find our way to God. The Greeks offer their way through their minds; the Pharisees offer theirs through external rules. This is Ophis's chief trick—blind us to how *close* the Lord is, closer than breath: we're in him, and he's in us. Ophis deceives the nations by one lie—separation. Our joy"—his face lit up like the rising sun—"is to tell the truth, let the light shine—and persevere the tribulation of enlightenment."

"Wow, that was a mouthful. And you make it sound so clear, even simple, but it's not easy for us to see your Jesus. There are millions who know and love him, but there are so many ideas that it's confusing, like we're dancing with someone whose face we cannot see. Sometimes, I'm afraid, we treat Jesus like an urban legend. I know I have."

"It *is* clear. You quoted it earlier. 'In that day, you will know that I am in My Father, you in Me, and I in you.' This is the simple truth."

"Simple? The word *in* alone blows my mind."

"Dear brother, either Jesus is *in* us or we are separated from him. If we are separated, then we must find a way to him, either through the *mind* with the Greeks or through the *law* with the Pharisees."

"Or through some sophisticated system that is a combination of the two," I responded, proud of myself, as a wave of peace washed through my entire body. I started relaxing. I thought of Jesus's words: "Come unto Me, all who are weary and heavy-laden, and I will give you rest." *That's it. Rest.* Not one day, not one second in my life have I ever known rest. Now I could see why. I had spent my life trying to get "in."

The old saint remained silent long enough for me to know that he was preparing something especially critical to say. He had that amazing way about him, like he was always several moves in front of my every thought. He held his words impeccably with the rhythms of my heart, and my heart yearned to hear him.

"Ideas are important," he said slowly, helping me savor every thought. "Ideas become our eyes. If your ideas are wrong, you cannot see what is."

Part of me was excited, and part of me squirmed. "Are you speaking generally or about me?"

"Perhaps both," he replied with a gleam in his eye but no hint of condemnation. "What do you do when you cannot see what is?"

I hesitated. His question was obviously rhetorical, but the answer was not obvious to me. I felt like I was trying to organize a bowl of wet spaghetti.

"When you don't see what is, Aidan, you create something you *can* see—in your imagination, of course. Then you defend with a vengeance whatever you have created, because it is all you think you have."

Good Lord, I have propagated ideas and defended them fiercely, only to see through them later. How many lectures have I thrown into the garbage and wished that I could start over, but I have never known how?

The apostle moaned, "A whole world, or *worlds*, growing out of the single lie of separation."

"Saint John, Apostle of Jesus," I exclaimed, shifting the subject away from me, "I do believe you just interpreted two thousand years of Western history."

"Your history is unknown to me," he said, his tone both compassionate and penetrating, "but this I know: the lie of separation from God is the chief of all lies. It may be like a mother spider with a thousand babies on its back, but there is only one mother spider."

"This mess, this historical quagmire of religions, wars, abuses, lust, and fear, all grows out of a single untruth?"

"Indeed, my son." He smiled, somehow proud of me. "The lie that we are separated from Jesus and his Father."

"So in your gospel and letters, you're trying to help us see through the lie of separation." The simplicity of what he was saying left me hungry and flabbergasted at the same time.

"Truly, I, and all of Jesus's disciples, proclaim him. My gospel is a series of stories that unveil Jesus, leading to the upper room—and to an encounter with Jesus himself in us. The Holy Spirit is working from the inside, and the faithful witness to the Word is working from the outside. It is about coming to behold Jesus in us."

What the apostle was saying made sense, perfect sense, and it was simple, like a daughter's smile, yet every bit as unfathomable. I thought of the celebrated "I Am" declarations in his gospel, and for a second I could almost hear Jesus declare, "I am the light of the world; the one who follows me shall not walk in the darkness, but shall have the light of life."

John, quietly pondering, looked into my eyes. "What happens when you discover Jesus inside your own heart?"

I marveled at the thought, longing to believe. "I could give you a good theological answer, but in actual fact I have no idea. I have searched my whole life, hint after hint, but have found that my heart is unsatisfied. Several times I was so brokenhearted and despairing that . . ." I dropped my voice to a whisper. "What I said before is true, I tried to take my own life and end it all."

He drew in a long breath, and I could see his compassion for me. Then a tiny smile appeared on his face, as if he had just solved another mystery or accomplished a mission. Then it grew wide and he proclaimed, "*I'll* tell you what happens, young Aidan. As you meet Jesus in you, you experience *his* life: his hope, his freedom, his joy in the midst of the darkness."

MACDONALD

The possibility of actually sharing in Jesus's own emotions took my breath away. Such an idea was too good to be true. I stumbled in silence, eventually asking, "Your gospel is a document designed to lead to enlightenment and *encounter?*"

"Indeed, and not one without the other. I wrote to lead people to the upper room and to Jesus's prayer, to discover him *in* them."

"Most letters are written to inform or explain, and the author assumes that the explanation carries its own weight. But you are informing so as to give us *eyes to encounter a person*. It's like writing something that won't really *say* what you want unless *something else* happens, unless the Holy Spirit transforms your words into an encounter with Jesus himself. Is that right?"

"Of course. We are created to think in the Spirit. Our minds don't work well without her. In truth, without the Holy Spirit doing what the Holy Spirit alone can do in us, no one will understand. We would be left with *lalia*, mere words or speech, and not able to hear the *Logos*, Jesus."

"'One can be in full possession of all the facts and yet miss their meaning,' to quote C. S. Lewis, a writer from our world."

"This Lewis, he gets the point," John responded with admiring enthusiasm.

"Lewis was one of the greats of our time. He learned from George MacDonald, a Scotsman. MacDonald, sir, now he was the best of the best."

The apostle studied my face as his hands came together like he was praying. "*Aye, laddie*," he said, rising with warrior's honor on his timeworn face.

"What did you just say?" I asked, stunned. A cool, wet wind swept into the room, and I shivered. Boy, did I shiver.

John turned toward me, his eyes flashing fire as he lifted his left arm. "'Good souls many will one day be horrified at the things they now believe of God.'"

I recognized the famous MacDonald quote immediately and jumped to my feet. "That is utterly remarkable! You have met George MacDonald?"

"I have indeed," he replied, satisfaction all over his face.

I shook my head, baffled, though less shocked than I should have been. I was beginning to realize such things were par for the course in his world.

"The Holy Spirit loves to share deep thoughts with us—and *through* us. George has keen ears, a good mind, a heart that cried out to the Lord—and sight to see what cannot be said with words."

My mind flashed back to the Grampian Hills in Scotland and to the little village of Huntly where MacDonald spent his youth, which I had visited several times. I pictured the heather and the wind-driven rain across an ancient path, which had become a road. Then I thought of King's College in Aberdeen—betwixt the Dee and the Don—the granite walls of the ancient structure overgrown with red ivy, where MacDonald took his divinity degree and where I studied as a postgraduate. Separated by a century, we had both stepped a hundred times on the same stone threshold that seemed an eternal passage into the theological world of King's College. Now I was on the isle of Patmos with the Apostle John, and he was telling me of his visit with the venerated MacDonald. *Good Lord, what is really going on?*

"Everyone," I managed to say, "who loves MacDonald knows he had a profound experience that changed his life in a library somewhere in the north of Scotland, but that is a mystery."

The apostle, unaware of my memories, at least as far as I knew at the moment, declared, "It is a mystery no longer. George was in a vast house, with more books than even I could imagine, standing in front of a look-glass."

"Sir, MacDonald is one of my favorites. Please tell me what y'all talked about."

"I suspect you already know," he replied, once again in tune with a conversation that failed to cross my mind.

"I would hazard a guess that y'all talked about Jesus's *Father*. I have read no one, not even my own teacher, who understood the Father's heart more beautifully than MacDonald. He was an amazing man and a very gifted writer, but I always felt that he knew more than I could see, which left me frustrated at his words, not unlike the New Testament itself and its grand promises, and to be honest, some of your own writings."

"George sees *what is* with Jesus's eyes. His heart *sings* of *Abba*." He tilted his head, apparently thinking about his fellow traveler for a moment. "He stood firm, did he not?"

"Oh yes! George MacDonald stood firm! He battled the Calvinists' vision of God till the day he graduated."

"That would be like the Holy Spirit," he replied softly but with a ring of joy and then motioned for me to continue about Calvinism.

"Among other things, Calvinists teach that God chose and predestined some people for salvation—the 'elect,' they call them—and abandoned all the others forever. And they teach that Jesus did not die for the whole world but only for these elect."

"Are they Pharisees, these Calvinists?" He glanced at me, and I could see his passion rising.

"I don't think so. Why?"

"Pride of a similar kind. We are the chosen people of God; the rest are dogs."

"I had never thought about that. I always assumed that such *skubala*," I said, proud of myself, "started with Augustine."

"You must tell me about all these men you are mentioning, Aidan. When did they live? What did they teach? And don't forget this Nicene Creed; I have a hunch that this creed is vital," he said, eyes bright with interest. Wisdom itself seemed to drape around him like a mantle.

"I will, my brother, but first you must try out your new handmade

attress; it turned out a little better than I thought. We will
on the lumps, but the lumps are much better than the

le walked over to his new bed. He was so taken that I think
even he would have lied if he didn't like it. But like it he did. He crouched
beside it, patting it with his open hand and feeling it give against his slight
pressure.

"Consider it a gift from the blessed Trinity to a highly favored son," I
said a bit shyly.

"Blessed Trinity?" He lay down and let out a sigh of relief. "This is
amazing, Aidan. Thank you. I think I will sleep well tonight."

"Make yourself comfortable, and I will tell you about the two streams
of thought I mentioned and the creed and Augustine."

"And those Calvinists, too. They must not have even *read* my gospel."

"They think they have. They are experts at selective reading, as I said—
like the Pharisees, and, to be honest, like the rest of us. They actually use
selected parts of your gospel to 'prove' their theology."

"What?" John thundered so loudly it echoed throughout the cave.
"How could anyone use my gospel to teach that God does not love the
whole world? The Father found us all, Jews and Gentiles, even the Romans,
in Jesus."

With that, the old man jumped to his feet, his passion unleashing.
He started pacing and preaching: "'In the beginning was the Word, and
the Word was face to face with God, and the Word was God. He was in
the beginning face to face with God. All things came into being through
Him.' *All things*, Aidan. I even repeated myself for emphasis: 'And apart
from Him nothing came into being that has come into being.' What, or
who, could possibly be left out of that? Jesus is the *arche*, the beginning, the
source and meaning of the creation of God, of *all things*."

He paused and seemed to gather steam. "*Not one thing* came into being
apart from him!"

I marveled at how the weight of his words seemed to alter the cave
itself. "I would love to see you in the room with the Calvinists." I chuckled.
"You would be surprised how they interpret your *all things*."

"You must get that *changed*. Such *nonsense* betrays all we live for and proclaim." He waved his arms. "This is the *point* of my gospel. Jesus was *face to face* with his Father before creation, and *all things* came into being *through him*. And he became flesh to meet us in our great darkness and death, so that he could be in us *inside our darkness*, and we could see with his eyes."

He was on another roll, this one even more powerful, the likes of which I had never encountered. This was conviction—pure, undiluted, passionate conviction. I was so discombobulated by his presence and the sheer weight of his words that I didn't know what to say. Usually when I get nervous I end up saying something that comes off as shallow as a birdbath, and here was no different.

"I do believe I read somewhere," I said. "'And the Word became flesh, and dwelt among us.'" At least it was on point, but I felt like a vapor when I said it.

"*In* us!" John corrected me, still breathing holy fire. He stopped and turned to look directly at me. "Such a small word, young Aidan, but it changes everything."

"I have never seen 'in' instead of 'among' in that statement until very recently. My friend François from South Africa has been translating the New Testament in a work called *The Mirror Bible*. He says, 'resides in us.'"

"Well, of course Jesus is *among* us. All things came into being in him and remain in being in him. How could he be separated from what he has made and sustains? Without Jesus the whole creation would vanish in an instant. Now Jesus has come to be *in* us, *in our darkness*, and *is*! 'In that day you shall know that I am *in* My Father, and you *in* Me, and I *in* you.'"

"As I told you, that is my favorite line in your gospel, but I feel certain now that I don't have a clue what you mean. To hear you preach it summons something very deep within me."

"That would be *the Word*, my son. *Listen!*"

The room, and the cave itself, shook.

"I am listening, my dear brother, listening with all my heart."

The apostle walked slowly around the room, still panting, but his passion was beginning to subside. "We must pray about this and rest. Your nap this afternoon will not be enough for what is coming your way. We will talk again tomorrow. Sleep on my new handmade mattress. I insist."

He was serious in his kindness, but I could tell he was preoccupied with more important matters.

"I would rather die than take your bed from you," I replied, completely ignoring his suggestion that something else was coming my way. "I will be fine on the pile of leftover rags. But it would be great to have a glass of wine."

"Well, now," he said, smiling, his demeanor changing as he grabbed one of the lamps and left the room. A few minutes later, he returned lifting a wineskin. "Not sure about a 'glass,' but I do have some wine. For the stomach, of course."

THE DEAD FLY

I awoke from the first night's sleep, if you can call it that, to the same sight and sound that had greeted me on waking from my nap—Saint John standing in prayer. Though I saw him sleep, I still wondered if he ever actually slept.

He pointed to the pitcher of water and some bread on a rock. "Don't drink the whole pitcher this time," he said with a grin. "Did you dream?"

"I did. Two dreams, in fact. They woke me up several times. The first one was more of a recurring nightmare and the second, a single picture."

"Tell me. I am good with dreams and visions," the old brother whispered, his eyes alight.

"I will be glad to tell you, but first I need to relieve myself of a certain burden."

When I returned, he met me at the mouth of the cave. The cloudy morning sky looked as if a storm was gathering.

"Now, your dreams, young Aidan. What did you dream?" He motioned for me to take a seat on the path. We sat with our feet dangling over the edge, looking over Patmos.

"Why are you asking me about my dreams?"

"The Holy Spirit, my brother, sneaks behind Ophis's madness in our dreams. She tells us things beyond our minds. And we eventually . . . *imagine* them."

I stalled. "As fascinating as that thought is, I'm still waiting to hear why you spoke of *the Word* instead of *the Son* in your prologue," I said, glancing at the apostle out of the corner of my eye and half ducking.

"Not biting," he replied, smiling. "Perhaps they are related."

"A recurring nightmare and the eternal Word of God?" I was fascinated at the prospect of his answer, then the thought struck me that perhaps he used "Word" instead of "Son" because Jesus is the eternal message of God to us.

"We will see," he answered, with a touch of a smirk on his face.

This will surely be interesting. "I do hope that you can help with my nightmare. It has plagued me for several years. Not sure what it means, but it makes me despair."

"That sounds like Ophis; he likes despair. He should get used to it," he muttered to himself. "But please, tell me what you dreamed." He cocked his head and listened, as if once again fully attuned to a conversation beyond my conscious thoughts.

"I was in a deep darkness for what I think was a long time. There was nothing, nothing at all—not unlike my first appearance in this cave. But there was a great sadness lingering in the air, maybe shame. It was scary."

"What did you see?"

"Nothing, at least not for a long time."

"Did you smell anything?" he asked curiously.

"No, not even rotting cucumbers. All was terribly nothing."

"Is that *all* you saw?"

"No. At length I saw a faint, almost square light. Somehow I was able to move toward it."

"Square light . . . hmm . . . That would be made by humans."

"It took me a long time, but I eventually made my way to the square light to discover that it was a window hanging in the utter darkness. There were no walls around it, no building, just a wooden window hanging by itself in the void. It had eight panes in it, the frame, and the window sill along the bottom. I was on the inside, looking out."

"That sounds apocalyptic."

"It certainly felt that way. Nothing funny about it," I replied.

"There is much humor in apocalyptic writing. That is often the key."

"Well, this was *not* funny. I felt horrible and had no idea why, although the window was the only thing I had seen or encountered for a long, long time."

"Did you see anything else, something on the windowsill?" he asked, as if he knew the answer. I suspected he did.

"I did. For a long time I did not see it, but as I studied the window, for there was nothing else to do, I scanned its edges to the bottom. I noticed that the white paint was peeling toward the bottom of the right edge. I thought the peeling was from water damage, and as I followed the peeling down, I saw a single dead fly in the bottom left corner. He was upside down."

"Do you recall your first reaction to the dead fly?"

"Oddly, it took my breath away. It was just a dead fly, yet I was shocked, then scared, then sad, as if it were a message to me."

"It *was* a message, for certain. But whether it was about you remains to be seen. What else happened? What were you scared of?"

"No clue, but maybe like I was being warned."

"Or enlightened," John said with his customary enigmatic confidence. As usual, it invited pursuit.

"Brother, do you know something about the dead fly that I don't?"

"Were there others?" he asked, instead of answering.

"How do you know that?" The alarm I had been feeling became a tight knot in my gut.

"I see the window, too, and the other flies," he confirmed.

"Why am I not surprised? I know you see things, but this is *my* dream."

"Of course, but it is also the Holy Spirit encouraging you."

"How on earth could a dead fly be encouraging to me?"

"The message is not about the dead fly alone," he answered gently, but his tone authoritative, "but about a great darkness."

"Sir, there were hundreds and thousands of flies, just behind the one fly—more than I could count."

"Perhaps millions?" He raised his bushy eyebrows.

"What does it mean?"

"History," my ancient brother announced. "History." As if that cleared anything up.

"You have gotten on your chariot again and left me in the dust."

"Did you think the single fly was *you*?" he pressed gently, fully serious, his compassion for me overflowing. I could see his deep and genuine desire that I understand and be encouraged.

"Not sure, but I felt that whatever happened, it was all my fault."

"Ophis," he whispered. "He slithers in on a dream of liberation and uses it, or tries to use it, to create despair. He uses the same tricks again and again."

"I'm lost here, and this is way too important for me to miss." I could see that much; it felt like my life depended on it.

"Your dream is not a nightmare but a *revelation*."

"A revelation of *what*?"

"Blindness. Think about the one fly, the leader. If he were a man, what would he be saying?"

"He would be *dead*," I retorted for a little comic relief, knowing that I had pulled one on the apostle.

"Before he died." John frowned; I knew that he knew I was avoiding something.

"I haven't really considered that. I suppose the man would've thought he was a Moses of sorts, leading his people out of bondage, convinced that he knew the way to freedom . . . *Good grief!* I can hear the man commanding, '*This* is the way, I know it! Trust me. Be faithful. Never give up. Stay true.'"

As the words came from my mouth, I heard Frank Sinatra singing "My Way," in my head. And a sarcastic ticker tape scrolled across my mind's eye: What a warrior . . . He left it all on his field of dreams . . . He never gave up . . . He stayed true to *his* cause . . .

"That is it," the apostle declared. "He was *determined* but *blind*. He could not 'see what is,' so he invented something that he could see in his own head and died of exhaustion pursuing it to what he thought would be freedom."

As I considered the tragic upshot of this, anguish rose within me. "Yeah, and thousands, if not millions, died following *him*."

Saint John stared at me. "Is this not sounding familiar to you?"

"Yes and no. *Determined* but *blind* certainly describes me, but—"

"*History*," he interrupted. "Think a little bigger."

"Okay, I'm good with thinking historically in general, but what do you have in mind?"

"What we talked about last night."

I racked my brain for the connection. "Um . . . specifically, what?"

"Union or separation," he replied cryptically like an old sage, with just a hint of surprise at my ineptitude.

"You have my full attention, but I'm as lost as a ball in high weeds."

He paused, reflecting, I supposed, on how to unpack the issue for me. "If we are separated from the Lord—and we are not—then we must find a *way back*. One's eternal existence would hang in the balance, would it not?"

"I get that, but how is it connected with a dead fly, a million other flies, and me?"

"Can you not see?"

As I reflected, desperately trying to figure out what to say, a thought finally came to me. "If we are separated from the Lord and have to find our way to God, then we are wide open to anyone's claim to know how to get back."

"Now *you* are on the chariot, my brother. *Ride!*"

"And since we are *not* separated, then any idea as to how to get back—"

"*Won't work*. And if they don't work . . ." He gestured for me to continue.

"We eventually *die* of exhaustion or of sadness and cynicism . . . or despair, even though we have been faithful and true to 'the' cause."

The instant the words came out of my mouth, my life's story was unveiled before me. My heart froze. *What a blind idiot I've been.* How embarrassing! Yet strangely I felt not a shred of condemnation. Instead, in fact, I was startled by simple compassion, which made me feel the security of a womb.

"Wrong ideas lead to destruction. Just as I expected."

"Expected? Sir, you are known for multiple meanings, layers within layers. I feel that you are speaking about me and at the same time about something much larger. I'm not getting all of this."

"Each person's story is part of a larger story—family, friends, nation, history. The Holy Spirit speaks in 'layers,' as you called them. Your dream *is* about you. The Holy Spirit is giving you eyes to *behold* Jesus and to know his freedom. Your dream also concerns the history of your people, and as I expected, it answers your questions about the Word and the Son in my gospel. I see the layers and their relationship now."

I suddenly felt known, really known, like I was understood, even accepted, and welcomed. *Come to Me*, I heard, *all who are weary and heavy-laden, and I will give you rest.*

John slowed and took a deep breath. "Why do you think I started with the Word, instead of the Son?"

"A moment ago I thought that perhaps you used Word because you wanted us to know that Jesus is God's message to us."

"Yes, indeed. Think back to your professor's favorite quote from Karli." I could feel his joy in leading me.

"I could never forget it; my teacher said it a hundred times. 'Not God alone, but God and humanity together, constitute the meaning of the Word of God.'"

"Now," he said, his voice quivering in anticipation, "substitute 'Jesus' in place of 'the Word of God,' and say the quote again."

"Not God alone, but God and humanity together, constitute the meaning of Jesus." I repeated it several times, my whole body shaking as I did.

The apostle watched me with delight, which made me proud.

I changed the order of the phrases several times in my mind, then cried out, "Jesus means that God and humanity are together."

The apostle covered his mouth with both hands, leaning back in joy. Then he cocked his head and raised his eyebrows, as if cheering me to continue. But he couldn't wait, and all but shouted, "What is the opposite of together?"

"Separated!" Then it hit me. "Jesus means that God and humanity are not separated but together in union! And this union," I said, fully aware that I was saying way more than I could possibly understand, "is the Word of God!"

"That is the Gospel According to Saint John! Well done, Aidan. The Holy Spirit loves to make us look smarter than we are."

THE BEAVER DAM

John stood in prayer and worship, nodding and raising his arms. His compassion for me was amazing. He did not know me from Adam's house cat, yet here he was sharing his heart and life with me, leading me. He turned without a word to walk into the cave.

I lay down on my back, overwhelmed by the light, my mind racing with a hundred thoughts. I stared into the storm clouds for a long while and could not help but notice the irony. On the inside Jesus was giving me real rest at last, but on the outside a storm was gathering. I thought of Mary, home, and all the unrest I had suffered and shared with her.

"Dear Lord," I prayed, "I hope you're meeting Mary like you're meeting me, and I hope that I can be good to her when I get home.' *I am only beginning, but I like where I am.*

In time the apostle returned and stood at the mouth of the cave, shining out like the full moon in the darkness behind him. "Young Aidan, tell me your second dream."

Part of me wanted to brave the risk of the Romans and go for a swim in the sea, but then how much time do I have with *the apostle*? I got up and joined him. "It wasn't really a dream. More of a picture. I saw a vast beaver dam. It was ominous, terrible."

"Beaver dam?" he asked.

"You don't have beavers here? Furry water animal, with a flat tail?"

"We have cats and dogs, lions, sheep and goats, and rats, but no beavers. At least I have never seen such a creature."

"Not even in one of your visions or meetings?" I pressed, with a touch of cheek.

"Not yet." He smiled, and I knew he was serious.

"Think of a huge rat, about three feet long, with a really wide, flat tail. It has two enormous, gnarly front teeth." I held out two fingers from each hand and performed a chomping motion. "It can chew clean through a tree, even a big tree."

"Do they eat trees?" He took a seat at the mouth of the cave and cupped his hand, inviting me to join him.

"The beavers eat the bark and limbs and leaves," I replied, taking my seat and looking out. Here we were, sitting outside in the stormy light . . . The Apostle John *himself* sitting with *me*.

"And . . . ?" he asked, waiting.

"Sorry. I was having a flashback to my first moment here, looking out at Patmos from this spot. I had no idea where I was or what was going on."

"These things happen." He smiled, gesturing for me to continue my dream.

"After the trees fall into the water, the beavers float them across to a carefully chosen spot and use them to build their dams. It is quite amazing to watch."

"Dams?"

"Beavers don't seem to like running water. So they build dams," I replied, interlocking the fingers of both hands to show the complex construction, "out of trees and limbs and rocks and mud to block the stream or creek. They particularly like to eat the plants that grow in the ponds that their dams create. Their ponds are usually great places to fish and for snakes to live."

"Hmm . . . I don't like snakes . . . So these beaver dams stop the water?"

"Not completely but almost. The beavers leave a little flowing water so their ponds don't stagnate."

"Or to thoroughly deceive good people," he muttered, stroking his beard. I had no idea what he meant. "You said your dam was vast?"

"I did. It was downright scary how big it was, so wide and deep it could block the greatest river in our world, a river more than a hundred times the size of the Jordan. The trees at the bottom of the dam were massive like your cedars of Lebanon, as big around as the mouth of this cave. Even bigger."

"Ophis," he whispered. "Same old tricks."

"I believe you, but you'll have to explain what you're thinking." My emotions were now settled, and I was dialed in for the new round of discussion.

"This beaver dam is holding back a great river indeed, *the* river of living water."

"But what *is* the dam? How did it get there?"

"History!"

He was running ahead of me again, but I was trying to keep up. "How could a beaver dam be related to history?" I asked, confused but enjoying this conversation with my brother.

He had energy and passion again, and his face betrayed the confidence of someone unfolding what he knew to be liberating insights. "The dead fly and all those other flies are related to this vast beaver dam. They are two ways of talking about the same thing, with a different emphasis. This is about ideas, ways of thinking."

I can't wait to see how this old saint connects the dead flies with the beaver dam. But I already learned not to underestimate him.

"I can see it now, your beaver dam." He cupped both hands around his eyes to imitate seeing a vision.

This brother lives in the Holy Spirit all the time.

"It is vast. *Ominous* is the right word. This dam is stopping up the river of living water from flowing through *the nations*."

Just his tone freezed my uncomprehending thoughts and triggered a range of emotions in my inner world; I had the sense that he was talking about something profoundly relevant to my own life. I thought again of little Aidan, but this time I was not afraid.

"The Holy Spirit," the apostle said, startling me, "is telling you that wrong ideas have taken hold of the mind of your people, exhausting them to death and blocking the life of Jesus in them from flowing."

"Roger that," I said, feeling that what he said was leading to something rather momentous. "But which ideas?"

"Roger?" he asked, smiling.

"Do you not know the expression?"

"No, I do not."

"'Roger that' is a military phrase. It means 'I hear you; I understand.' My brothers at Operation Restored Warrior use it all the time. I guess I picked it up from them."

"Roger that," the old man said, proud of himself.

I tried again. "Which ideas are we talking about?"

My brother looked at me like he smelled sour milk. "What have we been talking about all along?"

"Dead flies, beaver dams, the Word, history, the river of living water, my life—all kinds of things that aren't exactly tightly related that I can see. I think the conversation you're having in your mind is of another order than the one in mine."

"You left out something vital in your list."

"And that would be?"

"Union or separation," he said, raising an affectionately chiding finger.

"So the beaver dam, too, is about union or separation?"

"Indeed. That big cedar of Lebanon at the bottom of the dam is the main 'idea' I am referring to, the lie of separation. The rest are built upon it, carefully and with great cunning."

"Ah!" I remembered something. "Like the spider with its thousands of babies?"

"Now your mind is working, my young friend."

Was it ever. Thoughts tumbled over one another as the pieces came together, and I sucked in my breath, jumping from stepping stone to stepping stone in my mind. "I'm beginning to see it—I'm seeing history as one long battle between the truth of union and the lie of separation. That would be the second stream."

"Second stream? Did you see two beaver dams?"

"No, I'm talking about what I mentioned before, the second stream of

Western history. That second stream is really the beaver dam itself."

Before I could think, these words came from somewhere deep within my heart:

"We believe in one God, the Father Almighty, Maker of heaven and earth, and of all things visible and invisible.

"And in one Lord Jesus Christ, the only-begotten Son of God, begotten of the Father before all ages; God of God, Light of Light, very God of very God; begotten, not made, of the same being with the Father, by whom all things were made."

My ancient brother appeared stunned, his eyes expressing a query I had not seen before. "Beautiful! Did you write those words?"

"No, no, of course not. That is the Nicene Creed," I replied, anxious for him to know that I would never suggest that such a wonderful statement had originated with me.

"When was it written?" he asked eagerly.

"At the Council of Nicaea in the year 325 and finished at the Council of Constantinople in 381. Would you like to hear the rest of it?"

"Of course!" He moved closer and leaned in. "I would be honored." I loved the way he showed such respect for those who went before and after him.

I closed my eyes and remembered the church of my youth. I visualized the text of the creed as I heard "Holy, Holy, Holy" played on the organ by my aunt Polly.

"Who, for us men and for our salvation, came down from heaven, and was incarnate by the Holy Spirit of the virgin Mary, and was made man; and was crucified also for us under Pontius Pilate; He suffered and was buried; and the third day he rose again, according to the Scriptures; and ascended into heaven, and sits on the right hand of the Father; and he shall come again, with glory, to judge the living and the dead; whose kingdom shall have no end.

"And we believe in the Holy Spirit, the Lord and Giver of Life; who proceeds from the Father; who with the Father and the Son together is worshipped and glorified; who spoke by the prophets.

"And we believe one holy catholic and apostolic Church. We acknowledge one baptism for the remission of sins; and we look for the resurrection of the dead, and the life of the world to come. Amen."

I opened my eyes, marveling at myself but without a hint of pride. *I guess all those years in church mean something after all.*

"Or you are hearing the Holy Spirit," John replied, reading my mind, which no longer surprised me but always startled me. "I have rarely heard words so carefully crafted. You must excuse me." He rose to stretch, gazing out across the landscape, and I could tell he wanted a moment of solitude.

I eased into the cave, alone in Saint John's world, trying to imagine what it would feel like to be him and to hear the creed for the first time. He did not come back in for some time, so I lay down on his Mississippi mattress. I may have dozed. When I looked up, the aged apostle stood before me radiant, almost as if transfigured, his robe backlit by the light streaming through the opening of the cave.

"Would you write this creed out for me?" he asked, wonder filling his vivid brown eyes as he motioned for me to join him outside. "I want to study it; it seems so precisely written."

"I would consider it a blessing, but I have no pen and paper . . . or scroll."

"I have a special room. You can write it on the wall with some chalk. That is what I did with the Apocalypse. We will call it the Creed Room," he added, fully animated.

"Did you just say that you wrote Revelation on the wall?"

"I did, my young son."

"And you want *me* to write the Nicene Creed on a wall in the same room?"

He nodded, beaming with eager excitement like a little child on Christmas morning.

"Now, that will blow the archaeologists' minds." I laughed. "The Nicene Creed written *in English* on the wall of a cave on the isle of Patmos beside the Apocalypse! I can't wait to see what they make of that."

"Who were the people who wrote this creed? How did it come to be?

When I heard you quoting it my heart leapt with joy. I was overwhelmed with hope and needed time for gratitude. I will take you to my special place above the cave if the Lord wills, and we can see the world together from there. The brothers who wrote those words know the truth of all truths. They honor me."

"There were many involved, but Athanasius was the main author; at least, he was its greatest defender. Athanasius, influenced by Irenaeus, is one of the heroic brothers in history. This creed, my friend, flows directly from Patmos."

"They have read and know my gospel; that is certain," John said, amazement written across his face. "There is no beaver dam and no dead flies about this creed."

"If I read your letters properly, you were fighting the early stages of the same battle. It seems the truth in Jesus was being assimilated into the prevailing ways of thinking."

"The carnal mind of Adam cannot cope with *God* becoming *flesh*."

I thought of what he had said earlier about there being only one battle. I was beginning to see history in an entirely new light. As I pondered his words, I thought of Irenaeus. "Sir, what you just said about God becoming flesh reminds me of my favorite Irenaeus quote: 'Our blessed Lord Jesus Christ, who according to his transcendent love, became what we are to bring us to be what he is even in himself.'"

John put his left hand over his mouth. "What a beautiful statement! And you say that this Irenaeus was a friend of Polycarp's?"

"There is evidence that he was a *disciple* of your Polycarp; that's why I called him your grandson in the faith. His words certainly have the ring of Saint John about them, don't you think?"

"He knows the truth of all truths."

"Well, Irenaeus's statement, I am grieved to say, is largely foreign to the thought that has prevailed in the West."

My words were suddenly accentuated by a mighty clap of thunder and several frightening flashes of lightning. We both ran inside.

"That scared the willies out of me," I exclaimed.

The apostle smiled as we took our seats. "You have mentioned the West and Western. What do you mean?" he asked, sounding like a professor posing a leading question.

"Historically speaking, the one church officially split into two—East and West—roughly a thousand years from today, in 1054, but the seeds were there from the beginning. After your time several centers of the faith emerged: Alexandria, from which Athanasius came, Rome, Antioch, and Jerusalem, of course, and others."

"And there was a battle between these centers?" John asked, his brow creasing with bewilderment, if not a touch of anger.

"Not so much between *them* as between the different ways they dealt with assimilation or failed to deal with it."

"I see," he responded, a shadow of disappointment in his eyes.

I thought of Paul's great admonition, "'See to it that no one takes you captive through philosophy and empty deception, according to the tradition of men, according to the elementary principles of the world, rather than according to Christ.' Paul was clear in his letter to the Colossians, yet that's apparently what was allowed to happen."

"That brother was the most brilliant man I ever met," he declared, animated by fresh energy at the memory of his fellow apostle.

I, too, felt another surge of excitement running up and down my spine. "You must tell me what Paul was like in person."

John shook his head, I suppose remembering Paul's death. "Paul was a warrior in *Ruach HaKodesh*," he replied proudly.

Thunder rolled again outside as if creation itself were shouting in agreement.

The apostle hardly noticed. "Short, slightly humpbacked, but fiery like the Baptist, with long, dark red hair. He knew the tradition like none on earth, and none could stand before him in the Spirit. We were truly amazed, I am embarrassed to say, when the Lord revealed himself in Paul—or Saul, at the time—on the Damascus road. It took us a long while to believe him. But that brother loved Jesus and the churches like no other," he said, remembering Paul with great affection and respect. "His eyebrows touched each other, which, as strange as it looked, always suggested to me that in him the ancient tradition and the newly revealed truth in Jesus embraced."

Saint John grew quiet and stared into the void. I figured he was having another vision.

"I can see Paul now," the old apostle finally said, "standing with several scrolls under his left arm, his right lifted high, preaching about *the mystery*. That is what he called it, and he never tired of telling it. 'The mystery, the mystery, hid before the times of the ages, Christ in you, the hope of glory.' The gospel!"

"That, too, is in Paul's letter to the Colossians."

"I have read that letter many times and the ones to the churches at Ephesus and Laodicea. Those letters carry the thoughts of an expanded mind. We loved brother Paul deeply. His people in Ephesus have loved me in turn. They sent me here with oil for my lamps, bread, and fish."

"And wine for your stomach," I added, nodding and cocking my head as the apostle had done so often.

"They did not want me to return here, but they knew it was of the Lord. That was Paul's heart: *Christ in you, listen to him.* He saw that Jesus was the Father's plan all along and not just—"

"Hilary saw that, too," I interrupted like an idiot, "and Maximus the Confessor, among others."

"Hilary and Maximus? Tell me of these brothers, young Aidan."

I sorely regretted interrupting, as I wanted to hear more about Paul. But I was truly moved by how persistent and genuine John's interest was in everyone who had followed in his wake, how alert he was to every name mentioned.

I responded as briefly as I could. "After your time, which marked the end of the Apostolic Age, there were a hundred years or so of what historians call the Apostolic Fathers. Your brother Polycarp was noted among these men. Then came what we call the Early Church Fathers, and Hilary was one of these leaders, one of my favorites. Maximus came later. Not many in my day know about Hilary, but he was a brilliant defender of the truth, known as 'Hammer of the Arians,' a master wordsmith."

"Wordsmith . . . a smith of words. I like that."

"Of course you would," I said, laying a hand on his back in what I hoped was not too bold a gesture. "Hilary, like you, could turn a phrase that would take a lifetime to unpack. He should have been the Father of the Western tradition, and I wish he had; things for us would have been far different. But Augustine got that crown."

AUGUSTINE

"This Augustine," John mused, "surfaces again in our conversation. Must be a person of some importance . . ."

"Have you not visited Augustine?" I asked, thinking that surely Augustine would have made the cut for apostolic dream visitation. But of course I had no idea how such visits work.

"Before you arrived on Patmos, I had never heard of Augustine. Tell me."

"Augustine is called 'the Father of the West,' a real genius, and a prolific writer, but Calvin said that Augustine was excessively addicted to the philosophy of Plato."

"This is the one you spoke of before, the Calvin of your great Reformation?" he asked, seemingly hiding a half smile.

"Are you suggesting what I think you are? Did you visit Calvin, too?"

"Calm down and continue, please," the apostle replied in an avuncular tone, not necessarily avoiding my question but not answering it, either—which launched my imagination. I must have disappeared behind my mind's eye for a while, for he spoke my name rather loudly, startling me out of a flight of fantasy.

"You were speaking of John Calvin."

"Yes, Calvin was a son of the West but read all the fathers, East and West—Origen, Tertullian, Irenaeus, Athanasius, Hilary, Jerome, Gregory Nazianzen, and many more." I could see St. John making a mental note of each new name. "He tried to bring the Eastern and Western traditions together—with considerable success, I think. His followers are another story."

"What is the difference between these Eastern and Western traditions?" he asked, cutting through the haze.

"*That* is a doozy of a question. I need to think about it for a moment," I said, pushing my fingers through my hair.

"Take your time."

So I sat silent for a good while, leaning back against the cave wall with my hands behind my head, trying to frame a concise answer. The apostle waited patiently, giving me all the space I needed. I was almost lost in the labyrinth of history when I noticed a trail of ants making off with a piece of the apostle's flatbread. *That, too, is probably a message.*

"Many in the East followed your heart. Rome, too, early on, with Paul. But Roman law and Greek philosophy 'slithered' in," I said, carefully choosing my metaphor, "and began to shape the ideas of the Roman Church, which formed the mind-set that became the Western tradition: a dualistic mind-set occupied with separation, condemnation, legal justification that didn't really touch our broken humanity, certainly not mine. You talk about the lie of separation! As I think about it now, I see *everything* was separated: spirit separated from body, head from heart, heaven separated from earth, the Father separated from the Son, people separated from God, elected people separated from damned people, the saved from unsaved, the Word separated from the words."

As I caught my breath, enjoying this rather extraordinary burst of clarity on separation, I knew more was coming. Something monumental was right on the tip of my tongue. I could feel it. But then I became aware of an odd resistance inside me, a strong resistance in fact, as if there was something actually at work preventing my own thoughts from forming. The apostle's words *the wounds of war* echoed in my mind, and I sensed that all this amazing conversation about dead flies and beaver dams, history, union and separation was very close to home. This *was* about me—or at least *my life* was included in it. Then something broke, or was released, and the most terrifying thought struck me: *little Aidan separated from me.* I jumped back with fright, knowing the words were a revelation. My body reacted violently, and I tried not to show it as I struggled to calm myself and breathe normally. But terror choked my heart, and I felt that I would soon die right here in the room with John.

I looked at the apostle. He was clearly praying for me. He leaned toward me very calmly and patted me on the shoulder, and as he did this whole craziness inside me screeched to a sudden halt.

I couldn't believe it. *Does he know what's happening to me? How can this brother wield such power?* I thought of the Apostle Paul's phrase "peace beyond all understanding."

John nodded, obviously pleased. "That, my son, was the Holy Spirit. She is amazing, is she not?"

"Sir, I don't know what to say. What just happened?"

"As the Lord leads, all will become clear," he assured me, as if he really was privy to my internal episode. He rose to add oil to the lamps from his black wineskin. He seemed to know exactly when they were about to go out, and he seemed to know everything else as well. "Would you prefer a rest?"

"I don't know how you did what you did 'in the Spirit,' but I am right as rain." As soon as I said it, I thought, *It will probably start raining now.* And it did! Buckets, in fact, a real stump floater. My heart had a real chuckle, as I found myself miraculously back to normal, yet I knew that whatever was going on inside would have to be resolved. But I also knew, not yet. "Where were we?"

"East and West," he replied, gently trimming the third lamp. "You were telling me of the difference between the two traditions—holding forth on separation." I could hear pride in his words.

"I wish there were only two. The truth is that both the East and the West have a great variety of traditions within them. I am not as familiar with those in the East in my time. I grew up in the Western tradition, as I told you, two thousand years on, and while we honor the creed, most in my world have never heard of Irenaeus or Athanasius. Even though the creed is the only universally accepted statement of faith in all the churches worldwide, it is more or less a foreign language to us in the West; we haven't really understood the force of its meaning."

"How do *you* as a son of this West know Irenaeus and have such respect for what you call the East?"

This brother doesn't miss a thing. "That is a bit of a story," I answered, still wondering how the apostle had calmed my inner world with a simple touch. "But it starts with Athanasius and a treatise he wrote, entitled *On the Incarnation of the Word of God*, when he was still in his early twenties, which is shocking to me, how young he was at the time. I chanced across a copy many years ago and read it. It was the first time that my mind was blown. My heart has never settled since."

"*Chanced* across a copy?" He cocked his head, seizing on a word I'd used without thinking.

"Ah! Did you send him to me?" I laughed, not sure what to think.

"Perhaps Athanasius led you himself. He is not dead. How do you think he spends his time in the cloud?" he asked, spreading his arms and hands around us slowly, and adding, "which surrounds us now, as always." As he motioned the air shimmered like summer heat waves over a parking lot.

"I have no idea. I've never thought about that," I said, wondering again at what had just happened.

"You said that in your day you have some device, cell phones I believe you called them, through which you can talk to people all over the world?"

"We do. They are amazing. We can talk to anyone just about anywhere."

"I prefer the Holy Spirit."

I knew he was serious, and from what I had experienced with him, I had no reason to doubt him, but he kept stretching me beyond my comfort zone.

He whispered, "The Holy Spirit is everywhere, my son, in all times and ages and places—poured out on *all flesh*—in Jesus. You and I and everybody else are connected *in the Holy Spirit*. As we trust her, *truly* amazing things happen. Are you forgetting where you are?"

My mind froze in marvel at the apostle and his extraordinary perspective. Then I remembered Moses and Elijah meeting Jesus on the mount of transfiguration and that John was an eyewitness—and I was on the isle of Patmos with the Apostle John.

It took me several minutes to get my bearings. "I suppose it is naive if not outright arrogant to think that Athanasius and the cloud, who live in the Holy Spirit without shadows, are somehow less able to communicate than we are with our cell phones and the Internet."

"*Unbelieving* is a better word. Your perspective is limited, but it will not always be so." The joyful certainty in his eyes gave me hope. "Now, back to my question."

"And which question would that be?" I asked, half smiling.

"East and West."

I sighed and plunged in again. "Okay, then. When you visited Barth and MacDonald, you saw many books, sort of like bound scrolls. There are thirty-eight volumes of these books containing the writings of key figures from your day until after the Council of Nicaea. I have all those books in my library. I was blessed to study under a great man who had read almost everything in the history of the church, East and West. He directed us to the early fathers."

After a good while John turned to me and asked, "These thirty-eight books that you mentioned, you have read all of them?"

"Many of them—and some, like those of Irenaeus, Athanasius, Hilary, and Gregory Nazianzen, several times. You would be proud. These men were—or *are*—your worthy brothers."

"Are these the ones who wrote the creed?"

"Yes, in a way. It was essentially written by Athanasius, following Irenaeus and others and earlier creeds. Athanasius, Hilary, Gregory, and others defended it with everything they had. It was a war, my brother; the faith once delivered—and being with you is redefining my understanding of what 'the faith' is—was almost lost. I shudder to think what might have happened if Athanasius had not appeared."

"And these brothers were in the East?"

"In those days there was no division yet."

"Your Athanasius and the other brothers who wrote the creed understood God's union with us in Jesus. That is clear from what you said. What then happened in your West?"

"Hmm . . . That is another doozy of a question, and I don't think I am anywhere close to being able to give you a good answer. But it is clear that your bottom line is union."

"Roger that!" The ancient brother grinned.

"And that makes serious sense to me and sort of scares me at the same time. But taking that as the center, theologically speaking, I would say that the East—at its best, anyway—saw it and stood firm on union. Those men were awestruck by Jesus becoming what we are." I could feel St. John's pride and hope rising.

"But in the West," I went on, "we have been smitten, without always knowing it, with the Greek philosophy and with Roman law, as I mentioned. Not without protests along the way, mind you, and not least in Luther, Calvin, and later on your friends MacDonald and Barth and my own beloved teacher and his brother, among others. I don't know what you know or who all you have visited, but Barth coined the single most provocative and haunting word I have ever heard—*nomixophilosophicotheologia*."

"Now *that* is a word," he exclaimed, rising and clapping. "Karli cuts to the chase, does he not? I like that." He nodded with fresh intensity, his eyes shining. "No time for Ophis."

"Right! Barth was shouting no to the assimilation. He saw that the theology of the West had lost its way. I suppose you could say that in the West we have bought *separation*, hook, line, and sinker, and that has set the agenda for our family conversation for fifteen hundred years. I don't mean to say, of course, that we don't know and love Jesus, but we are a long way from knowing and *seeing* him the way you do. MacDonald and Barth saw and knew your Jesus. I see that clearly now."

"*Ideas*," the beloved disciple of Jesus replied, raising his hands with apostolic authority, "good or bad, shape what you see and do not. Perhaps your Augustine is the fly."

I looked at him blankly.

"In your dream. The one fly that led the others to exhaustion."

"Augustine is held in high esteem in the West, but there are many in my day, Barth and my teacher among them, who think he is the source of most of our Western theological ills. Recently one of our American theologians wrote that 'more than anyone else, Augustine shaped Western theology and made it different from the traditions of the East.' But there are many others in our West who think that Augustine was a genius, the greatest mind in our history."

"Perhaps both estimations are correct."

"Well, a similar thing has been said by others, too." I nodded, recalling things I'd read. "The great Reformation—when Luther and Calvin and Knox and many others, such as John Hus, John Wycliffe, George Wishart, and Patrick Hamilton, to name only a few, protested against Rome—has been described as the battle between the *two sides* of Augustine."

"A split mind?" John said, more suggesting than asking.

"That is exactly what many believe."

He sat stroking his beard for a few moments. As he did, something inside me began to squirm—what, or why, I did not know, and that made me nervous.

"Did this Augustine believe in Jesus's union with us?" he asked with no uncertain authority.

"Augustine," I said, my defenses rising, "was a great lover of Jesus and of the sovereign grace of God and a staunch defender of the Incarnation."

"Union or separation," John insisted, eyebrows raised. His tone was not interrogative but declarative. "Did your Augustine believe in union?"

As I considered his question, the kaleidoscope turned another notch in my mind, but it was too much for me to process. I suppose I sat in silence, and perhaps denial, a good while, for when I next heard the old apostle's voice, he was speaking my name quizzically as if suspecting I had lost my marbles.

"Sorry, sir. As you asked me about Augustine, my inner world trembled. I'm not sure why, but I have been starting to feel a bit frantic and anxious again."

"The darkness trembles at the dawning of the light. But the tremble is *Ophis's* fear, not yours—yet so close you feel it as yours."

His words carried such depth that I was not sure how to respond. So I sat quietly, letting my mind drift like a dandelion in the breeze.

"Augustine . . . ," he prompted.

"Oh yes. I would have to say that while Augustine was a passionate defender of Jesus, he did not believe in your union. His vision of God's election of only some and his arguments against Pelagius prove that point quite clearly." I hoped the apostle would ask me about Pelagius, but I knew that he would not. Something more critical was in his crosshairs.

"Ophis again," the brother groaned.

"Ophis is hardly ever mentioned in the same sentence with Augustine."

"If your Augustine failed to see union, he had Ophis's lies swimming in his head."

"But Augustine is revered as the genius of the West. He is sacred to the Western imagination and to many beyond such serious criticism."

"If he believed that we are separated from Jesus," St. John said carefully, "and if he, as you said, is the Father of your Western tradition, then his ideas led the West to exhaustion, no matter how much he loved and knew Jesus. Perhaps it was through the ideas he passed on that the deepest log in your beaver dam was put in place. But do not fear; the Holy Spirit always works to redeem our blunders," he whispered, resting a reassuring hand on my shoulder and sending something like an electric charge through my body, "especially our largest ones. Your Augustine is not dead but alive. I have a hunch that he is still fathering your West."

I wasn't sure what he meant by that, but his tone was respectful. I shook my head, full of questions. "When you frame it like that, it strikes me that the great Reformation was a protest against separation. To use your language, the Reformers protested the way the Roman church proclaimed separation and prescribed for people to get to God—accumulating merit by works or even by trying to purchase it."

"Union or separation, my son. Whenever people are led to believe they are separated from God, anyone or anything that offers a way back gets powerful."

"Yes. It is terribly shocking," I said, crossing my arms, starting to rock slightly.

"Now, in your great Reformation: these men and women, did they read my gospel?"

"That they did, with honor and care. They rediscovered the New Testament—you and Paul, Peter and James, the book of Hebrews, all the Gospels."

"Rediscovered? Was it *lost?*" he asked in disbelief.

"In a way it was. Not unlike before the time of King Josiah when the Book of Moses was lost. In the 1500s only the church's official leaders could read Latin, and apparently at the time of Luther, not many of them were even doing that. With his printing press, Gutenberg opened the way for the Bible to be translated into people's own language and distributed. Luther translated it into German, for example. Just as in Josiah's day, when the New Testament began to be read and understood again, many people were dumbfounded by how lost the church had become and were determined to realign it with Scripture. But it has been a wild and scary ride ever since, because everyone reads the Bible in their own way. In my time, right at five hundred years from Luther, we have thousands of factions within the church, as I told you. The fragmentation breaks my heart! It is *pitiful*. I have lost hope that we will ever come together."

It dawned on me that I was also talking about myself. Fragmentation . . . pitiful . . . lost hope . . . together. I thought of little Aidan, and I could see that my terrible despair was rooted in fear that I would never be whole or right or okay.

"Young Aidan," the apostle said, startling me out of my thoughts, then looking me in the eyes, "the Holy Spirit always works to reveal Jesus in us. Jesus is our togetherness, our union." I knew he was speaking to me and about the church at large and the world. "The revelation of Jesus in us is the way the church was born in the beginning; and that is the way it will be renewed. I have a hunch that your creed may be of great service to you and your West."

My heart flooded with relief, both for the church and for me. I actually allowed myself to hope that being whole was possible. "Perhaps it is time to write the creed in the Creed Room," I said, feeling an emerging sense that the creed held healing secrets for us all. "I would love to hear what *you* have to say about the most famous and celebrated document in the history of the church, East and West—apart from the New Testament, of course."

16

THE APOCALYPSE

"Follow me," the ancient brother said with a wink and a sly grin, as he grabbed one of the lamps and motioned for me to do the same.

We turned to the left into the main artery of the cave and walked about fifty feet. *I passed right by here on my way earlier*, I thought, *with no clue.*

As we entered another room on the right from the main passage, the lamps brought their light. The new room was much larger than the other and oddly shaped, more like an oval with a side room than a square, and there seemed to be no ceiling. Glancing around, I noticed that one of the long walls glistened. Then I saw it: there before me, not fifteen feet away, radiated the text of the Apocalypse. One whole wall was covered in writing, as far as the lamps would let me see to either side. My heart leapt with joy and silent awe.

St. John placed his lamp on a tall rock to our right as if he had done so a thousand times, which I suppose he had, and motioned for me to do the same on the opposite side. The room had a feel of its own, different from his living quarters; it was more like a sanctuary for warriors, its air thick with battle-tested honor, a truly hallowed space. I knelt, speechless, but my brother would have none of it. Putting a hand under my elbow, he drew me to my feet.

"In my time," I said, my heart quivering, "I have received a letter from the president of my country, met famous people, stood in the grandest cathedrals of Europe and Rome, and each commanded their proper respect. But *this room* in *this cave* with *you* and *this text* is too much for me to bear. I feel like a wild turkey at a beauty pageant."

Amused, the great saint simply shook his head at me. "Many hours have I sat in tears in this room. In fact, right where you are standing is where I stood praying in the Spirit on the Lord's day, when I heard behind me the loud voice like a trumpet." The room quaked, as did I as he spoke and pointed behind me. "The time is near. Today is the day of revelation, my son," he said without flourish, like a matter of known fact.

I had no idea what he was thinking, yet expectation flashed through my body. "You must tell me what this means, every single word. This is one of the greatest mysteries in history. Many people have spent their entire lives trying to understand your Apocalypse and fighting to prove that they had it right."

"Mystery?" he asked innocently.

"Surely you admit that the Revelation is not easy to understand."

"It is simple," he responded, distinctly puzzled.

"That would be the understatement of all understatements." I rolled my eyes. "You can't be serious. Your Apocalypse has left generations of scholars scratching their heads."

"I can't see how that would help," he mused.

"How what would help?"

"Scratching their heads." He shrugged.

"Just another expression. It means bewildered, unable to understand."

"Ah." He nodded. Then he turned and spread out both arms, taking in the wall. "*This* is about Jesus's victory over the darkness—the same as my gospel, only different. I had to find a way to get it past the Romans. They thought the letter was gibberish, written by a prisoner high on mushrooms."

"Mushrooms?" I asked.

"Patmos has special mushrooms. At least, I've heard that from other prisoners. I have no need of such. I have a hunch you will soon know why."

"Sir," I pressed, trying to keep him from going down a rabbit trail, "by some miraculous dispensation of exceeding grace I am here, and you *must* explain to me about the Revelation."

"My son, listen. Ophis was on the attack against my brothers and sisters. I wrote so they could see Jesus as the Victor, the *Lamb* on the Throne of the cosmos, so they would hold fast to the testimony of Jesus. The battle has been won. We must bear witness to the truth and persevere the tribulation of enlightenment."

He backed up and I with him, so we could see the whole text. He pointed to seven distinct sections of writing, indicating something of the structure of the book.

The first and the last sections are clearly the prologue and the epilogue. And the second from the left are obviously the letters to the churches laid out in the form of a chiasm.

"Each of these," John said, assuming the posture and tone of a teacher and pointing to sections three through six, "is a different picture of Jesus and his victory."

I took a deep breath, overcome by the sheer import of this opportunity. "There are so many questions, hundreds of questions. Let's start at the beginning."

"I am fond of the beginning." He gave me a look that I was coming to know as his boyish, apostolic look. "The *title* tells the tale: *unveiling*. The letter is about the unveiling of Jesus, same as my gospel. Study the ancient writings, and you will understand the Apocalypse. Everything I wrote is built upon the prophets' vision of the Christ as victor over darkness."

"That I believe, but you still have to explain *how* it all means that."

"As the Lord gives us time, we can talk until we fall asleep."

"There is no time like the present; I am all ears."

He stared at me like I had become Dumbo the elephant.

"Listening, it means completely listening." *If only I had my iPhone to take some pictures and record this conversation*, I thought, taking a mental picture of the beginning of each section. I noticed, or was somehow given to see, the strange variations of the word ανοιγω, "open," in the first line of the four sections following the letters to the churches.

"But now is your turn. The wall behind us is empty; we came in here for you to write the creed on it. You tell me about the creed, and I will share my heart with you as the Spirit leads."

"*And* your thoughts on your gospel, your letters, the Holy Spirit, the cross, Jesus and his Father, salvation . . . and your Revelation."

"It is not *mine*," John declared, slightly miffed.

"*What* is not yours?"

"The Apocalypse. Were you not listening to me?"

"With all my heart, but I thought it was you who wrote the Apocalypse."

"Of course I did." He laughed. "But it is the unveiling of *Jesus*, not of *me*."

"Right. Sorry. I got lost for a moment."

"Roger that." He winked. "Now, on with your writing," he commanded, handing me a white rock.

As I stood to write, I reminded him respectfully that I was hoping for a long discussion about his writings and thoughts. As if that wasn't what we had been doing!

"As the Spirit leads us, my son, as the Spirit leads," he responded, eyes twinkling like they did whenever he knew something I didn't.

"This has to be the most bizarre moment in the cosmos."

"No one knows, as I told you, how the Holy Spirit does things, but when we follow her, amazing things happen. Let us trust together." He patted me on the shoulder affectionately like a wise old master enjoying his student.

With his touch the lamps flickered in a gentle breeze, and the room was suddenly ablaze with light and fire as the ground began to shake. "*Behold,*" a voice thundered, "*the Lamb upon the Throne!*"

Awe shot through my veins like lightning, and every hair on my body bristled. The words echoed through the cave, hanging in midair as if they were taking material form. I was afraid to look, but that voice no one could ignore.

My whole body shaking, I turned and saw John the Baptist, standing in towering strength, white iridescent fire billowing around him as if he was in the burning bush or was even the bush itself. His eyes were aflame with the sun, his hair radiant. Then I heard the roar of many voices shouting, "*Worthy is the Lamb!*" It sounded like Niagara Falls, shaking the cave and surely the whole island, but I could see only the Baptist.

Like an ancient warrior, he lifted his right arm and pointed to the text of the Apocalypse. As I watched, the text moved and stood out from the rock, each letter and mark shining as though living gold. I stood speechless, staring in wonder at the Baptist and the living words.

Again he announced, *"Behold, the Lamb upon the Throne!"*

And again came the thunderous witness. *"Worthy is the Lamb!"*

Then a third time. *"Behold, the Lamb upon the Throne!"*

"Worthy is the Lamb!"

As the third witness reverberated, shaking the world, the room itself melted into the light of a sea of stars, as if the cosmos itself had come into the cave. A mighty wind rushed about, stars and planets and stunning suns swirling all around us, and I was lifted with them into the wind, suspended in midair. My eyes burned with searing light.

Then suddenly everything was calm, as if quick-frozen, and space itself and all its worlds were parted, like the bowing of trees in a grove before a blasting wind. Yet not a sound could be heard: it was as if the universe held its breath in awe. My gaze was drawn to the center, of what I did not know.

A sight unutterable rose before me. Legions of mighty angels stood erect, looking as one away from me—no lights flashed, no whirling wind, no noise could be heard. Then a tiny lamb, freshly slain yet somehow alive and standing upon the Throne of all thrones, appeared before my eyes.

My heart stopped. Every cell in my being stopped. I found myself *beholding* the *Lamb of God*: alive, not dead, on the throne at the center of all things. The cosmos flowed as a grand river from his wound; deep inside I knew that in the Lamb all things began and are. Surrounding him was the cloud of witnesses, the saints of old, even those not yet born—all the saints, myriads and myriads of them, a living ocean of men and women as far as I could see. They sang many songs, but all their songs became one:

From victory to victory the Lamb leads, worthy is the Lamb.
From faith to faith, the Word believes, worthy is the Word.
From Father's heart to Spirit's light, worthy is the Son.

Then everything in the cosmos joined the song—and I did, too—as life itself was spoken—glorious, abounding life—and beauty, bereft of any hint of shame or shadow.

The Lamb became two nail-scarred wrists and hands, holding a tiny sphere. The hands were held by another, a presence of care so true and good that I could scarcely imagine it. All around the hands and the presence, the song of light flowed, permeating everything.

I wept from the trenches of my soul, knowing my search, at long last, was over. Home had found me.

Then all creation grew quiet in joy unspeakable. I stood still, staring, when the hands, the presence, and the song moved around me, in me, through me. No human words can do justice to that movement—that harmony and beauty, energy, union, peace, and intimacy . . . Then the hands became Jesus, more radiant than a thousand suns, standing in person before me. I fell to my knees at once in adoration.

He placed his right hand on my shoulder. "Rise, my beloved; *hear me and live.*"

I awoke from the vision sobbing tears of hope, the ancient apostle holding me from collapse.

"Sit here, my son," John said, indicating a place with his hand, then gently helped me move.

I sat transfixed, my inner world as silent and peaceful as the falling snow. I must have fallen asleep sitting up, for as I came awake St. John was holding me in his arms as if to keep me from falling over.

"You saw *him*?" he asked, his eyes full of delight.

"I did, my brother," I replied, my breath catching in a sob as the tears welled up. "A sight only silence can tell. *The Lamb* upon the Throne of all thrones! Did you not see?"

"I have many times, but this was *your* vision," he said proudly.

"And did you not see the Baptist standing in majesty, pointing to your Revelation, and your own words coming to life, shining out the joy that went into their writing?"

"No. I have seen many things, but this was a vision for you. Tell me what you saw."

"Give me a hundred years. Perhaps then I will be ready to begin." How could what I saw ever live in words?

"I know the problem," he said and waited.

"It was all so beautiful, utterly breathtaking."

"And *simple*," the apostle whispered, smiling.

I looked at him. It *was* simple. More immense, rich, and deep than could be imagined but simple. "I saw a slain Lamb upon the Throne, alive, not dead, and the cosmos was flowing out of his wound, and the great cloud was singing a thousand songs, yet as one new song. Sir, you must help me understand."

"Can you walk?"

"I think I could fly to the heavens better than walk right now! Why?"

"It is best to take a walk after these visions, to let your mind settle. I know a place by the sea. The Romans are gone for now."

"My mind has exploded. How will it ever settle?"

"Your mind is beginning to know with your heart; your mind will never be the same."

I AM NOT

The beloved disciple helped me get up and steady myself. My heart was so full I could burst. The room shouted peace through its silence. As I rose so did more tears, these from places in me long buried: tears of hope, refreshed and almost singing.

"My son," John said, with honor and joy in his voice, "I see confidence forming in your eyes."

"Confidence?"

"Unearthly assurance, my dear brother, is taking flight in your heart like a bird from a hidden nest. You are coming to *know* the truth," he said, patting me affectionately on my shoulder.

"Sir, we cannot call this room The Creed Room. This is The Room of Revelation!"

"Indeed it is," he said with delight.

"Can we stay here for a while longer? I can't bring myself to leave just yet."

"Of course. This room is now yours, too; you can come and rest and *see* here. It is the Lord's gift to you." Then he added, with a wink and his wry smile, "A notch or two above Plato's cave, don't you think?"

"Nothing could be clearer to me now than how I, in all my years of struggle and faith and study, have so terribly *underestimated* Jesus. Everything is about *him*! Everything! I have missed the point entirely. Jesus is the center of the whole cosmos, yet we see him as so distant."

"Separated," he said, his voice strong and compassionate.

I thought back to the TV preacher we talked about earlier—coiffed hair bobbing, stage lights and music rising with perfect timing—passionately imploring his audience to receive *Jeeezus* into their lives. "We have it backwards," I said, as if he would know what I meant. I wasn't even sure I knew.

He did. "Your dead flies and your beaver dam shout to you that it is so."

"We believe that people are *separated from Jesus* and that it is our mission to persuade them to accept him into their hearts."

"I believe your word is *bizarre*." The great apostle grinned.

As excited as I was, I could see in his eyes that I had only just begun. He faced his Apocalypse as if gathering strength, not that he needed it. I noticed him staring at what we know as chapter five of the Revelation. He was thinking of the Lamb on the Throne of all thrones. I could feel his heart. I said nothing as I stood and waited, knowing that this dear, godly man was about to give me yet another gift.

John held up his left hand and looked at me. "Listen," he whispered, as his text seemed to follow his hand. "The gospel is not the news that *we* can receive Jesus into *our* lives. The gospel is the news that *Jesus* has received us into *his*—union, my son."

The room erupted with applause. I think it was the joy of the cloud. Everything seemed to shimmer and shake, and I knew that I had heard the undiluted truth of all truths. Never had a simple statement carried such shattering and liberating weight.

"Such a thought, sir, I know is true, yet it staggers my mind . . . all but inconceivable to us in the West." I felt freed and terrified at the same time, yet all that the apostle had been teaching me and all that I had just experienced declared that it was so. The real Jesus was way bigger than I had ever imagined. *Can we actually overestimate Jesus?*

"Are you having another brain glitch?" He smiled, knowing the path from darkness to light often requires a touch of humor.

"Are you kidding me? My brain is *fried*, burnt to a crisp, overloaded, reamed, steamed, and dry-cleaned!" I laughed. "But my heart—*my heart*— something in my heart, a great wound, is healing."

John turned quickly and dramatically toward me, as if the moment he had been waiting for had arrived and he was not about to miss it. Again he calmed the space around us and lifted his hands, as if pronouncing a benediction: "As we *behold* the Lamb, the weight of sin is lifted." He was always able, so beautifully able, I see now, to go with the flow of my frayed thinking, as he led me carefully to life.

With his words more tears rose from the deep places in my heart, and I sat down on the dirt floor, sobbing.

"Tears are the way of freedom. Tell me of your wound."

"I have spent my life trying to avoid it, running from it, being driven by it, or all of the above, but I see how I have believed—since I was a little boy—that it is not okay to be me. *I am not* enough." My own words now carried weight with my soul like the apostle's. "I am not there . . . yet, not worthy, not smart enough, not important."

"I, too, know that wound." He knelt beside me, and the light seemed to create an aura around his face.

"*You?*" I was a bit dumbfounded by the humanity of the apostle and thought he was simply being kind to me. "How could the Apostle John believe that he was not enough, not there yet, not worthy, not bright? You're the beloved disciple of Jesus, the wisest man in history."

"The Pharisees had a way of insinuating to us fishermen that we were unlearned idiots, and their endless rules overwhelmed every honest heart with the fear of never making the mark. Of course, the accusations came ultimately from Ophis, but they came through the Pharisees."

"What just happened in this room, with all this light and shaking and encountering, forever changes the definition of *education* for me."

"This word *education*, it is not Greek." John lifted his hands, and I could see his thoughts racing ahead of mine. "What does it mean?"

"It comes from the Latin *educare* or maybe *educere*."

"What does *educare* mean?" he asked, rising to his feet. I could see that detective look in his eyes.

"It means 'to draw out,' to draw out that which is within," I submitted, aware that out of my mouth had again come way more than I knew.

"As I suspected, my son," he said quietly, "as I suspected. In the great hour three times Peter was asked if he was a disciple of Jesus; twice he denied our Lord with the very words 'I am not.' I took note of that, such a sharp contrast with our Lord's 'I Am.' In time I realized that Peter's terrible 'I am not' was healed by Jesus's 'I Am.' I saw it with my own eyes, but I could not understand what Jesus was doing. It is the way for us all."

I was lost, wondering how Peter's denial and Jesus's "I Am" were related, how both somehow addressed me, and what any of it had to do with union and education. But I had learned something of the way the apostle's mind worked or his heart. He was always alert, listening, seeing connections, and pulling things together in the moment—in me—to help me. I knew the minute we met that I could trust him. Now I had every reason to give myself to his guidance even if it seemed like we were talking about ten completely unrelated things at the same time. I was sure he would lead me to understand what I had just experienced, heard, and seen.

"Now, tell me"—he shifted subjects, at least to my mind—"of the song you heard." I could all but see the wheels of his masterful mind turning.

With his question I could hear the cloud's song again in my heart. "That song, my dear brother, I will never forget. There were so many songs, myriads of them, but they all became one, and its harmony was beyond anything I have ever heard. They were singing:

> From victory to victory the Lamb leads, worthy is the Lamb.
> From faith to faith, the Word believes, worthy is the Word.
> From Father's heart to Spirit's light, worthy is the Son.

"Beautiful," he declared simply and then grew quiet. Lost in contemplation, he swayed from side to side.

I was grateful, as it gave me some time to get my wits about me. *I cannot begin to keep up with all that is happening. Who will ever believe this? How can I believe this?*

At length the ancient disciple spoke. "The cloud, those sisters and brothers . . . they can sing!"

"What are you thinking? What do you hear in the cloud's song? What is the connection you see with Jesus's "I Am" and Peter's "I am not" and me?"

"Aidan, what do you see?" John asked, striking a Socratic pose.

I tried to think, but all that came to my mind was The Grove and the Rebels playing on a Saturday afternoon. It took a few moments for me to discover why. "Sir," I answered, somewhat settling down and having no idea that I had just boarded the roller coaster again, "at home great crowds gather to watch football games in massive stadiums much larger than the Roman Coliseum, as I mentioned to you earlier. Anticipation charges the atmosphere. People are excited but nervous, very *anxious* in fact, because no one knows which team will win. The cloud is not anxious. They sing of certain victory unfolding in history, as if they know the end before it happens . . . But there is so much that is beyond my thoughts."

"You know more than you can say. The knowing of your heart will forever challenge your mind until they are one. It takes time." He was way beyond me, but I could tell my mind was actually expanding.

"Roger that." I remembered our first meeting when he opened his arms and said to me, "Welcome to *my* world." "I feel like a man smitten with a beauty I can scarcely bear, let alone talk about intelligently."

"Ah, the poet is born in you." John grinned as if letting out a secret. "Poetry is the best language of the soul. You must first see that which cannot be said. From the wounded places the words form, then comes the joy of saying—for yourself and for others. And to him."

"The poet? I feel more like the Scarecrow in *The Wizard of Oz* begging to get a real brain!"

"My young brother, you need a walk. You are sounding like you have been tokin' on the Patmos." John broke up laughing so hard that I thought he might embarrass himself.

I laughed, too, the laugher of relief of what seemed a thousand years of sorrow. I rubbed my head with both hands and took a long, deep breath. I was at peace, but inside I heard a voice saying, "Don't miss a word!"

18

FROM FAITH TO FAITH

I looked up toward the Apocalypse, and managed to get to my feet. Here I was in a cave with the Apostle John and the text of the book of Revelation, but my questions had changed. *How strange that the word* Apocalypse *has become a terror to so many people when it means the unveiling of Jesus himself.* I suddenly had an insight into the way Ophis twists things to create fear.

"Sir, the song, what does the cloud mean when they sing, 'From faith to faith, the Word believes'?"

A broad smile of pride swept his ancient face. "There is one victory, one faith, and One who knows the Father face-to-face."

"One faith. That is what the Apostle Paul wrote in Ephesians."

"Only one. The faith of Jesus himself—what he believes."

I had no idea how at this point I could think at all, but the notion of the faith of Jesus carried momentous encouragement, and I had a hunch that I was on the edge of "seeing what is," as the apostle liked to say. *But didn't the New Testament constantly call us all to faith and warn us of great sorrow if we didn't believe? And was not his own gospel known to many as The Gospel of* Belief?"

John could see the questions in my eyes, and said softly, "Aidan, without encountering Jesus, we are doomed to live in our own worlds—*Ophis's* madness."

Our own worlds. Lord, if ever anything summarized my life, that is it.

"Faith is seeing with Jesus's eyes, seeing *what is.* 'From faith to faith, the Word believes.'"

I looked down and noticed that the floor now sparkled as if some of the gold from the text had fallen into the dirt. The gold dust started to move, and I could see it in the air as well, even in the air that I breathed. The apostle saw it, too, nodding. I realized that as the gold filled the room and made its way inside me, somehow the faith of Jesus himself finds its way into our hearts." Anticipation rose in the Room of Revelation.

"My son, union or separation. If you are separated from Jesus, then—"

"Then all I have is my faith," I interrupted.

"But such separation exists only in our Ophis-infested imaginations. 'The Word,' as Moses teaches, 'is not far from you'"—John pointed to the particles of gold still in the air, moving his finger from the air to my mouth and then continued quoting Moses—"'but is very near, in your mouth, and *in* your heart, that you may believe.' Like this dust, Jesus is *in* you, and he *believes.*"

As I trained my overtaxed mind on the apostle's words, the confidence and joy of the cloud rose in my thoughts, like water rising in the stem of a plant, giving it vitality.

"The first faith of all is the faith of Jesus," he said, slowing down and speaking with patience and great gentleness. "As Jesus reveals himself *in* us, he is sharing himself, his eyes, his faith with us. Do you see? From his eyes to ours, from faith to faith."

I thought of Paul's comment in Galatians when he wrote of the Father being pleased to reveal his Son *in* him that he might proclaim Jesus *in* the Gentiles. I felt like I had suddenly come into serious white-water rapids that were beyond my ability to navigate. *Seeing with Jesus's eyes is too . . . too . . .*

"Beautiful for words," the apostle said, finishing my thought. "It takes time. Jesus asks us to take sides with him against the way *we see.*"

"Are you talking about repentance?"

"That is a strange word. I believe you mean *metanoia,* a real change of mind—a change in the way you see and believe," the beloved disciple replied excitedly, sounding exactly like my old professor, which startled and comforted me at the same time. "Jesus calls us to a change of the way we see, his Father first, then ourselves and others, until we believe what he believes."

"Sir, this change in the way we see is rather monumental! Everything is turning upside down."

"Indeed." John tried to hide his smile, but his eyes told on him.

"And without this change of mind or seeing, we remain lost in our own worlds or ideas?"

"Without Jesus you would only have what *you* do and do not *see*— imprisoned by your feelings, or lack of them, lost in your head . As we discover Jesus *in* us, we are given a way to change our minds and our feelings. With our 'Amen' to Jesus comes freedom to live from his 'I Am' from here," he said, pointing to his heart with one hand and placing the other on mine. "Aidan, living from Jesus' faith, from his 'I Am' gives us confidence to turn toward our Father. When we see the Father through Jesus' eyes, we experience life—eternal life."

"My heart is with you, but my mind, good Lord! You think about things almost the opposite way that we do in the West."

"It appears I do. How do *you* see things?" he asked pointedly.

I knew this was another defining moment in my life. "I am with you, at least in my heart, but in the West Jesus is external to us until we do something to bring him into our hearts. And then we try to live the life of a disciple from external information and principles by our own faith and sheer force of will. It's like we believe in the real absence of Jesus."

"Separation," he exclaimed. "How could you hope to believe anything that you do not already know?"

"Did you just say what I think you said?" I felt like a surfer who mounted an unexpected and gigantic wave.

"*Educare.* I believe that was your word—drawing *out* that which is *within*? The knowing, *his knowing*, his believing, his 'I Am,' is deeper in us than our own thinking and challenges our thoughts to expand. He calls us to hear him and say, 'Amen' to him, and to live out of his life within us. We take sides with him against the way we see."

I realized that when John speaks of Jesus's 'I Am' it is his code phrase for Jesus himself and the way he sees and believes, and all that Jesus is in his faith and faithfulness, victory and love, confidence and freedom, joy and life and communion with his Father in the Holy Spirit—eternal life.

I thought again of Peter and could suddenly see, and the sight filled me with hope unending. "Jesus's "I Am" met Peter inside the guilt and shame of his denial—his 'I am not.' And Peter believed; he said 'amen' to the way Jesus believed about him. He took sides with Jesus against the way he saw himself."

"Indeed he did. It is the same for us all."

"Wow! Sir, that is good. That is hope."

"'From faith to faith, the Word believes.'" John beamed. "*And* from faith to freedom and joy and life—in the midst of this terrible darkness."

I felt like I was an old wrinkled shirt that was being ironed. He made real sense, and what he was saying was breathtaking, but there were a lot of wrinkles in my thinking.

19

THE GREAT I AM

Hope raced in my heart and I was beginning to feel, but I knew I needed to slow down. My encounter with Jesus had absolutely blown my mind, and I desperately wanted to understand every shred of what it meant—personally, spiritually, psychologically, and not least theologically. My heart stopped suddenly in a moment of honest gratitude. I glanced at my dear brother with genuine praise in my soul for the way he had accepted me and loved me since I arrived. *He is a gentle man, a true apostle of Jesus.* I found myself tearing up again.

St. John had led me to meet Jesus as never before, and that encounter was turning everything I had believed on its head or exploding it from the inside out. But my left brain kicked in, and I needed this laid out logically. There were layers upon layers in what I had encountered and in what the apostle was saying, and I struggled to keep up. I thought of the three chairs I had seen, and somehow this helped me focus.

The apostle believed that Jesus was in us all with his eternal life with his Father. I had always thought that eternal life meant that we would go to heaven after we died and we would live forever—if we had properly believed the gospel. He clearly thought of life in more relational terms, not so much how long we live, or where, but who we know and the way our knowing shapes our experience everywhere. It certainly worked for St. John. I thought of Jesus's prayer: "And this is eternal life, that they may know You, the only true God, and Jesus Christ whom You have sent."

As I contemplated his prayer, a deck of cards came to mind, but I had no idea why. *Perhaps Jesus stacked the deck.* I laughed to myself. But uppermost in my mind was the way Jesus and the Holy Spirit were so real to the apostle. John did not live by applying Scripture to his life; he lived in a remarkable fellowship with Jesus and his Father, always in the Holy Spirit. Yet he clearly venerated Scripture. I was always taught that the Scriptures were holy and to be honored, but John was more enamored with Jesus himself and seriously believed that Jesus was present with us all, not absent up there somewhere, having left us alone with an inspired book. I decided to start with the question of Scripture, fully confident for the first time in my life that whatever was important for me to know would be unveiled.

When I asked him about his view of Scripture a quaint smile crossed his face, as if he knew what was happening and had every intention of honoring where I was in my processing. He tapped his left index finger on his lips. I could tell by his expression that he could see his way forward in my confusion, how all the dangling, disconnected thoughts could come together. He was inspired.

"The Pharisees believe that life resides *in* the Scriptures. They even eat pieces of the scroll. But Jesus told them, 'The scriptures point to *Me*. Here *I Am*, and you won't come to me for life.'"

My imagination ignited, and I envisioned Jesus squared off with the Pharisees.

"You should have seen their faces, Aidan, so twisted in fear and anger. But Jesus would not back down in his love. Again and again he said, 'I have come as Light into the world, so that everyone who believes in Me will not *remain* in darkness.'"

The apostle's eyes twinkled, and his lips widened into a shallow grin, and I knew that another one of his apostolic gems was coming my way. "Jesus *knew*"—his cheeky grin broadened into a full smile—"that he would find his way *inside*." John could hardly contain his pride. I held my breath in anticipation. "Jesus has a way of appearing in *unexpected* places, like inside locked rooms, darkened minds, and wounded hearts. Imagine their surprise, the Pharisees that is, when they began to discover Jesus not outside arguing but inside their own darkness!"

I gasped, clutching my heart. I could see what he was saying, but it was too simple to grasp.

He laughed, enjoying himself and me and this moment of revelation, knowing that I was close to freedom. "Without an encounter with Jesus inside our own hearts, we have no liberation from Ophis's lies and no freedom to *turn toward* the Father. Indeed, without the revelation of Jesus *in* us, we would never know we are in the dark at all."

"Slow down. A flood of wonder and light is shining in my understanding, but I can scarcely handle it. My only clear thought is that Paul said, 'The *gospel* is the power of God unto our liberation,' and I'm not sure how that relates to what you are saying."

"Of course, this is why we write and preach. As we proclaim the truth of all truths, Jesus, the living *Word*, the great 'I Am' reveals himself in us, shares his eyes with us."

"I do believe that I read somewhere," I said with a touch of cheek, trying to slow the hamster's wheel in my mind, "'What we have seen and heard we proclaim to you also, that you also may have fellowship with us; and indeed our fellowship is with the Father, and with his Son Jesus Christ. And these things we write, so that our joy may be made complete.'"

"That sounds familiar," he said slowly exaggerating his southern drawl, "from my first letter." He drew in a deep breath and looked into my eyes, then stood still as an owl, pondering depths, I suppose, that the rest of us only glimpse in our dreams. He finally asked, "Do you think Jesus needed the servants?"

"The *servants*? Are you having a brain glitch?" I asked, shocked that the words came out of my mouth.

"In my gospel . . . the wedding at Cana?"

I could not follow the apostle's thinking. It seemed to me that he had jumped ship altogether. I realized that I was praying and listening when the scene at Cana suddenly appeared in my mind's eye. "Do you mean when Jesus transformed the water into wine?"

"Yes," John replied quickly, seeing things coming together for me. "Do you think that Jesus needed the servants to get the water for him?"

"Well, I suppose he didn't. He is the Creator and Sustainer of all things. *Not one thing* has come into being without him, the Word of God, the light of the world, the *arche* of creation . . . ," I said affectionately, watching St. John, again surprising myself with my cheek and my newfound ability to keep up, sort of.

"Why would Jesus involve the servants?" he asked, unfazed by my comments.

"I have never thought of that. It could not have been because he needed their help. I saw the *whole cosmos* flowing from his wound."

"Place," he said quietly but with that now familiar apostolic authority.

"Now *you* are speaking in tongues," I replied, unable to control myself.

"Jesus has given *us* a real *place* in what he is doing. *He* could speak, of course, and it would be so, but our Lord, our blessed Lord, has no intention—" He stopped midsentence and raised his hands in quiet worship.

The room spoke peace to my soul, somehow admonishing me to silence. So I dared not open my mouth. In fact, I caught myself holding my breath, watching every twitch of his face, waiting, longing for light, as the great apostle saw things beyond the world's eyes.

When his heart, full and overflowing, was ready, John spoke. "Aidan," he said in a way that commanded every atom of my being to listen, "our blessed Lord Jesus has no intention"—he paused, almost unable to speak—"of being the *Father's Son* or the One anointed in *Ruach HaKodesh*"— again he stopped, with tears of stunned joy in his eyes—"or *the Lord* of all creation, *without us!*"

"That has the ring of things unspeakable about it," I said, realizing to my horror that I had actually dared to speak at all.

"Amen," he said in a hushed tone, humoring a good-hearted but unwitting son. "You say more than you understand, my brother."

"And it sounds like Barth," I blurted out again, wishing to find the pause button on my mouth.

"Jesus is the *living Word of God*, the great 'I Am.' He has found his way inside our deepest, most violent darkness. He has no need of apostles or preachers or evangelists."

"Sir, it is a massive shock to my entire system to learn that Jesus is in us all and we are in him, but I know it is true and love it even more. But now you sound like you are saying that Jesus doesn't care for us to know it. This cannot be."

"Of course not," John responded tenderly and with compassion for my journey. "Just as Jesus has no will to be the Father's Son without us, our Lord has no will to *leave us out* of his *letting people know* the truth."

"My dear brother, I am as lost as one of my tee shots. What are we talking about?"

"You quoted Paul: 'The gospel is the power of God unto our liberation,' did you not?"

"I did. That was a question, I think. Paul sees the *gospel* as very powerful."

John began to pace slowly. "The gospel is loaded, Aidan. Loaded with *resonance* with the *living Word*. That is how Jesus leads people to know the truth—through us."

"Good Lord! Jesus *has* stacked the deck."

The apostle looked at me like he had just taken his first bite of Spam. "Deck? Has this to do with ships?"

"Brother John, I think I see it! From faith to faith means from Jesus's presence *in* us to the *revelation* of Jesus in us, to our change of mind where we see with *Jesus's eyes, and we are free to live from his 'I Am.'* Now you are saying that Jesus will not reveal himself without our participation. So when the truth of all truths is proclaimed, the living Word resonates inside the hearts of the hearer, like a divine tuning fork."

"Deck? Tee shot? Tuning fork? You and your expressions." He laughed, bringing needed levity to our conversation but at the same time maintaining his focus.

"A tee shot is a term we use in golf when you hit the ball at the beginning of a hole. A tuning fork has to do with your resonance, like striking middle C on a piano, and the middle C vibrates inside us. A deck has to do—"

"Piano, middle C?"

"Sorry. I did it again. I mean something happens in here," I replied, placing my hands on my stomach.

As he raised his left eyebrow I could tell that another one of his enjoyable ideas was popping into his mind. He held his breath for several moments, then said, "Your own vision"—now smiling wryly—"was not outside you."

"My vision was *inside* me?"

"Of course, following our talk of union."

"Are you serious?

"I am indeed."

"All that I saw, all that happened, and all that I heard didn't happen out here but inside me. That is utterly amazing," I replied, raising my hands in the sheer joy of the moment and feeling a wave of new comfort in my inner world.

"'In that day, you will *know* that I am in My Father, and you *in* Me, and I *in* you.' It is our joy to tell the truth of all truths, and our honor to bear the scorn of others' enlightenment. The proclamation leads others to experience Jesus's 'I Am' within their own souls."

"But that rarely happens in my world. We have plenty of preachers, but—"

"Well, then, *what* or *who* are they preaching?"

"Not *Jesus in you*. Or not many anyway," I moaned.

"Then they preach *separation*, not *the Word*. Only the preaching of Jesus *in* us sings the song of light inside the human heart."

LITTLE AIDAN

Even though I was seeing the beaver dam again and feeling gloom, St. John's words quickened me. "Sir, I saw the song of light in my vision."

"Ah, dear Aidan," he replied, smiling warmly as his countenance shifted to satisfaction, "you saw *Ruach HaKodesh*."

"As I was *beholding* the Lamb, the Lamb became two nail-scarred wrists and hands, holding a tiny sphere. His hands were held by another, a presence of care so true and good I could hardly take it in. All around the hands and the presence, in and through them the song of light permeated all."

"The presence is Jesus's Father, Abba," the apostle replied, hands raised high in deep veneration. "Seeing Abba with Jesus's eyes, this leads into life abounding."

I felt relief rising like an irresistible fountain from far in the catacombs of my soul, moving into my heart and winding its way into my mind, then into my eyes. Before I could think, or even begin to understand what was happening, I suddenly saw *him*, Jesus's Father, Abba. I gasped and fell to the ground, not in fear but in astonishment and awe. Transfixed by the appearance, I felt a strange freedom take hold of my eyes, lifting them, and

I found myself turning toward the Father's face.

I could not take in the sight. It was too simple, too beyond my expectation, and too beyond the eyes of my fear. Sheer love poured into me through my eyes and all around me, containing *me*. I heard no mighty peals of thunder, felt no quaking of the earth, only calm and stillness, settling the squirming of my soul as if the stillness breathed in my own heart. I watched the calmness grow into silent peace, expanding. Facedown on the dirt floor, yet somehow looking up, I watched my own mind—the hamster's wheel—slow until it stopped. I marveled at the quiet.

Then a fortress of stone, impenetrable as hardened blue steel, appeared in my gaze. Helplessness seized my heart, and I cried, feeling the pitiful sorrow that comes when a prize is again and again just beyond your reach. As I shook my head in self-loathing, I heard the voice of Jesus, *the Word*, quiet as a clear whisper: "Take sides with me, against the way you see."

"Lord Jesus . . . this fortress is *me*, isn't it? I have built it, piece by miserable piece, but I cannot tear it down."

"I Am," I heard.

I heard at last, and all that was within me declared, *Amen!* I let go, of what I did not know. The fortress burst and vanished in a blast of purest light. In the light I could see, see beyond my own seeing. Two great eyes appeared, wide open and warm, clear as crystal, deep as a mountain lake and unclouded by any hint of shadow, and trained with affection upon *me*. In the eyes I saw myself reflected.

"This cannot be," I murmured. I wept and shuddered, convulsing in joy yet still not daring to believe. In his Father's eyes, *my* Father's eyes, I heard the song of light singing over me; I still cannot begin to describe what I was experiencing, except that it was a seeing that was also hearing. In the song flowed Abba's unsearchable care, all around me, in me, cradling me gently as a womb—*all of me*, every fearful, shame-riddled, guilt-ridden, war-torn fragment. All was *known* and accepted, embraced within and without—even, impossibly, *delighted in*. I felt a comfort and love more tender and beautiful than I ever dreamed could be possible.

Moving quietly, St. John, ever in tune with the Holy Spirit, left the room. He was giving me space to know, or as he would say, time for my imagination to *expand* until it was worthy of its theme.

I rolled onto my back with my eyes closed, marveling, when I felt Jesus's presence. I could *feel him—Jesus—in me.* I groaned as I realized that it had been a thousand years since I felt—or allowed myself to feel.

Then suddenly I saw little Aidan again. This time he wasn't in his swing or on the steps. He was packing a bag, as if running away. A cloud of sorrow filled his room and his heart. I saw hundreds of blackbirds flying in the sky. They became leaves falling in the wind, swirling, then the leaves became thoughts, whispers, accusations, and judgments. Most I could not make out, but some I could, like my grandmother's whisper, "Bless his heart. He's just dumb." And the words of my dad: "You were born trash, and you will die trash." I don't think they were intended as flaming darts, but woven with the hundreds of others they became a fiery pain in little Aidan—in me—and I watched myself shutting the door to my heart to protect myself.

"Oh, God!" I cried out, as I suddenly understood: little Aidan was the part of me that bore the sorrow, consigned as a scapegoat so the rest of me could cope with life. "Lord Jesus, what happened to me? What have I done? Have I become nothing more than a heartless brain?"

Little Aidan was leaving, but that irrepressible determination was a fire in his soul. He was setting out to find his real home. He looked back at me, straight into my eyes, and said, "I will meet you on Patmos." Then he was gone.

I fell over on my side, unable to move. Had little Aidan led me here? Had the sorrow that I gave him become my light? I could feel Jesus praying for me, as I thought of John's words about the Holy Spirit: "She specializes in using our sorrow to give us Jesus's eyes."

When I finally came to, I looked up to see little Aidan standing before me—clad in his embroidered cowboy shirt, Hoss Cartwright hat, and his prized boots—staring me down like it was the OK Corral. On my knees I reached out for him, and he ran to me. His eyes were alive with hope, eager, triumphant. I felt ashamed, as if I was guilty of murder or *suicide*! But little Aidan embraced me, and before I knew what was happening he disappeared in me.

It happened so fast that I hardly knew what to think. And I didn't think. *I felt!* I have no words to describe those feelings—whole is close, but only if you add full, integrated, together, right, at peace, and then forgiveness, joy, and goodness all overflowing together in love. I thought of Paul's prayer, "And to know the love of Christ which surpasses knowledge."

John returned. His eyes gleamed as if he had just spoken and a new creation itself had come to be. He was proud. "Jesus's 'I Am' trumps the 'I am nots', my brother. Freedom is necessary to our glory, and freedom may be the crack in the door that lets Ophis in, but Jesus has found his way inside our darkness!"

The presence of Jesus in me, our Father's eyes, the Holy Spirit's redeeming genius, little Aidan's return, the apostle's care . . . I was feeling things that I had never felt before in my life. "Now this is good! I like this! I will have more of this."

The beloved apostle held up his wineskin and some bread. "Now, my young son," he said softly with sacred warmth, "we celebrate and sing your song together."

St. John unfolded one of his purple rags and spread it on the ground like a tablecloth. He sat beside me, then grabbed the bread in silence and tore it into shreds, almost violently, dropping each piece deliberately onto his rag. The drama caught me off guard, but before I could say anything, he raised his wineskin above his head and poured it out onto the broken pieces of bread. Like water hitting a flat rock, the splatter was unmistakable. My heart, already raw with emotion and hope, was spellbound by the sight and sound. I couldn't see it at the moment, but his dramatic action was already preparing me for his final and greatest lesson.

The apostle soared into prayer:

> *Lord Jesus*, only begotten, beloved, and faithful Son of Abba, the living Word of God, anointed of *the* Holy Spirit, Son of Miriam, humble brother of the human race, Lord of all creation. With our whole hearts we honor you and bless your great name, the *arche* of creation, the Amen, the faithful and true Witness, the Lamb slain and seated upon the Throne of thrones, Heaven's Gate, the "I Am," Savior of the world, Victor over death and darkness. Worthy are you of all honor and glory and life, in this age and in all

ages to come. We rest in you. Bless you for finding us in the great darkness, for receiving me and my young son and the whole world into your life with your Father, for giving us *your eyes*. Worthy, Lord Jesus, are you of the summation of the ages; blessed be your great Name.

Holding up a piece of the wine-soaked bread, the ancient apostle whispered, "*This*, my brother, I give you in the name of Jesus, the great 'I Am' who is *in* the Father and *in* us. He has received you; hear him. 'From faith to faith,'" he declared with his wink, barely containing his sheer delight at sharing in all that had happened to me.

As he handed me the bread, I heard the voice of Jesus: "Rise, my beloved, *hear me* and live."

The apostle hummed the cloud's tune, as if he had heard the song himself. *He probably has a hundred times,* I thought, *but he said he did not see the vision I did.* Then I saw his face—radiant with the life pulsating within him, his hands lifted up as if receiving a cherished gift—and I realized that the beloved disciple of Jesus was not merely recalling the tune but hearing the song of the cloud then and there.

The room was aglow with dazzling light and unimaginable colors. No thunder or lightning, simply light and colors as if produced by many prisms at once, which gave me a momentary fright. Then the cloud's song gradually swelled till it filled the room. We both found ourselves singing, quietly at first and then boldly at the top of our lungs:

From victory to victory the Lamb leads, worthy is the Lamb.
From faith to faith, the Word believes, worthy is the Word.
From Father's heart to Spirit's light, worthy is the Son.

Again and again the song was sung, and each time we, too, sang with all our hearts. As we did, what looked like falling stars streaked across the room, falling one by one to the ground and becoming a billowing fire at the foot of the text of the Apocalypse. Two lines of text began to glow, alive, breathing, all but dancing:

> Holy, Holy, Holy, is the Lord God the Almighty,
> who was and who is and who is to come.

Together we sat mesmerized by the living words, speechless in adoration and hope, our hearts full of joy. Peace flowed as a strong, quiet river in and through us as the song of light comforted our souls.

There is far more afoot on earth than I have ever dared dream. Whatever happens to me, to us, to the world, to history, all will be well in Jesus.

21

SECRETS

"My brother," the apostle said, "it is time now for a walk. The Romans have come and gone."

"I will follow you anywhere," I answered, another sense of adventure surging in me, as we headed out of the room of revelation toward the mouth of the cave. It wasn't like I needed another adventure, but I wanted to know everything John knew, and I was not being left behind.

"Wait," he exclaimed, stopping suddenly. "I must get my satchel. We may need it." With that, he dashed to his room.

When he reappeared, he had his old leather satchel strapped over his shoulder, looking like Indiana Jones, ready for another exploit, and a staff, about six feet long, which I had not seen, which surprised me. The top of the staff was a carved eagle's head.

"Where did you get your staff?" I asked. As one who loved carving fishing lures, I was taken by the artistry and the detail of the eagle's head. I noticed the feathers immediately, then the beak with its fine detail. Then I saw a carefully carved talon gripping a serpent's head.

"This, my brother," he said with pride, pushing the staff toward me so I could have a closer look, "was made by a man born blind from Thyatira.

Well, he is not blind *anymore.* Jesus healed his eyes."

"Like the story in your gospel?" I thought it was significant that we were standing at the mouth of the cave again. A place that only a day ago symbolized my despair had now become a window into a new life for me. I didn't miss the irony of being with St. John himself talking about a blind man.

"Yes indeed, Aidan, just like the story in my gospel. He was born with no eyes. The minute I saw him, I heard Jesus say, 'Do what I did.' So I spit on the ground and made two little balls of mud, placed them on his eyelids, and prayed. Jesus gave him new eyes."

I was dumbfounded. "Are all your prayers answered?"

"Of course," he replied, smiling. "Jesus stacked the deck!" He could tell his answer surprised me; he was surely used to my baffled look by now. "Jesus never did anything that he didn't see his Father doing. That is the key. For a long time we were mystified at the way Jesus walked with his Father. But after the resurrection, when the Holy Spirit came we could hear Jesus speaking to us, just as he promised. Prayer"—he paused to look deeply into my eyes—"is listening to Jesus and sharing your heart with him. He will tell you what he is doing, and as he does you act on what he says. We get the water; he changes it into wine. Like Jesus with his Father, we share in what Jesus is doing. He is the Lord of all things, Victorious Lamb, Father's Son, Creator, Anointed One—and *he* refuses to live his life without us!"

He patted me on the back and indicated with his staff that it was time for us to head out. I took the lead, not because I knew where we were going but because I couldn't bear the thought of St. John, the apostle of Jesus, falling on my watch. The path was a touch treacherous at points, and I was on full alert to protect him; for all his authority and strength of character, he was an old man after all. At one point he stumbled, and I grabbed him, straining to hold him steady on the path; to my consternation, the strain caused a slight "accident" of wind, shall I say.

I turned red. "Please forgive me. That was a 'crop dusting' accident."

"Crop dusting," St. John exclaimed, faking a cough and waving his hands as though a swarm of mosquitoes were attacking. "You must be careful; the invisibles can be deadly!"

"Roger that," I said, glad he was not offended. Then I realized that the worst part of the descent was upon us. I felt concern for my ancient brother's potential difficulty on the return trip. But old as he was, he was not frail; he was still as strong as an ox, and I suspected that his pride would bring him home. With only a little work we eventually made it safely down the path toward the sea.

As we rounded a big rock covered in red- and brown-tipped lichen, the path flattened out, and a beautiful white beach summoned our eyes, all but sugar white. The water—twenty shades of green, blue, teal, turquoise, and even chartreuse—reminded me of Vivonne Bay in Kangaroo Island off the coast of South Australia. Blessedly, there were no snakes, at least that I could see. A single sailing ship appeared on the horizon to our right.

John let out a sigh of relief, smiling as if he had arrived at a cherished place he thought he would never again see. He fell to his knees in thanks.

"Have you been here often during your exile?" I asked.

"Many times. When the Romans poisoned me, the Lord brought me here in a vision. That was my first visit to Patmos and to this beach. This is a special place to me"—he winked—"born in sorrow, reborn in the Holy Spirit. *Listen*, the waves have the rhythm of the song of light."

He stood and started running, dodging the water as if it would hurt him, his feet kicking up moist sand behind him. I marveled at his freedom and joy—his almost childlike sense of plain fun—and tried to keep up. He ran for close to what seemed a mile before he stabbed his staff into the sand, threw himself down, and rolled over on his back. Breathless, he stared at the blue, now cloudless sky, panting a prayer of praise.

I sat beside the apostle in the sand, my heart at peace yet strangely grieving. "I see now that until coming here most of my days were spent in a fog."

"No longer, my son, no longer. You have new eyes. Use them!" He raised himself on his elbows, looked around him, and smiled. "Just look at this world! Amazing!" He lay back down, hands under his head.

"I feel like I have been asleep, almost dead, for years. I don't mean that my life was a waste, but it appears more akin to a coma than *life* to me now."

"Like one of your flies?" John asked with his half smile.

I shook my head in embarrassment, knowing it was true, and sat bereaved, but the sound of the sea refused to let me be sad. "I have searched—diligently—for the right thing in the wrong place or in the wrong way, neglecting the ones I love in my noble quest. I have lived in my head while Jesus dwelt in my heart, and I never recognized, never knew him. *What a fool I have been!* Brother, how stupid of me."

"You know now." He grinned, eyes dancing.

How can anyone feel forlorn around this man?

"You have heard Jesus's 'I Am' in the midst of Ophis's lie 'I am not' . . .Now comes a new battle. Ophis will attack again with a vengeance. Jesus will teach you of evil's schemes and empower you to stand firm."

"I feel free, home at last, alive, and—"

"Like a caged eagle thrown off a cliff into darkness but now beginning to soar?"

"Well, I'm not sure I am soaring just yet. I am beside myself with excitement at all that I now see, but it is so new to me I can hardly understand what to do with it. I feel like a proud traveler who strutted to his first-class seat, only to discover that he was on the wrong ship. Now I'm on the right ship—but I don't know how to sail it."

"You see the light of life. At first we all feel like fools in the light, ashamed of our folly and darkness. Then we rise in his 'I Am.' It takes time. 'From victory to victory the *Lamb* leads.'"

"It's obvious you walk with the Lord Jesus and in the Spirit all the time. How have you learned to do that?"

"Sticking close to Jesus and living in the Holy Spirit come when you have fought a few battles—and *lost* them to Ophis."

I looked at him in surprise. *Lost them?*

"Pretending eventually leads to despair, striving always ends in exhaustion," John continued. "Then Ophis strikes again with his 'I am not,' not whole, not there yet, as you said, not smart, not good enough, not important."

"I know from my own bitter experience that what you say is true. It was twice, I am not thrilled to admit, I tried to kill myself." My words hung in the air, but my guts were calm and I didn't feel ashamed.

"I knew before you told me that such had happened to you. When we first met, your eyes screamed despair. You were beaten down by Ophis. But the Holy Spirit, as I keep telling you, has a way of turning our sorrow into eyes to behold Jesus. The Lord appears in our darkness, as he has done for you. He knows all, my brother, and loves forever. And his Father, Abba, holds us with such unsearchable care, as you have seen."

Again John took my latest confession in stride. He was an amazing man, who had more wisdom in one phrase, in one look, than I had found in a hundred books. He knew the schemes of Ophis and how to live in Jesus's victory. As I reflected, I could not help but ask, "Have *you* ever failed, sir, really failed?" I was flabbergasted at my daring.

"Of course, many times." He nodded yet with no hint of embarrassment. In fact, he was almost proud. "If we say we have no sin, we lie. This is war. Ophis is doomed, and he knows it. His time is short, and he is enraged. He wants to destroy us. Like any enemy, he knows our weaknesses. He is ruthless, bitter, always seeking to devour. He whispers his 'I am not' to us, and as soon as we lapse into our old way of seeing, he exploits our blindness, and we fall on our faces in shame. It is overwhelming, as you know, until you learn to abide moment by moment in Jesus."

"I'm not leaving your side until you teach me," I replied quickly.

"There is more for you to see, but even now you are more ready than you know," he said confidently.

"That may be so, and I feel your assurance, but I don't think I'm ready. How do you fight something that you cannot see?"

"You understand now how Ophis led the flies to exhaustion, do you not?"

"The lie of separation?"

"Indeed, the assumption of separation is the darkness; sharing his shame with us is how Ophis keeps us blind," the apostle declared, then stopped abruptly as another thought came to his mind—one that I could tell he couldn't wait to share. But he started chuckling so he could hardly speak at all. He finally got out, "Shame is Ophis's *crop dusting!*"

His words caught me off guard. I could hardly believe the Apostle John was bringing up crop dusting. I burst out in a sudden fit of laughter, and my whole body shook. I fell backwards hitting the sand, and then I started pedaling my legs like a cartoon leprechaun. The apostle, too, commenced to vociferate. We found ourselves caught up in a spasm of spontaneous, hilarious cackling, then rolling around on the beach like we had gone mad.

I tried to compose myself, but I kept hearing, "Shame is Ophis's *crop dusting*," in my head, and each time I heard his classic quip I lost it, overcome with howling and shaking. I didn't know what was happening—never in my life had anything taken such a hold on my entire being. Out of the corner of my eye I saw the apostle try to get up, but he never even made it to his knees.

"The Patmos Shuffle," he managed to say.

With that we both heaved so hard I believe we actually levitated; at least the only things touching the sand were the backs of our heads and our heels.

I honestly cannot say how long our episode lasted, and I can only imagine what someone would have thought if they could have seen the two of us overwhelmed with such laughter. Had it not been for John's touch, I'm certain we would still be seized in a state of caterwaul on that beach. But something in me was released, relieved of duty, and I loved it.

As he reached to grab my arm, whatever was happening began to subside. Finally calming down, we sat up on the beach, shaking our heads, panting. I have known what it is like to live each moment on the edge of tears and the fight of holding them back, but I had never been on the edge of uncontrollable laughter. My only thought was that I needed to find a way to bottle this, and I said so to the apostle.

"I told you, did I not?" John grinned, still panting. "The Holy Spirit has a sense of humor!"

"Shame is Ophis's crop dusting! The Patmos Shuffle! Brother John, so do you."

"You came up with the Patmos Shuffle, don't you remember? I simply gave it a new twist." He grabbed his staff and tried to get up. But it was useless, and we both fell back to the sand.

It took us a good while just to be able to sit up again, but eventually he managed to employ his staff to stand, waving his right hand for me to follow. As I rose, I didn't know what to say. We walked slowly down the beach, quietly enjoying the scenery, watching the sea birds as they dove into the water to catch fish.

After ten minutes, or perhaps longer, the apostle stopped and looked hard into my eyes. "There are no secrets in the kingdom of light, not even a hint of shadows. This is the way of victory, no pretending or hiding or striving."

After what we had just experienced together, I thought it was a bit out of the blue, but I followed along. "Everyone has secrets, and most, I suspect, would not consider it a joy to have them known."

"That is what Jesus wrote," he declared, shifting subjects I thought.

"I didn't know that Jesus wrote anything," I said, my imagination piqued. "Did he write a book of secrets? Do you have a copy? Can I look at it?"

The apostle shook his head, enjoying me, and my imagination. His eyes betrayed the fact that he was on the verge of another laughing fit. But he held himself together. "No, Jesus did not write a book of secrets, but he did write with his finger in the dirt."

"Oh yeah, I forgot about our deal. So what did he write?"

The apostle leaned over and wrote *secrets* in the sand with his left index finger.

"Secrets?" I moaned, intrigued.

"That was Jesus's first word." Then the ancient brother wrote in the sand, *I know yours*. "This," he said, with a hint of humor, "is what Jesus wrote the second time. You would have enjoyed the look on their faces."

"I would have never thought of that, but 'Secrets . . . I know yours' makes perfect sense. No wonder they all walked away, beginning with the oldest."

"The victory is in knowing that all is known. That is how the war is won," the apostle replied and sat down. Closing his eyes and lying back on the sand he said, "When we met Jesus on the first day, at the first moment, we knew that he could see right through us. Believe me, that rattled us. But Jesus has a way of letting us know that shame has no place in his presence. His 'I Am' banishes it, and in its place rises Jesus's fearless peace."

I stared out over the water as I sat down, then leaned back with my hands behind my neck. "Now that I think about it, when I encountered Jesus in my vision and then again just now, I felt no fear or shame."

"Indeed, my son, meeting Jesus and hearing his 'I Am' in our darkness is how we stand firm and defeat Ophis for ourselves. Not just once, but moment by moment, hour by hour. As we behold the Lamb in us, the weight of our folly is lifted. Then we stand and walk in his light. The burden of sin depends on secrecy, darkness, hiding, pretending. Confessing our secrets opens our ears to hear Jesus's 'I Am' within us more clearly."

"Our secrets—the very things that we hate and loathe and pretend are not so—they become the way of victory?" I asked, dumbfounded and hopeful at the same time. I noticed a buzzard circling high above us.

"Once exposed, my brother. Ophis's power lies in our secrets, in things we have done wrong and hide or in how we pretend to be right when we are not. And in the very disclosure of secrets comes the experience of Jesus' victory."

"That gives confession an entirely new meaning."

"Confession spoils Ophis's shame and its power. He lords our failure over us to build his beaver dam, and we, ashamed, dare not face what we have done or our pretense that all is well. As we do, Jesus manifests his presence in our darkness. 'In that day, *you will know* that I am in My Father, and you in Me, and *I in you*.' Then comes joyous freedom."

My vision of Jesus returned. I could see him in me, and I could feel the embrace of his Father's heart again. I thought of Paul and how he said that we now look in a mirror dimly, but we will all see face-to-face. Now we know in part, but we will know fully, as we are fully known. Then I remembered John's words from the first day: "We humans are a blind lot. We have been terribly deceived, but the Holy Spirit is here."

"Sir, I know Jesus is in me; I have no doubt about that. I guess it is dawning on me that the me he is in is really *me*, if that makes any sense."

"'I in *you*.' Which *you* were you thinking?"

"I suppose the Sunday me, the me that I have tried to present to myself and to the world, the me that I assumed was always being watched and carefully evaluated. *Good grief*, what a load! How exhausting! But underneath that disguise, or that persona, was the me that always felt a complete failure, a loser. And *that's* the me he honors with his presence. Wow!"

"Of course, my brother: *you*, as you are in the great darkness. Jesus is not ashamed to call us his brothers, never ashamed of us, and neither is his Father."

"*This* is hope, real hope," I said, amazed at both the love of God for me and how blind I had been to it. "I think I can see something of the schemes of evil. Ophis's whispers of shame, his 'I am nots' are intended to keep us from looking at our sorrow. His fear"—I felt the apostle's encouragement as I struggled to find the right words—"Ophis's fear forms a resistance within us to face our pain."

I shook my head as I pondered. "That's it! I could never discover Jesus inside my darkness and never know his union with the real me or his Father's love while I refused to acknowledge my sorrow. That is how we get trapped in pretending, hiding, medicating, and seeking salvation in our heads, and that is why we create an external religion. *Oh, Lord!* That is why we conjure up scapegoats to blame for our own misery, even scapegoats within us!"

I covered my mouth with one hand and my heart with the other as I thought again of little Aidan. I sat still feeling my feelings, not disappearing this time into my head. I could hear Jesus again: "Rise, my beloved, hear me and live."

"Well done, my son, well done," the apostle said with pride. Then he shifted quickly to being very serious. "Now listen carefully: When Ophis attacks, he is attempting to get you to feel his own evil conscience as your own. Lies and accusations are all that he has to fight with. Be on guard, especially when you are alone and exhausted. Remember: Jesus, who is face-to-face with his Father, is in you. Turn to the Lord with the accusations and with your folly, and you will hear his Word of affirmation. The Paraclete, the Holy Spirit, too, *endorses* the truth within you—no shame!"

I thought of Paul again: "And the Spirit himself bears witness with our spirits, that we are children of God." "Sir, you have blown my mind more times than I can count, but this, this is . . ."

"*Freedom*, Aidan! 'And you shall know the truth, and the truth shall set you free!'" he declared with a grin as wide as the sea."

"This I love," I shouted back, sharing in his enthusiasm and letting it carry me. "I have no idea how this has happened, but being here with you is the highlight of my life! You have saved me! My heart is thrilled. When I first got here all I wanted was to get back home, and I can't wait to be with Mary after all this and to pass on, or at least try to share, what you have given to me. Thank you for caring for me, for taking time to love me, and for letting me pick your brain."

"Pick your brain? Have you been in the mushrooms?"

"It means 'to get inside your thoughts, to hear you.'"

"Pick your brain," he mused, Charlie Chaplin eyebrows dancing. "I will definitely use that one in my next letter."

Then the ancient apostle drove his staff in the sand and slowly rose. I rose with him. Once on his feet he turned to me, leaning his staff against his chest, the eagle's head right over his heart. He placed both hands on my shoulders. "You do know, my son"—I loved it when he called me that—"that *this* is eternal life?"

"Forever a book or two ahead of my thoughts you are." I smiled, waiting for more.

"This freedom gives us *eyes* to see Jesus *in* his Father *in* all things *in* the song of light."

"My dear sir, I will never forget this moment or your words."

"We will, I tell you," John said, stretching out his arms and turning around completely, lifting his staff like Moses, and declaring with his apostolic smile, "we will enjoy this without end, as we graduate—no shadows."

He poked me in the chest three times with the eagle's head of his staff. "Jesus has given you his own eyes. Hold no secrets from Jesus, and you will see everything with his eyes."

22

APOSTOLIC FISHING

We meandered on the beach after that, enjoying the Lord and his good creation for a long while without any more words. I was amazed at the life I saw all around me. Then St. John drew symbols in the sand with his staff, and as I watched, most intrigued, something in the distance caught my eye. I looked up to see a school of fish, *big* fish, exploding the surface of the water not fifty yards from shore.

"Look," I shouted. "A school of fish! I wish I had my rod and reel and my lures or one of your nets. We could have a fine supper tonight, a feast, a *large* time!"

"No need for nets or your rods and reels," he declared in a way that only he could do, peremptory and affectionate at the same time. "I have a fishing lesson for you." He sounded like a Cajun starting a Boudreaux and Thibodeaux tale.

I didn't know what to think or expect, especially after the last couple of days.

"Professionals," he said with his characteristic wink, "don't need nets. We are masters of the art."

"St. John," I replied, knowing by his tone and his eyes that he had something up his sleeve, "what in the name of Patmos are you up to?"

"Aidan," he commanded, thrusting his staff forward in the air like a general, "go climb that rock, and you will see."

"Rock?"

"Yes, that big one over there." He pointed down the beach about a hundred yards.

"On it, boss," I said, like I was on *NCIS*, afraid that Jethro would thump me if I hesitated.

I ran down the beach and climbed the rock—or at least started to before I tired more quickly than I ought, but no way would I show it. The rock was rough as a cob, with sharp edges, and over seventy feet high. But when I made it to the summit, I understood. St. John watched me proudly, like he had led me to the holy grail of fishing secrets. As I turned around I spotted below me a smaller rock that had been hidden by the one I was on, connecting it to another larger one almost as tall as mine. Behind the small rock was a tiny sandy beach with a pool.

Then I saw the apostle's tale. The big waves would come in over the smaller rock, trapping water behind it, forming a pool in front of the secluded beach between the larger rocks. Then I saw fish.

"Good Lord! Trapped fish!" I turned again to see my brother.

He beamed, as if to say, "I told you so."

I climbed joyfully down the rock in haste, though with care, as every rock fisherman knows. In the small pool were a dozen baitfish, frantically swimming as if they would soon be eaten. A huge wave crested the small rock, and before my eyes three large fish crashed into the pool.

I threw myself into the shallow pool, determined to catch the larger fish. It took some work, but I soon learned that if I got next to the small rock, the fish would flee shoreward in fear. One, two, then all three of the big fish beached themselves in front of me. Full of pride, I thought of the smile I would see on my brother's face when I climbed down the rock with three fish.

Then the question hit me: How will I carry the fish? *I need both hands to scale the rock.* I stood pondering the problem when a sudden inspiration came to mind. *Seaweed, make a stringer out of seaweed.* I smiled, knowing the idea was not my own. Glancing about, I noticed long strands of seaweed strewn over the small beach. They looked like strips of kelp from off the coast of San Francisco, which made me think of crab, which made me think of Fat Tuesday's, my family's favorite restaurant back home, and of fresh oysters, gumbo, andouille sausage, and soft-shell crabs—all of which made me hungry and determined to get my fish to the apostle and find a way to cook them.

Gathering several strands of seaweed, I braided them together till they were about six feet in length. It took longer than I thought, and for some reason I felt under pressure of time, though the sun was a ways from setting yet; perhaps I was afraid John would be getting impatient. The stringer finished, I grabbed the three fish one by one and ran the stringer through their gills and mouths, tying the whole tight around my waist. Then I set myself to the task of climbing back up the rock with the fish dangling.

As I topped the rock, my heart rose in my throat. Roman soldiers marched on the beach, half a mile or so behind St. John. *Dear Lord!* I gasped.

St. John, never one to miss a thing, was already in a full sprint, his robe flying like a cape behind him.

By the time I reached the bottom of the rock, he stood panting beside me.

"What do we do?" I yelled.

"Fear not, my brother," he declared, sounding like Joshua of old.

The Roman soldiers bore down on us like a swarm of praying mantises ready for the kill.

John grabbed my hand and started running like he was half his age, away from the beach toward the cliffs on our right. It seemed fruitless to me, as a wall of rock a hundred feet high rose before us, but there was no other option except to climb over my rock to the tiny beach, and even then it would only be a matter of time before the Roman soldiers surrounded us.

"In there," he directed with calm urgency.

I saw nothing but rock. "In where?" I asked, scared out of my wits but ready to follow my brother with all my heart.

"Follow me."

"Roger that," I cried out, as if I had a choice.

He led me between two rocks, one in front of the other, which formed an optical illusion appearing as a single solid stone. As we entered, a rogue wave crashed behind us, and I hoped it would wash away our footprints. We sprinted up a narrow, sandy path, clearly worn by centuries of erosion. His staff in his left hand fired like a piston toward me with each step, so I lagged behind about ten feet. I heard the soldiers behind us, swords and shields clamoring against the narrow pass. As quick as a cat, the apostle ran, and I thought of how he outran Peter to Jesus's tomb. *How can he possibly run like this at his age? I guess those years in hard labor have kept him in shape.*

As we reached a plateau, a labyrinth of passageways emerged in front of us. Without hesitating John took the one on the far right, which led into what appeared to be a tunnel. I could see light at the other end, but the tunnel was darker than the open path, so we slowed to a fast walk until we came to a pool of still water.

"Follow me," he shouted, as he rounded the pool.

I could still hear the Romans, but I couldn't see them, which meant they couldn't see us, either. *My brother knows his way like he knows the gospel.*

The apostle quickened his pace until he stood inches away from a dramatic ravine at least two hundred feet deep. I thought we were doomed. There was no way to cross it. For a second I wondered if the apostle might actually jump. But he turned to the side of the tunnel and lifted himself up about three feet from the ground, then started edging down a small ledge back toward the pool, motioning for me to do the same. Our footprints stopped on the ledge as if we had both jumped or climbed down.

The apostle made his way backward and then jumped into the pool. I was right behind him, the fish flying in the air behind me. The water, not freezing but cold, was clear for about two feet, then it turned inky black. John poked his staff toward me, and I grabbed on for dear life. He swam down and then to the right for about ten yards. Then he popped straight up like a cork. I, too, broke the surface, gasping for air. I was dazed and couldn't figure out what had just happened.

John pulled himself up on a bank of stones and rock and reached toward me with his staff. I could barely see, but somehow he was on dry ground. "Quiet, Aidan," he whispered. I finished my climb, threw the fish on the bank, and sat beside the apostle, breathing heavily. *Well, we both needed a bath*, I thought.

It took a while for my eyes to adjust. We were in another cave. I was surprised that I could see at all, but then I noticed two tiny shafts of light coming in from the top right. The place reminded me of his sleeping quarters in a way, but here the walls were more jagged and the top of this cave was much higher.

"They don't know about this place," he assured me.

"You certainly know your way around, and I for one am glad for that."

"The Holy Spirit knows the way. I thought the Romans were gone for the day, but I guess time got away from me."

"Time is a strange thing these days, brother John. I thought you said the Romans were predictable."

"Only once before have they deviated from their routine. I was having a swim in the sea when I saw them, and they chased me down the beach. The Holy Spirit led me here."

"How?"

"I ran the same way we just did. It was closer to dark then, so I had to move more slowly, but when I got to the pool, I heard the Holy Spirit say, 'Swim deep,' and I did. There are two more caves similar to this one, so it didn't matter which way I swam. I have come here many times. We will wait till the Romans get back to their quarters, then we will make our way to the cave. But first we need water."

"First, I need to calm down. It is not every day I time travel, meet an apostle, have extraordinary visions, and get chased by Roman soldiers." I could tell that though he was still panting he was praying. The room calmed, or more likely it was me that calmed. I drew in a long breath, finally feeling safe.

John lifted his staff across the pool.

"Are you going to change it into wine?" I laughed, and so did he, but then again maybe he was! Then I realized he was pointing to water running down the side of the cave, gathering into a hole about twice the size of one of my crawfish pots, which made me hungry and miss home again. I looked at the pool, then back at the apostle.

"That water is better, trust me."

"That I do. That I certainly do. How will we know when the Romans

171

are back to their camp? They were scary, and I have no intention of ever encountering them again." I got up and headed toward the water. "I thought for sure we were toast."

"Toast?" he asked, looking askance. "Young brother, you are full of strange words."

"I do believe that you could take the entire collection of my strange words, and they would not equal two chapters of your Revelation. Speaking of which, how did you get the Apocalypse off the island? And for that matter, how did you return to Patmos afterwards?"

As the apostle knelt to drink, he stopped and replied, "Some of my brothers brought me in a boat."

"But how did you get by the Romans?"

He grinned. "I dressed as an old woman, peddling fish."

"Brilliant. I wish I could have seen that: St. John dressed as a woman, long beard and all."

As we both drank our fill, sudden fear gripped me, and I bit my lip. "How will you return to Ephesus?" I asked, not sure I wanted to know his answer.

"The Lord will find a way," he said, hope sparkling in his eyes. "Or I may stay in the Room of Revelation and pass into the cloud in his arms on your mattress."

"I still have my fish and my Leatherman. Do you like sushi?" I changed the subject, grieving, not wanting to face the fact that my mattress could well become the very place where St. John would "graduate."

"Sushi? Not sure what that is."

"Raw fish. It seems to be the craze these days. Sushi is actually quite good, a Japanese delight that has now, or in my day, swept the world."

"I wouldn't eat raw fish with a Pharisee's mouth. These Japanese, do they not know how to cook?"

"Can we build a fire then?"

"Here? I don't see why not, but we have no wood."

"You are the beloved apostle of Jesus," I chided playfully. "Only the Holy Spirit knows all that you have done and seen. Can you not start a fire without wood?"

"We could start a fire with your seaweed and melt this sand," he retorted, pointing to a small patch near him, "to make silicon for your computers."

I held up my hands in surrender.

"I have no clue about your silicon, but the Holy Spirit gave me that one as a joke. She can fill your Grand Canyon with her humor, as you are beginning to know," he said, eyes twinkling again.

"Have you seen our Grand Canyon in one of your visions, or have you actually been there?"

"I have no idea what your Grand Canyon is. As I told you, the Holy Spirit delights in making us sound smarter than we are! She gave me the words, and I felt her joy in doing so. She was letting us know that it is safe to go back. Trust me."

"Good. It's starting to get really dark in here, but I don't want to die at the hands of Roman soldiers two thousand years before I was born. And I certainly don't want to be the man responsible for the death of St. John the theologian."

"That would be an anomaly in the space-time continuum," he announced, beaming with playful smugness.

I sat speechless, shaking my head.

"No need to ask. I have no idea what it means. The Holy Spirit's penchant for humor strikes again."

"Sir, sometimes you can be too much. But I will hang in there! I have three fish, what kind I do not know, and a Leatherman to clean them, and I am determined to find a way to cook up a feast for us. Do you know of anything we can use for spices?"

"Sea bream. Gut them, wrap them in your seaweed, and let's cook them on a fire when we get to the cave. That will be a 'large' time!" He clearly enjoyed borrowing my expressions and being carried along by the timeless wit of the Spirit.

"Well, this 'trip' has redefined a 'large' time for me."

"The Holy Spirit, my son, redefines all things. Now, grab your fish, and let's 'get out of Dodge,'" he said, full of delight. "You have some writing to do tonight."

I didn't even ask about Dodge, but as we began our trek to the cave, I asked the aged apostle how he knew about the fish. "Did you pray for a special miracle?”

“Many times I have sat on that beach, and many times I have seen schools of fish. One day I noticed the baitfish swimming close to the rocks for safety when a great wave swelled and swept them over the smaller rock. Several of the big fish chasing them were swept over as well. I wasn't sure it would happen today. The tides and the waves have to be right, but I had a hunch.”

“I have grown to love your hunches.”

“The Holy Spirit gives everyone hunches all the time—and much more, Aidan. Ask her to teach you to notice her.”

“That I will, my brother,” I replied, pausing to mumble a prayer to myself. *Holy Spirit, I am as blind as a bat. Please help me see and notice you.*

“Bats are not really blind, you know,” the apostle said, grinning, and I couldn't help but chuckle. “They have different eyes.”

“Roger that, and so do you, my dear friend.”

Once out of the pool, we walked slowly back to the beach. We emerged from the rocks to a night sky that took my breath away. We both stopped to take in the sight.

“I have never seen stars like this. At home we have so many city lights, and even if we stopped for a moment in our frantic lives to notice the sky, we would never see this. Out here I can see the Milky Way plain as day!”

“Milky Way?”

“The system our earth is part of has so many stars and planets in it that their light makes a vast band of white haze in the sky. I guess it looks like a swirl of milk if you use your imagination. It is said to have as many as two hundred billion stars, and some say a great many more. And our Milky Way is only one of millions of such systems in our universe! Utterly amazing!”

“Indeed,” he responded, marveling. “I have enjoyed looking at the stars for years but have little knowledge of them. They stir the soul's yearning for the Lord, don't they? So immense! So beautiful! And all created and sustained by Jesus.”

“In my day we have placed telescopes . . . Uh, think of a long tube with special lenses in it that help you see distant things . . . It is a way of seeing into the cosmos. We have placed these telescopes beyond the earth, and they send back pictures, astounding pictures of planets and solar systems, exploding stars, unimaginable beauty."

"I believe I have seen some of those pictures," he responded, knowing I understood that he meant in one of his visions.

As if right on schedule, a giant meteor flashed across the sky, then another and another, reminding me of the Room of Revelation. We stood riveted, watching the dazzling show in the heavens. Meanwhile, without our noticing, a large moon had risen above the cliffs behind us, and as we turned to walk, we saw the oversized giant hanging in the star-filled heavens, full, radiant, and so close that I felt I might be able to touch it.

"That, my young friend, is a wonder of wonders, is it not? It speaks of the Father's constant heart," John whispered. "It reminds us that we are watched over with great care in the darkness."

I could tell from his eyes that his imagination was kicking in again, and things were connecting that were new even to the apostle. "The time is right for you to write that creed on the wall. After we eat, we can talk into the night."

"Till the cows come home." I said, anticipating a wonderful night in the cave. I figured my ancient brother had no idea what I meant by the expression, but then, who knows? He didn't even nod.

We lingered in the light of the moon, staving off the end of our shared adventure. Somehow we both knew that we would not return to this place together; I could tell that the same sadness, mixed with wonder and hope, stirred his heart as it did mine. I knew this was a special moment and treasured it without speaking.

Then I turned to him, studying his face as if to seal it in my memory. "I have fished in a hundred places, and I have my own fishing tales, some of them even true, but this afternoon tops them all. When I return to my time, I will tell this tale again and again," I said, smiling, but sadness tinged my words.

"Of course, my brother! What fisherman doesn't tell a few tales?" He winked. "Tell me your favorite."

"Before we leave the beach, I think it best to clean the fish and rinse them off in the sea. Then I will tell you a fishing tale worthy of your time."

"Roger that," the apostle said and wandered down the beach, hands lifted in prayer.

My Leatherman Micra proved to be a real help. "But not exactly what I need for these monsters," I mumbled, already stretching the truth. I gutted the fish and washed them in the waves, St. John still walking and praying.

GATOR!

On his return he invited me to tell my fishing tale. He didn't actually say a word; it was more in his eyes, one fisherman to another.

"Well, brother John, my best fishing *trip* to date has to be Australia, two years ago in the remote northwest, north even of Broome. We flew in on a seaplane. But my favorite *tale* involves Captain Jason Shilling, a boyish forty-year-old Cajun from south Louisiana, which is about a four-hour drive by automobile from where I live in Mississippi or almost a week's walk by foot. For you, sir"—I winked—"only a second or two. Redfishing is my favorite—until today, of course.

"I remember it like yesterday. The captain had us on some huge reds, and I hung one as big as Moby Dick; he all but spooled me, rippin' off drag like a scalded hyena. But with *consummate skill*," I said, tongue in cheek, "I finally turned him. I had him headed toward the boat when the monster made another run. Then the line went slack, limp as a dishrag, and I yelled a few choice words, thinking for sure that he had broken my line.

"As you know, when brothers lose a giant fish like that, they console each other with both exaggeration and endless *skubala*. Captain Shilling listened quietly for a while, then started telling a Boudreaux joke, but all at once he noticed my line moving, slowly but steadily. He pointed to my rod, shouting, 'Aidan!'

"I reacted with a jerk of my rod, like a professional," I continued, imitating setting the hook like I was jerking the fish's lips off. "That monster fish responded with a jerk of its own, which almost broke my arm. But I, my friend, being a seasoned veteran of fishing wars, managed to hold on. It felt like I was hooked to a whale! Even the boat started to turn toward the beast!"

"Do you catch whales?" the old brother asked.

"Not until I met you that first day."

"One never knows about you, young Aidan."

"I assume that the Holy Spirit is giving you an interpretation of all this."

The old fisherman nodded. "But your eyes tell the tale."

"Well, the best, or worst, was yet to be. Captain Shilling fired up the motor, and I held on for dear life. Whatever was now on my line felt like a cement truck, and it was headed straight for the marsh. No way was I giving in, of course, but we all noticed that between us and the marsh lay a rock pile less than a foot below the surface. The captain turned the boat to the right and shouted for me to hold on as he fought to keep the boat off the rocks without losing me in the process. Both hands firmly gripping the rod, I was holding on with absolute determination when before I could think I found myself flying through the air, screaming. The captain, looking to find a lifeline, shouted, 'Let go, Aidan! Let go!' I thought of a mule."

St. John's blank face was a wordless query.

"Mules are considered stubborn in our world. It's an expression."

"That much is plain. Go on."

"I hit the water like a bowling ball—uh, a big rock—but still holding on to my rod. As one of the submerged rocks gashed my left leg, I managed to find a footing with my right one to fortify myself for the fight of a lifetime. But then my line went slack again, followed by more choice words from me, and a moment or two later, utter dejection.

"I stood on the rock muttering, my friends, of course, laughing. I started reeling line, convinced that this time it had broken, and what had held such promise as a fishing tale had now ended in abject failure." I paused just long enough for the feeling to sink in to John's imagination before ripping in to my story again.

"But before any of us could see my line, it tightened twenty feet in front of me on the other side of the rock pile! I was as confused as a butter bean, trying to make sense of this, when Jason shouted, 'Gator!' As soon as he screamed, a massive alligator—think of one of your road lizards but eight feet long and three feet wide—surfaced, thrashing about and heading *for me.* My entire life flashed through my mind, letting me know that my end had come.

"To my eternal shame, I have to tell you that I dropped the rod and started swimming madly for the boat. A lifeline was already flying through the air towards me from the captain. As I grabbed it, my friends hauled me in, and I skirted across the water just out of the gator's reach—but not before it snapped at my left leg, taking my tennis shoe and part of my little toe. I can show you, if you like."

"I believe you," St. John said over his laughter.

"The instant before what I anticipated as the second snap of the beast's teeth-lined jaws and the loss of at least one of my legs, I heard a shrill, 'Not on my watch!' followed by a flash above me and what seemed to be an explosion behind me. My friends hoisted me onto the boat, and as I turned around, I caught a glimpse of a single blow from Captain Shilling and his ball-peen hammer. For a moment or two we could see nothing. Then the captain broke the surface of the water, hammer in hand, dragging the dead gator behind him. Smiling from ear to ear, Captain Jason Shilling shouted, 'Gatah Piquante tonight!' I have a pair of alligator boots at home to prove it," I said, laughing.

The ancient brother shook his head, smiling at me in fisherman's affection. We laughed together, like old men remembering grand times.

"*That* is a worthy tale! I will tell my favorite."

"Sir," I said, catching my breath, "how could you top Jesus's calming the sea?"

"No one can top that, but I do have a story about Peter *parting* the sea . . ." The fond memory brought another smile to his face. "But first we have to climb this summit."

We began our ascent with no further words, as we both knew that all our energy must be channeled to the climb, except for moments now and then when my beloved friend stopped to gather sticks and leaves for the fire. *I see now why he insisted on bringing his satchel*, I thought as we moved soundlessly along. Although the Romans were long gone now, we were instinctively careful not to make any unnecessary noise.

"We must be cautious here," I said when we stopped to rest before the steepest part of the path. "This is a bit tricky."

"Indeed, my son, especially with your crop dusting."

"Yes, I suppose I am a bit embarrassed about that."

"I am a 'son of thunder' myself"—he grinned—"or at least I was back in the day. Peter, that brother could part the sea, as I told you. He made us laugh to tears many times. Our best fishing trick was to throw Peter over the side of the boat. He had a way with wind! All we had to do was gather the gasping fish."

Shocked and laughing, I hardly knew what to think or say. When I finally collected myself, I said, "It is a strange gift to me to hear you tell such stories."

"Why so?"

"In the West we have not been so comfortable with our humanity. I reckon it has to do with the way we have split the world between the sacred and the secular. Holy men are not supposed to be very secular and certainly not enjoy their humanity."

"Union or separation—we see our humanity as separated from the Lord or as a living union. There is no secular, only perversion in Ophis's madness. Do not forget the crown of thorns."

His words stopped me in my tracks. I felt strangely relieved of a burden, though I hardly knew what the apostle meant. As I started to ask, something like streams of clouds came into my mind, one stream on the right, the other on the left, racing away from me like they were being blown by a hurricane at full force. The clouds met at a point in front of me, billowing. Then they faded slowly, and I could see an ancient city. I heard mocking shouts. Then I saw Roman soldiers beating Jesus, spitting on him, driving the crown of thorns into his head with contempt as blood rushed down Jesus's face and ears. With bitter cruelty they hoisted Jesus on the cross, the sweating crowd calling out obscenities. The scene was hideous, as was the crown itself, woven it seemed from Adam's fear and the broken earth. The crown moved like a dying snake, but then suddenly it became a garden, expanding in beauty and life from Jesus's head to his outstretched arms and into all the earth and beyond.

I remembered my vision of Jesus in the Room of Revelation, the cosmos flowing as a grand river from the Lamb's wound. *There really is no secular world at all; Jesus has filled the whole creation with himself.*

We talked little as we climbed, St. John grabbing a few more sticks. Once at the mouth of the cave, we caught our breath and stared at the moon, now smaller than when it had first appeared but still strikingly beautiful. St. John at once began preparing the fire.

"What about the Romans? Won't they see the fire and come after us again?"

"They are back at their fort, a good ways over those cliffs. Probably high on mushrooms." He chuckled. "The wind will blow the smoke out to sea. Besides that, we could see their torches from the minute they appeared in the pass. We are safe."

I unwound the seaweed stringer and wrapped the fish with the seaweed. The old brother suggested that I stuff some of the seaweed into the cavities, and I did, then finished wrapping them as best I knew how. As I turned to find two small sticks to carve into makeshift forks, he started the fire. How, I could not tell, and when I asked, he only smiled.

"How do you think we should cook these?" I asked, thinking we would skewer them on a stick and roast them like marshmallows.

"As the fire dies, we will place your miracle bream on the coals. Trust me, young Aidan."

"Roger that. I could eat a horse," I replied, watching his eyes. "A col'beer would be mighty fine about now."

"You drink them cold?"

"As cold as ice," I declared proudly.

"I have had beer but never a col'beer," he responded, imitating our Southern conflation of the two words into one.

The stories, the fire, and the mention of beer in my own dialect evoked thoughts of life back in Mississippi, and I suddenly missed home again.

"I'm certain that my wife has called the police and my brothers at

ORW. Only the Lord knows what they'll be doing." I smiled, thinking of their stories of "hot extractions."

"Perhaps not."

"What are you thinking?"

"Perhaps our time together involves little of your time."

"Are you doing another space-time continuum thing?"

"Thinking of Phillip," he answered. "Philip said that his travel to and from the Ethiopian involved none of our time. Perhaps it is the same with you."

"You said three days. Do you really think I will make it home?" I asked, not exactly sure I wanted to know the answer.

"For certain, Aidan. The Holy Spirit brought about our meeting for your healing, not to die. You have amazing things ahead of you—in the Holy Spirit."

"When I met you and began to believe that you really were the Apostle John, I hoped that the Lord was answering the prayer of my life."

"It is time," the old brother said definitively.

"I'm going home *now*? But we haven't finished our conversation; we've hardly talked about your gospel and the creed and—"

"To cook the fish," John said, and I swear he muttered, "Bless his heart." Then he smiled, with his palms up and shoulders raised. "I have no idea," he answered before I could ask.

"Those three words would take me a week to explain. They can be good, but in the mouth of a Southern belle they can mean any one of a hundred things," I declared, thinking of my grandmother. "Here are the fish, stuffed and wrapped as you requested."

He handled them like they were a rare treasure, laying them carefully on the glowing coals. As they cooked he asked me about the creed and whether I still had the energy, after such a day, to write it on the wall in the Room of Revelation. His stamina amazed me.

"I will rest when I die, my brother. Nothing could keep me from sharing the creed with you," I replied, realizing that here was a chance for me to give a real gift to the apostle. I had no way of knowing that I was about to see what is.

The apostle and fish chef turned the bream only one time on the coals after about three minutes. (I was watching carefully.) We sat in silence waiting, counting the seconds as we watched the fire and the fish.

Eventually, he looked up at me. "It is time for supper! A little fried okra and kawnbread would be good, don't you think?"

"Sir, you are *killing* me!" I managed between snorts of laughter. "It's not easy to keep up with *you*, but when the Holy Spirit gives you those zingers, it is more than I can take. I think I lost ten pounds laughing these last couple of days."

"Well, Aidan, you carry a little extra!"

I tried to retort, but my body was shaking too hard, and I was certain that a new episode of the Patmos Shuffle was upon us. "If you don't stop, I'll never be able to eat a bite," I said finally, wiping my eyes.

The apostle folded out some of the seaweed to make a mat onto which he rolled the fish. He broke serious for a moment and offered a prayer, thanking the Lord for such an astounding day, but the undertone of his prayer was longing to be home.

The moment was too dear to me to allow sadness to spoil it. "Who will ever believe this story?" I murmured, lifting my hands toward St. John.

"Here, my young brother; you deserve the first taste," he said, motioning for me to come closer.

Hungry as I was, I took the first bite without hesitation, and it melted in my mouth. I thought of my mother. "That is the best thing I ever put in my mouth," she would always say. In this case, it was. "That is as good as Chilean sea bass. Do you have some butter you're not telling me about?"

"Butter?"

"The fish tastes like it has butter on it."

"It is as you prepared it. Perhaps the Holy Spirit is doing a few things through you. She approves of good food, you know."

"I'm sure that's true, but I'm glad you took over the cooking detail; I would have roasted them over the fire on a stick. This is awesome."

"They are good that way, too, but wrapping them in seaweed keeps them moist."

A new thought popped into my head. "What were the fish like that Jesus cooked on the shore?"

"*He* had *butta*!" he replied, amusing himself.

We finished off the fish, leaving not a speck on any bone. As St. John rose to go into the cave, I sat still, wondering how on earth any of this could be real and thrilled that it was.

He returned with his wineskin. "Now, a toast to a blessed day and a prayer for even more tonight," he said, handing me the wineskin.

"This was the day of all days for me. I never saw it coming. I didn't see *any* of this coming—it's just been one striking, liberating, life-giving surprise after another. And I will have to get me one of these when I get home," I said, holding aloft his wineskin. I handed it back to him, then wiped my mouth with the back of my hand.

"Now, my son, to the Room of Revelation and some light on this creed," he declared with new urgency.

NEAR DEATH

As St. John threw a few remaining sticks on the fire, the mouth of the cave brightened, shadows dancing on the wall behind it bidding us to enter. I thought again of Plato's cave and his shadows and of my brother's comment earlier in the day. Stepping into the cave it was instantly clear that the Room of Revelation had a light of its own; the glow from it lit the stony corridor. Anticipation rose in my heart as I half expected Athanasius himself to make an appearance. *Perhaps he is already in the room,* I thought.

As we turned into the hallowed space, I saw the lamps burning, which of course stirred my imagination, but then I remembered that the ancient apostle had gone into the cave earlier to get his wineskin. So I figured he lit them then.

"Now, my young son," John said somewhat dramatically, "here is the chalk. I think it is time to write the words of this creed." He handed me the piece of limestone and took his seat expectantly.

"Why don't I get your mattress so you'll be more comfortable? It has been a long and rather grueling day."

"You are starting to think like you have a brain," he teased.

"Well, according to an ancient fisherman I know, I have the mind of Christ. And I think I just used it," I replied gleefully before I left the room.

It took me longer than I expected to fetch the mattress, as the sleeping quarters had only the light of the moon coming in from the mouth of the cave, and I handled the mattress with care like we did the fish, keeping the large and unwieldy thing together. As I made it back and laid it on the ground, the entire text of the Apocalypse shimmered, as if awakened and ready to speak again—or hear a bit of history.

The apostle seated himself on his mattress, his face lit with anticipation.

When I turned to write, I was astonished to see the first part of the creed already written on the wall. *We believe in one God, the Father Almighty, Maker of heaven and earth, and of all things visible and invisible.* Turning around, I discovered John smiling like a child.

"I got it right, didn't I?" he asked.

"Your memory and the Holy Spirit are an amazing duo."

"It is so carefully worded," he replied, ignoring the compliment.

"What do you see?" I asked eagerly.

"I see *oneness*, and I see the way these brothers carefully placed creation within the Father's heart." He pointed with his staff to the phrase *Maker of heaven and earth*, then pointed to *Father*. "Creation flows from the relationship of the Father and Son. *And*," he added, his intensity growing, "I see *all things* there!" He was fully pumped now, rising. "'Maker of heaven and earth, and of *all things* visible and invisible.' *All things*!" he repeated, beaming. I realized that he was seeing his own gospel in the creed.

"My dear brother, at last I have something to give to you. Not even a hundred years from this day, about 180 AD in our time reckoning, Irenaeus, bishop from Gaul—or France as we call it in my day—wrote against the Gnostics. His book is a difficult one to read as he details at length their strange beliefs, and believe me, the Gnostics would have tripped you out. Irenaeus saw himself as defending the one faith handed down by the apostles. That would be you, sir. He wrote:

We believe in one God, the Father Almighty, Maker of heaven, and earth, and the sea, and all things that are in them; and in one Christ Jesus, the Son of God, who became

incarnate for our salvation; and in the Holy Spirit, who
proclaimed through the prophets . . .

"The Nicene Creed is essentially the careful expansion of what Irenaeus handed on in the context of condemnation and confusion."

John listened, eyes wide with approval, his face all but glowing again.

"I told you the creed flows from Patmos. I see that on a new level now." *This must be a thrill to his heart to see his own thoughts handed on and defended.*

Smiling, he motioned for me to continue.

"The Jews and the Greeks, in all their variations, accused the Christians of being polytheists, worshiping three gods."

"Ah, of course," the apostle mused, rubbing his chin, "thus the opening statement about oneness."

"The creed says, 'one God,' then 'one Lord Jesus Christ,' then 'Holy Spirit.' True to their worship, all Christians believed in one God and knew that Jesus was from the Father and that the Holy Spirit was in the midst of the Father and Son. But they were torn as to what it all meant."

"Ophis," the apostle chimed in, "the dragon of old always attacks the vision of Jesus and his relationship with his Father. Anyone who denies that Jesus has come in the flesh is antichrist."

"I will admit to you that those words from your first letter always sounded a bit harsh to me but no longer."

"If Jesus is not *from* the Father, he cannot give the Father to us. He would only have wisdom to share, like the prophets. Everything depends upon that relationship—*everything*—even the very air we breathe."

"That was the burning question that emerged: What exactly does it mean that Jesus is *from* the Father?"

"Hurry, Aidan, and write the next part of the creed. I want to see exactly what they said about Jesus and his Father."

As I wrote the paragraph on Jesus, the apostle eagerly watched each word being formed, at points gasping with joy, almost shouting.

And in one Lord Jesus Christ, the only-begotten Son of God,
begotten of the Father before all ages; God of God, Light of

Light, very God of very God; begotten, not made, of the same being as the Father, by whom all things were made. Who, for us men and for our salvation, came down from heaven, and was incarnate by the Holy Spirit of the virgin Mary, and was made man; and was crucified also for us under Pontius Pilate; he suffered and was buried; and the third day he rose again, according to the Scriptures; and ascended into heaven, and sits on the right hand of the Father; and he shall come again, with glory, to judge the living and the dead; whose kingdom shall have no end.

Somewhere about halfway through the paragraph he started rocking slightly and whispering repeatedly, "Holy, Holy, Holy is the Lord."

Isaiah 6 and the famous throne scene came to my mind. Then it hit me. "Good Lord," I cried out. "Brother John, you wrote that Isaiah saw *Jesus*, did you not?"

He cocked his head. "I did indeed."

As I stood there, chalk in hand, focusing on what that meant, the ancient brother rose and grabbed the chalk from my left hand. With it he circled five words or four words and a phrase, actually: *incarnate, man, of* in the phrase *begotten of the Father, of* in the phrase *very God of very God,* and the entire phrase *of the same being as the Father.*

"Was this creed written in Greek?" he asked.

"It certainly was. Why?"

"Do you know these words in the Greek?" He pointed to the ones he had circled.

"My professor hammered us with these words almost every day," I declared with pride.

"So what Greek words did they use?" His voice quivered with restrained excitement.

"*Sarx* is here," I said, pointing to *incarnate.* "And this word *man* is *anthropos.*"

"As I suspected," the brother said, tears welling up in his eyes.

"Suspected what?" I turned to him, eyes wide.

"These brothers know my gospel."

"Sir, you must be proud!"

"*Sarx* became *flesh* in the *Holy Spirit*, my brother, became *flesh* in the *Holy Spirit*," he shouted, running about the room like he had just scored the winning touchdown. It would not have surprised me if he had given me a high five. "*The light of life! The light of life! The end of Ophis!*"

I stood there marveling at my brother's contagious excitement, knowing this was important but not really getting all that he was thinking. I could tell that he knew I didn't understand.

"Young Aidan, if the Word became human—and he did—that would be beautiful but would not help *us*."

"It seems to me that the Word becoming human would be a *good* thing."

"Of course, but that was not all that was needed."

"Why not?" I asked, trying to understand.

"Becoming human, *anthropos*, is itself a gift of grace abounding, but Jesus already had a relationship with *all things*. His mission was to reach *us*," the great apostle said, eyes full of fiery love. "We are *flesh*: humanity bound in the madness of *Ophis*—blind as bats, as you said."

I could see in his eyes his heart rejoicing, as the lights of the lamps seemed to gather around him.

He moved his arms and hands rhythmically like a conductor. "Jesus established his union—his existing union with us—in our darkness. Remember how it dawned on you that 'the me he is in is really *me*,' I believe were your exact words? And then you said, 'Wow!' when you realized that it was the broken you that Jesus honors with his presence?" His hands kept moving as if he were wafting the light in the room into my soul.

"*Sarx!* Not simply human (*anthropos*) but humanity as broken and blind—flesh (*sarx*). *That* makes me proud, proud with Abba's heart. I prayed that people would understand 'and the Word became *flesh, sarx!*'— the heart of the truth of all truths—and the brothers who wrote this creed, they understood it indeed!" John sang out, waving his arms wildly, and then danced what looked like a Scottish jig.

I listened solemnly, stunned all over again that I should be on Patmos hearing St. John himself talk about the Incarnation.

As if sharing the apostle's joy, the text of his Apocalypse came to life, each letter again shining like diamonds in the dark, and some words and whole sentences moving as if directly connected to St. John's heart. The beloved disciple of Jesus suddenly stood transfixed and all but transfigured before my eyes; I thought he would be taken to the cloud on the spot, and I suppose he was. Though I couldn't see what he was seeing, it was enough for me to stand beside my brother, enjoying him enjoying his vision of Jesus.

"Holy, Holy, Holy is the Lord," he whispered three times, each time lifting his palms higher. Then he sang the song of the cloud.

> From victory to victory the Lamb leads, worthy is the Lamb.
> From faith to faith, the Word believes, worthy is the Word.
> From Father's heart to Spirit's light, worthy is the Son.

I joined the song, finding my hands and arms lifted like the great apostle's as another wind swept into the cave. We sang and sang until I could tell his vision was ending.

This time it was I who held St. John and gently helped him to his mattress. "I will get water."

"Thank you," he whispered, his breathing shallow.

By the time I returned with the water, St. John lay motionless on the mattress. At first I thought he was simply resting from the long day and even thought of running my fingers over his chest like a spider to scare him as a little joke, but something inside me said, *He's gone.*

My heart called out, *Dear Lord, No! No! Not yet! Not yet!* Then I realized I was shouting it. Even as I did so, my brother did not move a muscle. Still unsure what was happening, I looked for signs of breath, but even in such silence I could not hear him breathe. Tears dropped from my eyes as I knelt to grab his hand to check for a pulse, terrified of the outcome. St. John lay silent, as though entombed, his hands folded over his chest; the text of his Apocalypse grew dim, as an unbearable sorrow filled the Room of Revelation.

Rubbing my head and then the back of my neck, stunned in disbelief and trying to absorb the shock, I buried my face in my hands, sobbing, hoping against hope that this was not happening. Again and again I tried to compose myself, but I couldn't stop shaking and crying, my mind hysterical, my heart overwhelmed with anguish that St. John was suddenly *gone.*

I sat quivering at his side, holding his hand, rocking back and forth as my body heaved under the weight of such devastating loss. Of all the thoughts running wild in my mind, the one that kept recurring was the idea that John's passing was my fault. Waves of guilt washed over me. Then I remembered his words: *Be on guard, especially when you are alone and exhausted.*

"Sir," I said through my tears, "I would never keep you from Jesus and the cloud, but don't go just yet. Don't go! I don't understand, Lord Jesus. Why now? *Why now?*" I asked, traumatized, more tears rising from the depths of my heart. "I have grown to love this man, the greatest man I have ever known . . . Lord, you brought me here, apparently to learn from him, and I've only just started. Why take St. John now?"

Still rocking and praying, gathering my wits, I gazed at the ancient apostle, who lay still as a statue. *What on earth do I do now? St. John is gone, and I cannot bear to face it . . . I cannot just leave him on this mattress . . . and I have no way of digging a grave in this rock.* Then I thought of burying him on his beach. *That I can do, if I can manage to get him down the path. I will bury him on his beach, on his mattress. I will get a rock from this room as a marker.*

As I sat crying, a prayer emerged. "Lord Jesus, my heart has broken with sorrow and grief. I kneel here holding your disciple's hand, feeling the wretched anguish that he must have felt in the upper room. Yet even though I am drowning in tears, my heart is full, and I thank you with all my being for giving me this time with your beloved apostle. I am honored beyond words, and were it not for my wife and family, I would gladly lie down and die beside this great saint. Thank you, Lord." As more tears flowed, I added, "I could use another revelation."

When I looked up in the utter stillness of the room, I noticed a new light, blurred by my tears. Eventually I noticed four words from the Apocalypse glowing like polished gold:

ΑΝΑΠΑΥΣΟΝΤΑΙ ΕΤΙ ΧΡΟΝΟΝ ΜΙΚΡΟΝ

My heart quickened with hope at the sight. Drying my watery eyes with my shirt, I rose to get closer to the glowing text. I recognized the last two words without much trouble. *Chronon* is "time," and *micron* is "little." *Time little*, I thought. *A little time.*

"What does 'a little time' mean?" I asked, as my eyes focused on the first two words. I mouthed them slowly, *Ana-pau-sontai eti.* As I did, hope hit me like a hammer between the eyes. "Good Lord! *Ana-pauo* . . . 'to give rest!' '*Rest for yet a little while!*'" I could scarcely believe what I read. *Could it be that St. John is not dead but resting?* I was afraid to hope, but hope I did, for I knew at the core of my soul that it was not I who had made the text shine.

"Lord Jesus, can this be? Are you telling me that John is sleeping for a little while?" As I prayed, a single word of St. John's text lit up like a firework exploding to my far left.

AMHN

Amen. That means "truly." "Oh, Lord, thank you! Thank you, thank you, thank you! There will be no beach burial today," I shouted, running around the Room of Revelation like John himself. I told myself to calm down and let the brother rest. "Yes, yes, I will," I sang out. "Rest, my brother, rest all you need."

I took my seat beside the apostle and stayed there for a long time, holding his hand. *My goodness me, what a day! I hope I can remember all this when I get home . . .*

An idea popped into my head. I stood up, grabbed the white rock, and wrote the rest of the creed on the wall, thinking I would surprise my brother when he woke.

> *And we believe in the Holy Spirit, the Lord and Giver of Life;*
> *who proceeds from the Father; who with the Father and the*
> *Son together is worshipped and glorified; who spoke by the*
> *prophets . . .*

EK, NOT APO

"Did you think I had graduated?" The familiar voice broke the silence behind me.

"John," I cried out as I spun around, my call echoing through the cave. "Brother! You're back," I shouted, running to hug his neck, relief pouring into my soul. "When I came back you were out cold. I knew for sure that you had left me and were with Jesus in the cloud. You lay there for an *hour*, still as a watermelon in a field. I was beside myself, crying my eyes out, shaking, alone. But Jesus spoke to me . . . through your text." I jumped up and darted to the Apocalypse to show him the words that had appeared to me in my sorrow.

He slowly rolled over on his side to watch, smiling. "*Amen*. That word is the word of the Kingdom. I am sorry, dear friend, that I frightened you. I laid down for a quick nap but found myself in a deep vision. I left my body for a little while in the Spirit. I have seen the unfolding of the next stage in your people's history." His eyes were wide with intrigue.

"Whoa! Sir, slow down. You've just seen the future for people living in the 21st century? You must tell me, but take it easy."

John continued quickly, as if we were running out of time. "I saw multitudes of the dead flies being quickened in the Holy Spirit, but their resurrection will come as your beaver dam is destroyed. The truth of all truths is the secret, and your creed is critical. You have done well here, but your mind must be expanded before you can see the mystery more clearly. We have work to do."

The Room of Revelation grew intense, and I could see profound depth in the apostle's eyes. What I thought would be a chance for me to give to the apostle was turning into new levels of learning for me and the prospect of an unfathomable mission. I wanted to press him for details, but I decided to trust him. "Lead me, brother John." *Holy Spirit, I am in over my head, but I trust you now more than ever.*

"That I will, but first how about some water?" he asked, sitting up. As I grabbed his pitcher, he whispered, "*Sarx* and *anthropos*, my son, *sarx* and *anthropos*."

"Settle down. I am listening carefully, but it would be best if you drank some water and relaxed a bit."

"I am fine, but I will have a stretch."

I helped him to his feet, and he stretched as if he were Rip van Winkle waking from his twenty-year sleep.

"I like that," he said, pointing to the new text I had written. "'The Lord and giver of life.' That sounds familiar. Now, what of these two words?" He gestured to the paragraph on Jesus and the two prepositions meaning "of" that he had circled earlier.

"I am proud to be able to identify those two words as *ek*, meaning 'from' or 'of.' My professor talked about them, but I admit to not processing what he said."

John's smile betrayed his excitement about the truth he wanted to share. But before he could get too animated, I motioned for him to stay calm and took a few deep breaths myself to make sure he got the idea.

"*Ek*," he said with a flourish, ignoring me, "is not simply 'from' or 'of,' my son. *Ek* is 'out of, out of the center, from the interior outwards.'" He spoke earnestly, sounding every bit the seasoned apostle. "*Ek* is not *para* or *apo*."

"You and your prepositions. Slow down, please. I'm still trying to catch up with your *en*, 'in,' and now you're adding *ek*, *para*, and *apo*."

"*Ek* means 'from the center or interior'; *para* means 'from the side of,' often implying fellowship. And *apo* is 'from' and sometimes 'away from.' Prepositions are small, but they are important words, as I expect you know."

"I think I do, but you have to give me a minute. I thought you were *dead*, and now you're rippin' off a dissertation on prepositions."

"Now, what of this phrase? Do you know this in the Greek?" John asked, pointing to the three words that were the central profession of the entire creed.

"Yes, sir," I answered with all the pride of my Scottish ancestry, translated through the heart of the Deep South. "It's *homoousion to Patri*, 'of the same being as the Father.' My professor and his brother never tired of talking about *that* phrase."

"Your professor was right." He smiled. "'Of the same being as the Father.' *Brilliant!* You must tell me what you know about how and why this came to be part of the creed."

"As the gospel traveled into the world, there were those, as you know, who simply could not *conceive* of the Son of God becoming flesh, becoming what we are. Some taught that Jesus was the first and greatest of all God's creation, that through him all things were created and redeemed. Athanasius, almost alone, realized that—"

"Jesus is no creature," the apostle interrupted firmly. "He was in the beginning face-to-face with his Father, out of (*ek*) God's being. Now he is also in us in *our darkness*. That is the gospel," he said with calm and uncompromising authority.

"Yes, sir, and it is *loaded*, and I feel its resonance," I replied, smiling. "The Greeks and the Jews, though for different reasons, could not abide the idea that Jesus is the eternal Son of the Father. For the Pharisees that could only mean that there is more than one God. For the Greeks it meant that God's *being* was divisible."

"Of course," John murmured, stroking his beard. "*Ek*, out of, out of the *being* of the Father."

"Everyone believed that Jesus was *from* the Father, but for most, that only meant he had been *sent*—like any other prophet, I suppose. But that did not sit right with the *worship* of Jesus, the Father, and the Holy Spirit. Athanasius and a few others realized that the apostolic vision of Jesus—and

I can see now, Jesus's union with us—was being eclipsed, assimilated by the alien mind-sets."

"Of course, young Aidan," he responded, again sounding like a professor. "If Jesus is only *sent from*, and not *ek*, out of the being of the Father, he cannot give us the Father. The stakes were high at this Council of Nicaea."

Yes, they were. And after my experiences in this room, I had a much clearer idea why. "It is said that Athanasius saved the Catholic faith. After the creed was written, he defended it with a passion until the day he died. Through him, Gregory Nazianzen, Hilary, and others, the vision of the blessed Trinity was developed. Or as you would say, the church's mind was expanded until it was worthy of the theme."

"Tell me more about what is meant by this Trinity," he pressed, clearly fascinated, his intensity holding fast. I could see his mind working as if getting another clue.

I remembered that *trinity* was not a biblical word, and unless John had another one of his revelations, it would be unknown to him. As I reflected, it seemed that the entirety of our conversation—going back to our first words, including our discussion of Jesus's union with us—was sharpening my focus on the importance of the relationship between the Father, Son, and Holy Spirit, although for us in the West the Trinity had been little more than an orthodox prefix, a largely irrelevant idea.

"The condemnation of the Jews and the Greeks forced the church to think very carefully about Jesus's identity. On one hand, the church, in agreement with the Jews and most thinking Greeks, believed that there was only one God. On the other, the worship of Jesus, the Father, and the Holy Spirit exposed the church to the charge of worshiping three Gods. *Trinity* was a way of expressing in a single word the reality of the one God with an intrinsic threeness: Father, Son, and Spirit." I was about to say more when he asked another question.

"How many churches were involved in this battle?"

"All of them. Well over three hundred bishops gathered in Nicaea. The whole church was in an uproar."

"You must tell me all that happened."

"You would be proud of the Fathers. They rejected the logic of 'the abstracts,' as you called them, and followed the *logos* of worship. Your introduction," I said, smiling, "and I see now your *out of, in,* and *begotten,* led the Fathers to perceive in spite of Athens, Jerusalem, and Rome that the *one* being of God is *relational*—one eternal, divine being, three persons, dwelling in one another in unspeakable love and oneness." I thought of the three chairs moving around one another, then face-to-face. "Your *en* and *ek* helped lead the brothers in time to *perichoresis*—mutual indwelling without loss of personal identity. This is the doctrine of the Trinity, flowing *out of*—I nodded and winked—"determined fidelity to your gospel."

I was suddenly overcome with adoration. I had taught about Nicaea off and on through the years, and the doctrine of the Trinity had always been meaningful to me, but now to speak of the Father, Son, and Holy Spirit was sacred, personal. Reverence filled me. *The blessed Trinity is no doctrine! This is God!* I found myself unable to speak.

"Oneness," St. John repeated. "The womb of the creation of all things. The Father is *in* the Son, the Son *in* the Father, and the Holy Spirit *in* the Father and the Son. It has always been so and always will be. And *we,* my dear Aidan, every broken *fragment,* are *in* the Son and he *in* us. *All will see,*" he declared with his extraordinary confidence. "'In that day, you will *know* that I am in My Father, and you in Me, and I in you.'" His gaze radiated life and love, and I felt entirely enveloped by them.

Flipping the white rock up and down in his hand while contemplating the mystery, he turned toward the Apocalypse. He walked to the far right of the room, passing the tall rock and its lamp, and stopped near the end of his text. There he circled the phrase ΑΛΦΑ ΚΑΙ ΤΟ Ω, (alpha and the omega, the equivalent to A to Z in English, meaning "the beginning and the end"). Then he walked a little farther to the right and circled the exact phrase again.

I stood behind him, still unable to speak.

John pointed to the circled text to his left. "This is the Father . . . and this," he said, pointing now to the other, "is the Son. This has always been so and always will. The Holy Spirit took me to Genesis and to the place where Adam and Eve were ashamed in hiding. They heard," he said in a low voice, "the sound of *Yahweh Elohim* walking in the *Ruach.*"

My heart was so captivated that I could scarcely take in what my brother was actually saying. So I repeated what he said to myself: *They heard the sound of Yahweh Elohim walking in the Ruach.*

"*Ruach*," I was finally able to say, "the Holy Spirit is in that verse in Genesis?"

"Indeed, my son. I had not paid attention to the readings. But *ruach* is there," he replied simply.

"The Lord God was walking *in the Spirit?*"

"Yes, it surprised me as well, but then I made a sudden connection with the word *Elohim*."

"I'm not following you."

"*Elohim* is plural. Literally, the text reads, 'the Lord *Gods.*' Of course I'd always known the word was plural, but until then I made nothing of the fact, because I wasn't able. Now, after all that I had learned from being with Jesus and being taught by the Holy Spirit, it took on an utterly exciting meaning for me. Why do you think Moses wrote, 'Let us make man in *our* image'?"

"That has been a question to me and many others. It sticks out like a sore thumb."

The apostle shook his head, amused again at my expressions.

"What I mean to say is that it seems so random, out of place."

"It appears so, but it is intended to prepare us. Then the Holy Spirit took me to the first words of Genesis. 'In the beginning God'—*Elohim* again—'created the heavens and the earth . . . and the Spirit of God (*Elohim*) hovered over the abyss . . . Then God (*Elohim*) spoke.' So there in Moses in the ancient text itself, we have one God Yahweh who is at the same time 'Gods,' we have the Spirit, and we have God speaking: the Word!"

I could only look at him in astonishment, sharing his wonder, nodding slowly for him to continue.

"As I marveled, young Aidan, the Spirit brought to mind the sacred *Shema*: 'Hear, O Israel, The Lord our God is one Lord.'"

"Is *Elohim* used there?" I asked, even though I knew the answer. I was seeing the truth speeding at me like a train. I chuckled, thinking back to my first moments in the cave when I thought the faint light might be a train. *Well, it is a train after all, but one that I welcome.*

"Yes, and the word for 'one' is *echad*, which simultaneously carries plurality within it. *Oneness.*" He nodded, pointing to the creed. "Amazing, isn't it? No one has thoughts or words for such beauty and relationship. We must expand our thoughts . . ."

John continued. "Wave upon wave of light flooded my mind. It was almost too much to bear, but the light kept shining in the darkness of my mind. The Holy Spirit was not yet finished with this lesson; she took me to Aaron's blessing, and my imagination ignited like fire."

The *Lord* bless you and keep you;
The *Lord* make his face to shine upon you, and be gracious to you;
The *Lord* lift up his countenance on you and give you peace.

"There are *three* divine blessings in *one*, my young brother. And then the prophet Isaiah: '*Holy, Holy, Holy* is the Lord of hosts.' And he writes again of the Lord asking, 'Whom shall I send, and who will go for *us*?' And the Psalm of David: 'The *Lord* says to my *Lord*: Sit at my right hand . . .' And King Solomon: 'Remember also your *Creators* in the days of your youth . . .' Once your eyes are opened, you see it *everywhere* in Scripture!

"The Spirit was bringing all this to my mind, preparing me to receive the revelation of Jesus. 'In the beginning was the Word, and the Word was face to face with God.' And out of this relationship, which stretches back before creation into the very *being* of God—who has words, my son, who has words?—*all things* have come into being!" His breath came quickly with excitement, and I was caught up in it with him.

"Grab your rags, Aidan; let's sleep in the Room of Revelation tonight."

"There is nowhere I would rather be, my brother, nowhere in the whole world," I responded, my mind now deep-fried like a Sunday chicken. But still in the game.

SUBMISSION

As I returned to the Room of Revelation with my sleeping rags, the ancient apostle was pacing slowly in prayer.

He motioned for me to sit. I could see in his face that he regarded what he was about to teach me as the linchpin of everything else.

"The Pharisees," he began, picking up his pace and intensity, "in their snide way, accused Jesus of being a child of fornication and claimed that they, on the contrary, were the children of the Father. Jesus retorted, 'If God were your Father, you would love me; for I proceeded forth and have come from (*ek*, 'out of,' 'from within') God, for I have not even come on my own initiative, but he sent me.' As I said before, we were dull of mind, but when I heard those words I had a sense that something profound had been said. Later in the upper room just before his prayer, Jesus was speaking to us about the Father's affection for us, and he said,

> I proceeded forth from (*para*, 'from the side of, from fellowship with') the Father. I proceeded forth from (*ek*, 'out of the being of') the Father, and have come into the

world; I am leaving the world and going to (*pros*, 'turned toward, face to face with') the Father.

Unsummoned tears rose to my eyes.

"My son, I have pondered those words for years. The best we could understand Jesus, when he spoke them to us, was to say 'we believe that you came from (*apo*) the Father,' and that was true in terms of his mission. But Jesus was speaking of divine mysteries, a much deeper connection between himself and the Father. I use that conversation in my gospel to prepare my readers to hear Jesus's prayer, moving their hearts to receive his final words:

> *I have* made Your name known to them, and *I will* make it known; that the love with which you have loved me may be in them, and *I in them.*

As he quoted Jesus's prayer and his own gospel, the air thickened in the room as if hallowing itself. I felt the witness of the Spirit and focused on the last three words—*I in them*. I knew they were the key. "Why did you end the prayer at that point? I mean to say that in your gospel, immediately after Jesus finishes that prayer, he turns toward the cross. I feel dumb as a post in asking, but were you being intentional, mentioning the one right after the other like that?"

"Everything I wrote was intentional, and everything was also true to how I witnessed it. Jesus's last words to his Father were 'I in them,' and the next words in my gospel are 'when Jesus had spoken these words, he proceeded forth.'" His hands trembled.

I sensed a light beginning to dawn and leaned forward in anticipation. "Sir, what exactly *was* your intention?"

"To relate Jesus's *I in them* with his *crucifixion* in the reader's heart, of course. *I in them*, our blessed Lord Jesus was finding his way *inside the great darkness in us* to make his Father *known to us*," John declared with pride, joy, wonder, simplicity, and hope. "'I have made Your name known to them, and *I will* make it known . . .'"

I was afraid to ask but compelled to do so. "How did Jesus do that on the cross?"

"Submission," he cried out in holy awe.

"Submission? To what or to whom?" I trembled, trusting that my pressing was not offensive to the beloved disciple.

"*To the world*—Jew and Gentile—trapped in Ophis's madness, twisted blind by his dastardly lie."

"But how? How does Jesus's submission to us make the Father known to us?"

"Union, Aidan, union. The Word became *flesh* to dwell *in* us."

"But how could union be related to the crucifixion?" I blurted out, increasingly frustrated at my own incompetence.

John paused, his intensity calming, and I could see a gentleness within him. He then turned to me and whispered, "Gather up the fragments; see that nothing is lost—"

His use of the word fragment made me think of little Aidan. But the apostle and I had not talked explicitly about little Aidan, although I knew by now that he missed nothing. Then it dawned on me that he used that word in his gospel. "Sir, are you referring to the story of Jesus feeding the five thousand with fish and bread?"

"Yes, Aidan. Think, now. Think with your heart."

I tried with everything I had to connect the dots.

"When Jesus spoke those words, I heard many things in *my* heart . . ." His voice trailed off into a whisper, laden with emotion. "All the fragments, *the broken pieces*, my son . . . shattered in Ophis's madness! But I did not yet see. It was only as the Lord bowed before their betrayal—" He stopped, scarcely able to say the words because his voice was quivering so. He looked away, then turned toward me again. "As *Jesus became a lamb* before their treachery and *submitted himself* . . . ," he said, closing his eyes and covering his mouth with his shaking hands as if to stop himself from speaking of such darkness. "As he allowed himself to be mocked and beaten . . . and tortured to death—" Once more the great apostle could no longer speak, his body convulsing with a memory so vivid it was breaking his heart all over again.

Silence filled the room as the ancient warrior relived the heinous scene. The moment was so holy for my brother—his emotions so raw in remembering Jesus's sufferings and so overcome by the light shining in them—I dared not say a word. I stood beside him, beginning to feel my own heart tear apart with the strange and unfathomable combination of bereavement and hope I saw in his eyes.

At last, when he was able, John looked at me and resumed. "The light shines in the darkness. I saw the light shining in the world's *darkest* hour. 'When Jesus had spoken these words,'" he repeated quietly, "'*He proceeded forth.*' He proceeded forth out of the being of the Father and into the great darkness itself. Do you now see, my son?"

"I see Jesus's heart as never before," I replied, uncomprehending emotion stirring in me as I walked toward the Apocalypse—unconsciously hoping that the text would somehow help me. "I feel Jesus's heart, feel it in you, through you. I see Jesus now as a little lamb before a monstrous mass of insane cruelty." I realized that I was once again standing in front of the scene in Revelation where the Lamb is in the center of the throne in heaven.

"Do you see his joy?"

"As the Lamb upon the Throne of all thrones, I do, sir, but not in his suffering on earth," I answered with sincere and painful regret. If ever I wanted to see it, it was now, but I couldn't; it was just beyond me.

"I heard Jesus's joy in his voice when he prayed. Even in the horror of his suffering, I saw his joy. Jesus knew that the way of the lamb was the way of his entering our flesh, the great darkness."

I tried with all my might to visualize what the ancient apostle was seeing. But I couldn't conceive of joy in Jesus while he suffered such agony or what he meant by entering our flesh.

"As he hung there, his body writhing in torture, I saw his joy shining," John said, his voice resonating hope even as he wiped his nose on his left sleeve. "*He knew* he was finding his way inside our blindness and that he would bring us to see his Father with his own eyes—as he has with you."

Like a curtain being drawn aside, I suddenly glimpsed a redemptive genius I could barely apprehend. "*Submission*," I gasped in a whisper. "Jesus had to go right inside our darkness and let it do its *worst* to get to the rock bottom—and yet he knew our blindness couldn't destroy him; he knew that only from the inside could he give us his eyes to see, heal our believing. So he rejoiced. Is *that* what you meant all along?"

The grin that broke across his face set it alight like never before. He nodded. "The Lord knew that *all things* were coming upon him. His *hour* at last had come, and *he proceeded forth*. Such confidence I had never seen: Jesus, bowed in humility before the hatred of the world, to be brutally murdered by the Jews and the Gentiles in collusion with Ophis's madness. *He knew!*"

The text of the Apocalypse radiated as if applauding, the Room of Revelation quickening with the apostle's heart. I stood riveted in awe at his words, holding my breath for him to continue.

"My son," he said, growing solemn, "Judas came with the temple police and with hundreds and hundreds of Roman soldiers, with lanterns and torches and weapons. It was a show of strength, they thought in their lunacy: the might of the world's great empire and the power of religion, joined as one against the Father's Son, the Creator of all things." The apostle stretched both arms wide, then moved them forward at the same time to a focus in front of him, indicating the joining of all the dark forces against Jesus. Without a shred of fear, Jesus proceeded forth," St. John said proudly, his speech slowing with the sheer drama of it.

"'Whom do you seek?' Jesus asked. 'Jesus the Nazarene,' they declared contemptuously." The apostle smiled through tears of sorrow and elation. "They got more than a Nazarene, my young Aidan; they got more than a Nazarene!"

"I had no idea that there were so many."

"A cohort, at least six hundred soldiers. I can see it now, the proud police from the Sanhedrin posing with their self-important smirks of disdain and the pompous Roman army with their menacing array of weapons, glistening in the light of the torches, marshaled as a great horde in formation to intimidate him and us. But the Lord spoke two words, *Ego Eimi*, 'I Am,' and sudden fear fell across the valley. Some knelt instantly in awe; all the others, every last one, fell to the ground like stones."

I knew I was standing on hallowed ground but could not help but ask: "How did things move from that moment of triumph to the horrors of the cross?"

"Jesus was letting them know that their murderous mission would only be fulfilled with his consent. 'No one takes my life from me, but I lay it down on my own initiative.' Peter thought that we should fight, and there was a part in all of us that rose up with him, but that wasn't the way. Jesus bowed as a powerless *lamb* before the slaughter, knowing it was the way into 'the flesh.' 'The cup which the Father has given Me, shall I not drink it?'"

All three lamps flickered at the same time, and I recognized that the lights would soon die. John gestured to the opening to the room, commanding me without words to fetch the oil. In a flash I grabbed one of the lamps and was on my way, carefully protecting the flame. I knew the event was a metaphor. I could hear the apostle saying, "All of life is a living parable, my son, for those who have eyes to see."

I returned with the oil and replenished the lamps, though not as skillfully as the apostle, and quickly took my seat in front of St. John. "I have not forgotten where we were or where I was. You said that Jesus was letting the Romans and the Pharisees know that only by his consent would they be able to take his life, *but why* did it have to be so horrific? The reviling, the mocking and insolence and bitter disdain, the scourging and beating to the point that Jesus was hardly recognizable as a human being? It was all so sickening. Couldn't Jesus have simply *died*? Why the cross, that ruthless Roman torture machine, and the cascades of violent wrath from everywhere?"

"'Gather up the fragments; see that nothing is lost,'" he whispered. "The crowd shouted, 'Away with him, away with him, crucify him!' Pilate smirked, 'Behold, your King!' The chief priests blasphemed, 'We have no king but Caesar.' Do you see, Aidan, the gathering of the final, hostile fragments of the great darkness? And Pilate delivered Jesus up to them to be crucified."

Still as a cat, I sat speechless, my heart soaring, knowing that I was hearing from the Apostle John himself the undiluted truth that could set me—and the whole world—free forever. Unimaginable grace whispered all around me, in me, everywhere, but I was still missing something.

The beloved apostle reached up, as if touching a small knob in the air with his thumb and index finger. Then he turned it half a turn and smiled. "What would be left out if Jesus had stumbled, hit his head, and died on the way to Golgotha?"

"Brother John, my heart is overwhelmed, but I'm seeing it now; this is the opposite of everything we in the West have been taught about the cross . . . I am seeing not *God's* wrath, but *ours*, the wrath of the human race, *our* anger, scorn, bitterness, hostility, and enmity toward God—*O Lord Jesus!* This is awful!"

"All of Ophis's madness," John said, picking up where all thought failed me. "His madness, as it had *poisoned* the mind of Adam's race, gathered into one act of terrible *iniquity*, the complete rejection of the Father's Son. The deepest darkness, the last broken fragment. Isaiah saw it: 'He was despised and forsaken by men, and the Lord caused the iniquity of us all to encounter him.'"

"*Sir!*" I fell to the ground in tears. "*We* cursed and damned and *crucified* the *Word of God!*"

"And *the Word* became *flesh* to dwell *in* us," he whispered, embracing me with tears of joy flowing down his ancient face. Never had such a quiet voice sounded with such power! St. John's whisper thundered through the cave, through my heart, and probably through the entire cosmos.

Yet I cried out, "But what about the *Eloi*? Didn't the Father forsake Jesus on the cross as he encountered our sin? That is what I have always been taught."

"Forsake?" he growled, obviously appalled at the thought, anger flashing in his eyes. "Who could think that the Father would ever forsake Jesus? He was with him, in him, through it all."

"Sir, is that not what the psalm says? Matthew and Mark quote, 'My God, My God, why have You forsaken Me.' And even in your gospel you quote from the same psalm."

"Do your people not know how to read?" John frowned, almost dumbfounded yet not losing his joy. "Jesus could hardly breathe as he hung on that cross, but he was able to speak the first line of that psalm in victory. We all knew it by heart. Read the whole psalm, brother, and you will see. 'For He has not despised nor abhorred the affliction of the afflicted; Nor has He hidden His face from him; But when he cried to Him for help, He heard.'"

He leaned forward slowly and embraced me again. "Jesus *entered* our iniquity by submitting to our insanity. Our blessed Lord made his way inside Adam's broken eyes; that is why he cried out, and as he did his Father held him in his arms, even as I do you now—yet from the inside. Union with his Father and with us in darkness. 'It is finished,'" he whispered in triumph, holding me as if he wanted me to feel the truth.

My mind swirled like one of Ezekiel's wheels. I understood what the apostle was saying, but this was so foreign to all that I knew. Then the universe inside me slowed, and I could see a single neon sign flashing before my eyes. It was the title of Jonathan Edwards's famous sermon "Sinners in the Hands of an Angry God." My guts wrenched. But I heard the song of light and knew to watch carefully. As I looked the words *Sinners* and *God* changed places in the sign. I gasped as "God in the Hands of Angry Sinners" appeared, pulsating with the rhythm of the song. "Oh, God! What have we done?"

At last I could see. "Jesus's submission to our hostile rejection of him was his way into our . . ."

"*Flesh*," the apostle finished. "The great darkness. *Sarx!* Where Ophis had his hold," he shouted, lifting his hands and jumping to his feet. "Oh! Lord Jesus, yes! Amen! Union with us in our sin!"

I thought his heart would burst in joy, as he let out a mighty sigh of relief. I think he believed he had lost me at this critical moment. He drew in a deep breath, then stared dramatically into my heart. "Listen carefully. The Son in whom all things are, who dwells face-to-face with Abba in *Ruach HaKodesh*, now dwells face-to-face with Adam's race *inside* Ophis's madness. Heaven's gate," he called out, raising his hands in worship. "The great 'I Am' inside the violent world of 'I am not.' All will see! This I know. In that day you will *know* that I am in My Father, you in Me, and *I in you*."

The penny finally dropped for me. I could see that Jesus bowed before our hatred to enter into our darkness—and he did—but instead of his Father forsaking him at that moment, his Father was in him and in the Holy Spirit. That is what John had been trying to help me see. On the cross Jesus brought his union with his Father in the Holy Spirit into His union with me, with us, with the world in our sin. The divine embrace. Heaven's gate! In that moment all my questions stopped, and I wept at the genius and the stunning humility and the love of Jesus for me, for us all. I in them—I, with my Father and the Holy Spirit—in them and they in me.

Then the great apostle slowly stood as if to conduct a mighty symphony, and as he did the song of light filled the Room of Revelation with holy calm, his beloved Apocalypse shining as the sun itself, while every hair on my body rose with expectation. St. John's face was suffused with light as he opened his arms wide in adoration.

Behold, the Lamb of God, who takes away the sin of the world.
Behold, the slain, yet living Lamb upon the Throne of all thrones.
Behold, the Lion through submission enthroned, the Lord of all creation.

Then all around us a song rose, the cloud and many thousands of angels singing of the Lamb.

Worthy is the Lamb that was slain
to receive power and riches and wisdom
and might and honor and glory and blessing!

The wondrous song echoed for a long while through the cave. Then all was quiet, St. John still standing in worship. After a moment he raised his arms high, as if summoning the whole of creation to join in a final triumphant chorus, and every created thing—in heaven and earth and sea, the cosmos and all it contains—shouted as one invincible voice:

To Him who sits on the throne, and to the Lamb,
be blessing and honor and glory
and dominion forever and ever!

St. John sat down on his mattress, spent in the joy of the light of life. I went to his side, watching his face carefully as he whispered to himself, his head moving slowly with the song of light. He lifted his hands in front of his long beard, turning them slightly toward one another as if to receive a treasure from someone standing over him, like a child from his father. Then he began speaking, veneration in his voice, savoring the words as tears of joy flowed down his face. I listened with every fiber of my body and soul.

The glory which you have given me I have given to them; that they may be one, just as we are one; I in them, and you in me, that they may be perfected in unity, so that the world may know that you sent me, and loved them, even as you have loved me. Father, I desire that they also, whom you have given me, be with me where I am, in order that they may behold my glory, which you have given me; for you loved me before the foundation of the world. Righteous Father, although the world has not known you, yet *I* have known you; and these have known that you sent me; and I have made your name known to them, and I will make it known; that the love with which you loved me may be in them, and *I in them.*

I sat in awe as the beloved apostle lowered his hands, stilling the Room of Revelation in the glory of Jesus.

A NEW DAY DAWNS

I awoke on the third day to the apostle in prayer, not standing but kneeling—kneeling *above me*—whispering words I could not recognize, words with tears.

"Sir, why are you crying?" I asked, surprised, as I sat up. I adjusted my vision with effort, trying to orient myself. "For the first time in my life I feel as though the earth itself, and all that is, has hope beyond our wildest dreams."

"Hope we have, my son, and forever." John composed himself and found a smile as he rose. "The Lamb of God, slain by Adam's race, lives now inside our abyss of *shame*, and is not swallowed by it: the light shines in our darkness, and our darkness cannot overcome it. This is our hope."

He really didn't need to speak, as his eyes preached by themselves, and joy leaked like a sieve from every pore of his being. For several moments he stood in silence, his face and body so radiant I thought he might transform into the burning bush like the Baptist. Then he looked directly into my eyes and sang the song of the cloud.

From victory to victory the Lamb leads, worthy is the Lamb.
From faith to faith, the Word believes, worthy is the Word.
From Father's heart to Spirit's light, worthy is the Son.

As I became more awake, I joined the song, and we sang out our great hope together. At the same time I felt a trace of inexplicable sadness, which my mind steadfastly refused to acknowledge for fear of what it might mean.

"Did you sleep well?" I asked in my nervousness. "After yesterday I slept like a log until a start in the night awakened me."

"My dear Aidan." He turned toward me, his brown eyes still vibrant yet not without a creeping shadow of something I thought I recognized. Did he feel the same as me? "I have news. Good and sad together."

O Lord! I cried out inside, a knot forming in my stomach. *Not now! Not yet!*

"The Holy Spirit," he said, forming the words with much effort, "tells me that it is time for you to return to your own time."

I felt my heart rip apart. "*No! No!* This cannot be! There is so much more to talk about! We have spoken only a little about your gospel and scarcely at all about the Revelation and your unknown letters. And there is so much more history I have to share with you."

"My dear young Aidan, I have a hunch," he whispered, punctuating the words with his familiar wink, "that *I* will visit you *again.* The Holy Spirit is a mystery beyond words. As we trust her—"

"Brother John, I do not want to hear this. Not now! Not yet!" I buried my face in my hands.

"Calm down," he whispered, sitting beside me. "We have time yet to see the world together."

"The world?" I asked warily, looking up.

"I told you I would take you to a special place above the cave. We can see the world from there."

"So I am *not* returning?" I asked, confused and barely daring to hope.

"Not just at this moment. We have time yet to talk. Tell me of your dream."

"I didn't say anything about a dream."

The apostle shrugged and cocked his head.

"I suspect that you already know more about my dream than I do. I would surely love to hear your thoughts about it."

"The Holy Spirit never shows me all, as I have told you many times. There are things that only you can see. We discover together; it is the way of the Kingdom."

The apostle grabbed his staff, and I scrambled to my feet and followed him out of the Room of Revelation. At its doorway we both stopped and turned for a final look, and as we did, a portion of the Apocalypse on the far left became prismatic:

ΜΗ ΦΟΒΟΥ ΕΓΟ ΕΙΜΙ Ο ΠΡΟΤΩΣ ΚΑΙ Ο ΕΣΧΑΤΟΣ

"'Fear not, I am the first and the last,'" I read out loud.

St. John continued, without looking, "'And the living one; I died, and behold I am alive forevermore, and I have the keys of Death and Hades. Now write what you see,'" he finished, patting me on the shoulder with an air of satisfaction.

"Sir, it is amazing how things change and sometimes so quickly."

"What are you thinking?"

"A few days ago I walked through this cave scared out of my mind. Now it has become a sacrament of hope and of utter wonder to me."

"As a son of your West"—he laughed, raising his bushy eyebrows—"you *needed* to be scared out of your mind."

"Roger that," I replied, finally able to find a little humor in the proceedings.

We had been heading down the narrow path for only ten feet or so when the apostle turned right and started up a small trail almost hidden between two boulders, a trail I had not noticed before. Though we were walking uphill, it was surprisingly not difficult, and after a short walk we arrived at the summit, marked by a solitary rock over six feet tall and eight feet wide on the left edge of the trail. The view was shockingly beautiful: the blue-green sea, dotted with white-capped waves, stretched out in all directions, reminding me of the evening sky as the stars begin to appear—or a delta cotton field in late October.

"I told you we would see the world together," the apostle declared, grinning. Spreading his arms out to catch the breeze, he turned around, inviting me to turn with him. I thought of the first time he had spread his arms wide in front of me as I stood traumatized on my first day on the island, telling me unbelievably, "This . . . this *is* Patmos."

"I've been here before," I said eagerly, with all the cheek I could muster. I couldn't wait to see his reaction.

After a few seconds he raised his eyebrows quizzically.

"In a vision," I added, nodding and smiling, "of course."

"Get used to it," he responded with equal cheek. "I mean, visions—of course!"

"It was in my dream last night. Over here"—I gestured to a plateau about twenty feet below where we stood—"I saw the Garden of Eden, at least what I could bear to take in. Its trees and fruits and flowers—thousands of different kinds, and I recognized none—pulsated with the splendor of your Apocalypse when it came alive in my vision. In the air I could see the song of light everywhere. The animals, only a few did I know, lived as one. In the eyes of every living thing shined the glory of Jesus.

"Then I saw Adam and Eve, their bodies broken, hiding from the Father, Son, and Holy Spirit in terrible shame. A man stood a great distance away," I said, pointing across the sea, "yet he seemed to be beside them at the same time. Then I saw another man at a greater distance and another out beyond him, almost on the horizon, yet they were together."

"West, my son. West."

"What do you mean?"

His eyes said it all, but he lifted his arm anyway. "You are pointing due west."

"Why am I not surprised?"

"Did you see a great darkness?" he asked, confirming that he did know my dream, at least part of it.

"It was terrifying: an abyss of darkness, like a massive black hole swallowing up the whole earth. I saw the cosmos with all its stars and suns and planets and moons, worlds within worlds, universes within universes. As a bright light flashed in the void of space, I saw millions of strands, like a spiderweb, moving out in every direction, connecting all things. At the center was the earth itself, and within the earth, the garden, and in the garden, Adam and Eve. The earth—and all that is—was being sucked into Adam's darkness. The fear awoke me. I could sleep no more."

"Perfect love casts out all fear. This is Jesus's creation. He is Lord." John spoke in his confidence, in which I had been sharing, but I thought he could see on my face that my dream had shaken me deeply. "Did you know these three men?"

"I couldn't see their faces, but I had a pretty strong impression as to who they were or what they represented."

"And . . . ?"

"The first, the closest to Adam, was definitely a Greek philosopher, perhaps Plato, though I had the sense he was more a symbolic figure than a specific person. The second, in the middle but at a great distance from the philosopher, was a Roman lawyer—"

"And the third?" the apostle interrupted, most intrigued, I thought, as we had spoken of Greece and Rome.

"The third, at a greater distance still, was a scientist. It may have been Sir Isaac Newton, who, until the last century in my time, was heralded as the most brilliant scientist in our history."

"And what did you feel?"

"Sadness and *panic*, not unlike what I felt when I thought you had graduated."

"What do you think Adam and these three have in common?" he asked, assuming the pose of a professor trying to lead his student to an insight.

"Adam and Newton have the apple in common," I replied, trying to calm my growing anguish with a touch of levity.

Turning toward me with warmth and gentleness, the old saint motioned for me to sit on one of the three flat rocks in front of us, then he sat down beside me. I felt like I was before a doctor about to deliver bad news. He tore off a piece of the bread he'd brought along and handed it to me. We said nothing for at least five minutes as we chewed.

At length I looked at the apostle with an unasked question in my eyes, waiting.

"Young Aidan, did you learn from your other dreams?" John asked without a trace of impatience, probing, reminding.

"Of course I did. Too much to tell, that's for certain."

"What was the main—?"

"Union or separation. I don't think I'll be forgetting that."

"Adam hid in the bushes, torn in the madness of Ophis's lie of separation."

"Yes, but how exactly do you think that relates to the Greeks?"

"Young Aidan, did the Greeks teach union?" he asked, cutting to the chase.

"That is a broad question, but Plato and then Neoplatonism—which emerged not long after your day—taught separation. God, or the One, is infinitely removed from us, unknowable, unreachable, unmoved by anything that happens in the world."

"And where do you think this Roman lawyer fits in?"

My insides lurched as if a final, stubborn root was being pulled from my soul. "Roman law . . . Good grief! *Separation* is the hidden assumption of the Western mind, and *law* is our default setting as to how to get back to God!"

"And this Newton?" the apostle asked, uncharacteristically quickening the pace, which made me nervous.

"Newton gave birth to the modern scientific vision, which is not so modern now, but still dominates our thinking."

John closed his eyes and stroked his beard. "I see our blue world hanging in the black void, with a great shield around it. Does that mean anything to you?" he asked, no doubt knowing that it did.

A shiver ran down my spine. "Do I need to explain?"

"We discover together."

"Well, Newton believed in God, to be sure. He even taught at Trinity College, which is ironic, as he had no time for the Trinity. In his vision, the solitary God created the cosmos as a vast machine run by unbreakable laws. As you saw, however, the machine was closed to all outside influence; not even God could enter his own creation or violate any of its laws—the meaning of your shield, sir."

"Did this Newton believe in Jesus?"

"Perhaps in a general way as a prophet or a teacher or as a good example. But *your,* or *our* Jesus"—I could not help but smile—"was *inconceivable* to Newton, and therefore could not be."

"Your science has continued the blindness of the Greeks." The apostle stiffened, and I could see fire in his eyes.

He must be summoning his chariot, I thought.

But he said nothing more in reaction to my summary of Newton's grand vision of a cosmos closed to the presence of the Father, Son, and Spirit. The irony hit me: Why would we call it a vision when it blinds us to Jesus's union with all things?

I sat biting my right thumbnail while both legs bounced up and down in nervous anticipation, aware that the world around us had suddenly become as quiet as an alligator sunning himself. Not even birds squawked. Then I noticed that St. John was having another vision.

His head and upper body jerked backwards as his hands rushed to his face, as if something had exploded and the debris was coming right at him. Whatever it was apparently moved swiftly down and to his left, and his head and upper body followed to the point that he was completely turned about on his rock, looking the other way, his hands cupping his eyes as he carefully "watched" something move off into the far distance.

The ancient brother drew a long breath and let out a low moan; I couldn't tell if the moan was good or bad. Eventually he turned toward me but still did not open his eyes. Then his hands were beside his upturned face, trembling in exultation, and he opened his arms ever wider and raised them ever higher till they were completely extended in praise. At last he opened his eyes, smiled, and winked at me.

"You must tell me what you have seen, please."

"My son," he replied with earnest joy, moving his head from side to side, "your beaver dam appeared before my eyes, vast and deep and solid."

I found my heart quaking at his words.

"But I saw the living Word, with many words within it, become one great hand"—the tone of his voice was one of resolved hope—"and the hand laid hold of the cedar at the bottom of the dam, slowly prying it out, till at last with one mighty heave the cedar was dislodged and flew through the air."

"What happened next?"

"The earth shook as the water rumbled and tore the dam apart, and a mighty river swept away a third of the world—a sight fearful and full of awe."

"Is *that* it?" I said without thinking. "I mean, did you see nothing more?"

"I did indeed."

"What did you see?"

He lifted both hands as if giving a benediction. "The great river flowed out of the abyss of blackest darkness that you saw in your dream and into the spider web. And then I saw the appearing of the bright Morning Star—the Lamb upon the Throne of all thrones, his light permeating the cosmos. All things breathing the song of light, held in the unsearchable care of Abba."

John sat quietly for several moments, then nodded, looking fully satisfied, as if he had finally finished writing a long book. He stood and motioned for me to do the same, then scrounged around in his satchel like an old man frantically searching for his false teeth.

I couldn't help but smile, even though I knew that my time was near.

"Aha! I found it!" He held up something that looked like one of those fat pencils children use in kindergarten. "The Lord wants me to stay here for a few days before my journey continues. There is more to write," he said, eyes dancing before they filled a moment later with sadness.

It's a tug-of-war for him, too, I thought, grief growing in my heart. Unable to contain myself, I blurted out, "This is not right. Lord Jesus, why are you doing this? Why now?" On the roller coaster of my inner world I knew that it was time to go, but I couldn't bring myself to believe it; I didn't want to leave.

In my turmoil I heard the *Word* underneath my knowing, calling me to take sides with him against the way I was seeing. I said yes or wanted to. An inexpressible tearing wrenched my heart.

"Sir, you must promise to make a copy of whatever you write and leave it behind the tall rock in the Room of Revelation. I will return and find it. All the powers of hell could not keep me from coming back here and finding whatever you leave behind for us."

"That, I believe, my son. I will leave you the way to what I write as the Holy Spirit leads. Perhaps tell you in a dream."

I was speechless. Tears formed in my eyes, and I felt a lump the size of a golf ball in my throat; I couldn't swallow.

"I will watch over you with serious care," he whispered, "in the

Father's heart."

A beaver dam in my own soul burst. I thought I had been sad before, but now a river of sorrow flooded my heart. "What on earth am I to do now?"

The beloved apostle stood silent in his thoughts, peering into my soul. "Young Aidan, I believe you are having another brain glitch," he replied, intending humor and, I suppose, comfort.

"I don't know about my brain, but my heart is being drowned by waves of sorrow and fear." I held both hands over my heart. "I want to do what is asked of me, but I can't seem to avoid this pain."

The ancient apostle embraced me with tender strength, holding me like a father holds his beloved son. "Abide in Jesus. Do not avoid the sorrow; turn *toward* it, lift it to Jesus, and listen. Hear Jesus in the middle of it, and live. You have seen me at prayer each morning. As I wake, I listen to hear Jesus, just as he always listened to his Abba."

"I do hear Jesus, but . . . this is a battle . . ."

"Take sides with Jesus against Ophis's madness."

We held each other and wept together, for how long I do not know, but long enough for us both to find a measure of calm.

"So how do I return?" I finally asked, restored. "I have no ruby slippers."

"Ruby slippers?" he asked with his look, and I took a mental picture of his face.

"It would not be fitting for me to leave without one last opaque expression. That one is from one of our most famous stories," I answered, trying to relieve the trauma in my heart. "I will miss you, my dear brother, St. John of Patmos, the beloved apostle of Jesus. I will miss you for the rest of my life. How can I thank you?"

"My son, there is no need for thanks. Stand firm in the truth," he said, big tears trickling down both cheeks to shine in his long beard. "Aidan from Mississippi, you have been a gift to me from Jesus himself, and I look forward to the day when we will be together again—and we shall! I am not far from the cloud. I will pray for you every day, with new eyes. And while I am here I will sleep on my Mississippi mattress."

He tried to smile but couldn't, and neither could I.

St. John stepped back and looked at me with kindness, then handed me his pencil—which was not a pencil but a tiny scroll, held carefully in his cupped hands.

Afraid to look, I put it in my pocket; at the same time, I reached in and found my Leatherman Micra and with trembling hands laid it in the open palm of my dear friend. "I hope this may help you in some small way, but be careful not to cut yourself with it. This should give the archaeologists something else to think about!"

He took the Leatherman and managed a smile, then hugged me again as only he could do.

In the arms of the Apostle John, I thought.

"Lord Jesus Christ, Father's beloved and eternal and faithful Son, *homoousios to Patri*," he said with his characteristic wink, raising his voice, "as you sent me, so send I my new son." And then to me he said, "Preach the *Word*, the truth of all truths, persevere the tribulation of enlightenment."

A fine mist began to fall, though there were no clouds in the sky. Surprised, I watched the droplets burst into a million prisms as a rushing wind rose around us.

A second later I was standing in my foyer at home, staring at my front door with twenty-eight panes of beveled glass. I froze in disbelief. Grabbing my chest with both hands, I looked around. *This cannot be! This cannot be!* I shouted inside my head, stamping my right foot on the wood floor to see if I was really home. It was solid. I stood still, lost in ten thousand questions, when I smelled coffee brewing.

What in the name of Patmos has just happened? Have I completely lost the plot? No way. I must have had a spell of some kind and imagined the whole thing or gone to sleep standing up and dreamed it. No way could I have really been with the Apostle John. Time travel is simply impossible.

Gradually I started to trust that I was home at last. The clock on the wall read 6:13. *Not a second has passed*, I thought, then wondered what John 6:13 might say. I looked down and noticed my tennis shoes—orange, with no strings except the one loop at the top—and my cutoff khakis. Before I could think, I felt in my pocket and discovered the small scroll where my knife had been. Trembling, I opened it slowly. As I read, I cried. Oh Lord, did I cry! My heart grieved, yet it was full of joy.

On the scroll was written:

"In that day, y'all will know that I am in My Father, you in Me, and I in you."
A *large* time awaits us all—no shadows.

John

AIDAN'S PARAPHRASE OF ST. JOHN'S "PROLOGUE"

Before the time of the beginning the Word was face to face with God. He was there before the ages in intimate union with God, and fully God. Everything that is came to be in Him. And not one thing has existence apart from Him. In the Word life was and came to be, and this life is light, the true origin and meaning of human life. And the light of life shines in the gloom of darkness, and the darkness does not understand the light, neither can it stop it shining.

Suddenly in the darkness a man appeared, sent out from the presence of God. His name was John. He came to be the witness, the witness to the Light of life, that everyone might see and believe. John was not the Light, but its witness.

The true Light who enlightens every person born into the world was already in the world, and though the world was made through Him, the world was unaware and did not perceive Him. He came to His own people, and they did not recognize Him or receive Him.

Yet those who embrace Him, who believe in His name, find His Light, His I AM setting them free to become their true selves, free to live as children of God in the darkness, discovering their origin beyond their earthly parents in the Word in God.

And so the Word became flesh and entered the darkness in person, and found His way within us. And we perceived His true identity, His glory as the only begotten out of the Father, an overflowing fountain of grace and truth.

This is what John was sent to show us about Jesus, that He existed from the beginning, ages before John himself. Out of His fullness we were born and now are being liberated.

For the Law came through Moses. Through Jesus Christ has come the true exodus into grace-filled reality, into the very bosom of the Father where the only begotten Son dwells face to face with His Father.

ACKNOWLEDGMENTS

From the time I can remember my heart has been fascinated with the idea of "union with Christ." I have always believed that Jesus is the answer to our ills, and somehow knew that his union with us was the key to understanding how. That fascination became an obsession, which led me into theology, history, psychology, and a life-long study of the Gospel of John. The wounds of my childhood and my own sorrow have never let my pursuit reside in the ivory tower of the intellect. This has been a heart quest for healing and life.

I discovered that though I was a devout Christian, I was blind as a bat, and that my blindness was exacerbated by the framework of the Western church itself, with its distant deity, external performance, and horrific vision of the death of Jesus. In the early church I found a different framework, one focused almost entirely on Jesus having become what we are. Those brothers understood the incarnation to mean that Jesus's union with the human race was not a goal but an accomplished fact, a stunning and simple reality from which we could live life here and now. While I did not see *Patmos* coming, it is the fruit of my heart's cry through years of wrestling and reading and tears.

One morning the scene at Aidan's front door hit me out of the blue. I wrote it not knowing where it would lead at all. A few months later I thought of the scene again and I heard the word *Patmos*, in my mind. I told my friend Larry Bain, Jr. about it and he immediately encouraged me. Larry has walked with me from that moment through the terrible first drafts all the way till the end. Thank you, brother. Without you this book would have never seen the light of day.

Reading George MacDonald and C. S. Lewis has stirred my imagination for several decades, but nothing like reading *The Shack*. Two days after I finished it, Paul Young phoned me. What seemed a random phone call turned into a priceless friendship. I cannot imagine undertaking such a project as *Patmos* or finishing it without Paul's endless reassurance. What a brother you have been to me. Thank you. And thank you for adopting me into your ever-widening family, and for introducing me to John Mac-Murray and Wes Yoder. The four of us have had one long, inspiring, and thrilling conversation for the last several years. That conversation cross-fertilizing with the years of insightful discussion with Ken Courtney, Julian Fagan and John Novick in my Tuesday morning group has proven to be the seed bed out of which *Patmos* has grown. Thank you all. Our friendship I regard as one of the highest privileges in my life. Ken, we stayed in the game.

Editors have a special gift. I sent what I thought was close to the final draft of *Patmos* to Debbie Sawczak in Toronto—who did a fantastic job editing *The Shack Revisited* but somehow, to my eternal shame, was not properly acknowledged for her amazing contribution. When I got her edited version of *Patmos* and her suggestions my mind exploded with new ideas, which took the manuscript to places I had not foreseen. Reading the updated version again, Larry, Paul and Wes, and my wife, Beth, suggested that I submit the expanded manuscript to Becky Nesbitt and her team for further editing.

Meantime my friend Ted Dekker, who not only read several of the drafts, but helped me understand the process of writing stories, raised more good questions than I can count, and prepared me for the editor's scythe. No blame, of course, goes to Paul or Ted or Debbie or Becky or anyone else for whatever may be weak about the book. But more credit than I can say goes to them for it being what it is.

Special thanks to Christy Jones who has been my dear friend for over twenty years. Christy read all the drafts and would not let me give up.

Your friendship means the world to me. Thank you.

I am profoundly indebted to Paul Lavelle and the team of Operation Restored Warrior. Their Drop Zone Program is the most amazing ministry I have ever experienced. To date over seven hundred warriors have been healed and restored. I was honored to be one of the first civilians to go through the Drop Zone. In those five days my heart was healed and I had the greatest encounter with Jesus in my life. I am privileged to be the theologian and honorary team member of ORW. Brothers, it is difficult to imagine writing *Patmos* without those five days, and your friendship and prayers. Thank you.

There have been so many people around the world who have helped me in the long and winding road leading to this book's final draft. A sincere thanks to Linda Smith and to The Posse for your prayers! To David Jennings for your generous and overflowing heart. To Dr. Harry and Robbie Phillips for a life-long friendship of great care and laughter. To Randy Baxter and Ed McNamara, Jason Hildebrand, Michael LaFleur, Dr. Jim and Kay Sawyer, Francois and Lydia du Toit, Rod (Papa Smurf) Williams, Craig and Jenny Bowes, Tim Brassell, Bill and Davina Winn, Sherrie Moore, Mike Rough, Dr. Darrell Johnson, Dr. Ken Blue, Dr. Kevin Freiberg, St. John Walker of the Motherland, and the Perichoresis family around the world, thank you all for your hearts, and for your laughter and comments, and for your determination "to see what is". Your friendship keeps me getting out of bed and soldiering on.

To Beth, my wife of 34 years, you know what an ordeal the journey has been. It is the simple truth that without you there would be no ministry of Perichoresis, no books, no lectures, no Baxter. I owe my life to you. Thank you. The best is yet to be.

To our son, James Edward Baxter, and daughter Laura K. Moore, thank you especially for being ever present in my life. Your support, and knowing you are always there, sets me free to go.

Finally, I dedicate *Patmos* to Kathryn, our child of joy and color. You are the daughter every dad wishes to have. You make me glad to be alive. I kept my promise. I love you forever.

Holy Spirit, grant that all who read this book would have as much fun as we did writing it.

OTHER BOOKS BY
C. BAXTER KRUGER

The Shack Revisited

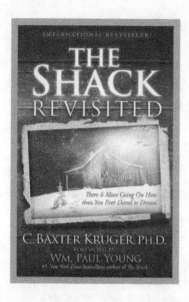

Millions have found their spiritual hunger satisfied by William P. Young's #1 *New York Times* bestseller *The Shack*—the story of a man lifted from the depths of despair through his life-altering encounter with God the Father, God the Son, and God the Holy Spirit. Now C. Baxter Kruger's *The Shack Revisited* guides readers into a deeper understanding of these three persons to help readers have a more profound connection with the core message of *The Shack*—that God is love.

"Baxter Kruger will stun readers with his unique cross of intellectual brilliance and creative genius as he takes them deep into the wonder, worship, and possibility that is the world of *The Shack*."

WM. PAUL YOUNG
Author of *The Shack* and *Eve*

"Baxter Kruger brings his typical down-to-earth charm to this masterful job of laying out in clear, layman's terms the rock-solid historical Christian theology behind Paul Young's best-selling novel. Fans of *The Shack* are going to love *The Shack Revisited*."

DR. JOSEPH TKACH
President of Grace Communion International

"Among the theological books available to the broader market *The Shack Revisited* asserts itself like a battleship in a marina full of fiberglass boats. In this book, Baxter Kruger has done more than merely put forward a theological framework for Paul Young's bestseller; he has gathered threads from the entire width of the Christian tradition, and from the depth of two thousand years of history to weave together a clear and compelling restatement of Christian belief, which, for me at least, makes me proud to be called 'Christian.' I cannot imagine how anyone could possibly refute the logic or the weight of scholarship in this book. Yet it is eminently readable and enthralling. The last chapter on the Holy Spirit is, perhaps, the most remarkable thing I have ever read on the subject. A 'must read' for any serious thinker or church leader."

REV. DAVID KOWALICK
Author of *All About Glory*, Adelaide, Australia

"Throughout the history of the church, the Living God, in His grace, has raised up men and women who are given special grace to understand who He is for us and for the world. One such person for our time is C. Baxter Kruger. Very few people can so winsomely articulate God's Self-revelation as Father, Son, and Holy Spirit, the way Baxter can. I think it is because very few people have been gripped by the Trinity the way Baxter has been! What a fortunate human being he is! Whenever I read his work I am moved to tears; tears of joy as Baxter helps me realize that I too have been included in the inner-life of the Trinity. Everything Baxter writes pulsates with the extravagant, healing, life-giving love of the Trinity. Oh how grateful I am for this blessed theologian ... and brother."

DARRELL JOHNSON
Preaching Pastor for First Baptist Church, Vancouver, Canada
Author of *Discipleship on the Edge: An Expository Journey Through the Book of Revelation,* and *Experiencing the Trinity.*

PURCHASE HERE:
www.perichoresis.org/shop

Jesus and the Undoing of Adam

In *Jesus and the Undoing of Adam*, Dr. C. Baxter Kruger takes aim at what he considers to be the sin of all sins in the Western Church. If you are a Bible believer yet feel uncomfortable with the ideas that our Father had to be appeased to accept us, and that Jesus' suffering on the cross was from His Father, then this book is for you. Concise, clear, tightly argued and compelling, *Jesus and the Undoing of Adam* offers a biblical and inspiring vision of Jesus' death as an act of the Father, Son and Spirit in complete unity reaching us in our great darkness. Includes an exposition of Ps 22:1, "My God, My God, why have You forsaken Me," and a sermon on Good Friday.

"Theology is a vehicle created for exploring the wonder and depths of God with us. Sadly, many driving the vehicles are prone to taking the same safe roads, in their all too familiar economy sedans. Thankfully, from time to time an adventurer comes along, who in obediently choosing to leave the main thoroughfare leads us into the deep, vast mysteries of the glorious triune God. Baxter Kruger is just such an adventurer, and *Jesus and the Undoing of Adam* is his latest all-terrain transportation; I have benefited greatly from the ride."

GLEN SODERHOLM
Pastor, Singer/Songwriter, Toronto, Canada

"In the fall of 2009 I came across the book *Jesus and the Undoing of Adam* by Dr. C. Baxter Kruger. Looking back, it was a pivotal moment in my life. Every once in a while you read a book or discover an author whose writings turn the kaleidoscope through which you view, not just the world, but God, relationships, and even yourself. In *Jesus and the Undoing of Adam* I found a God of beauty, grace, compassion and love. Jesus has indeed undone what Adam did. The light of Jesus has shown in Adam's darkness, your darkness, my darkness, and the darkness cannot overcome the Light. The Light is here to stay. I highly recommend you read *Jesus and the Undoing of Adam*. But be prepared to have your world shaken."

RANDY BAXTER
Retired CFO of a Michigan Nonprofit
and current Secretary-Treasurer of Perichoresis

PURCHASE HERE:
www.perichoresis.org/shop

Across All Worlds: Jesus Inside Our Darkness

Drawing from the early Church's vision of Jesus, in *Across All Worlds*, Baxter Kruger brings us face to face with the astonishing fact that Jesus has established a very real and personal relationship with us in our darkness. Jesus is present, not absent, and he is present with and in us as we are, not as we pretend to be on Sunday morning, in the very places where we are ashamed of ourselves and where our demons hide. For Jesus refuses to be the Father's Son and the One anointed in the Holy Spirit without us, and the us He refuses to leave behind is the broken us, the obstinate, hiding, blind us. We are in for a wild and liberating ride, but Jesus will not let us go until we see what He sees, know what He knows, feels what he feel, and live in His freedom.

"Across All Worlds is a superb book which I shall be recommending . . ."

PROFESSOR ALAN J. TORRANCE
St. Andrews Scotland

"For those who are compelled to 'kick at the darkness till it bleeds daylight,' *Across All Worlds* is a steel-toed book."

STEVE BELL
Singer/Songwriter, Winnipeg, Manitoba

PURCHASE HERE:
www.perichoresis.org/shop

The Great Dance: The Christian Vision Revisited

Many people can't see the relevance of theology to everyday life. In *The Great Dance*, C. Baxter Kruger takes the historic doctrines of the Trinity and Incarnation, shakes them free of their academic dust, and shows how they unlock the hidden truth of our ordinary lives.

From motherhood to baseball, from relationships and music to golf and gardening, Kruger shows how our human existence needs to be understood as participation in the life of the Father, Son and Spirit. Step by step, Kruger walks us through the stratagems of evil and the messes we make of our lives. More importantly, he explains why we hurt, what we are really after and how to get there, and why faith in Jesus Christ is so critical for abundant life.

Written with pace and poetry and winsome grace, *The Great Dance* is the voice of the ancient church speaking to us across the ages through the pen of a Southerner who loves life. This is theology at its very best—steeped in tradition, yet unfamiliar and exciting, even revolutionary; deeply personal and honest, yet universally relevant.

PURCHASE HERE:

www.perichoresis.org/shop

God is for Us

The sequel to Baxter's short but internationally acclaimed *Parable of the Dancing God*, *God is for Us* leads us into the heart of the gospel. This book is composed of five outstanding lectures, clear and accessible, yet, as usual, challenging. Dr. Kruger is a son of the West who kicks against the goads of what many know cannot be the truth. The opening chapter, "The Eternal Gospel of the Father," remains Baxter's personal favorite.

"That God should be 'for us' will be a remarkable and transforming discovery for those who have grown weary under the whiplash of a theology that drives us to 'do something for God!' I wish that overburdened pastors could read this book before ever preaching another sermon, and uninspired Christians could inhale its fragrance before going to church!"

RAY S. ANDERSON, PH.D.
Former Professor of Theology and Ministry, Fuller Theological Seminary

"When I first picked up *God is for Us* I read it through in one sitting, in an hour. I could not tear myself away from the sheer goodness of the triune God that Baxter Kruger conveys in this short book. But then I had to go back and read it carefully through again, in order to allow the deep truths to penetrate my life afresh. Here is a clearly presented exposition of the profound truth that we are created to be with God forever."

GRAHAM BUXTON
Senior Lecturer and Head of Ministry, Tabor College, South Australia

PURCHASE HERE:
www.perichoresis.org/shop

For More Information about Baxter and the Ministry of Perichoresis, go to:
PatmosTheBook.com
Perichoresis.org

For More Information about Speaking Engagements, go to:
AmbassadorSpeakers.com

Over 300 hours of Dr. Kruger's Lectures are available at Perichoresis.org

Portuguese (Brazil) and Spanish Language editions of
The Shack Revisited and *Patmos* are also available.